THE EXHAM-ON-SEA MURDER MYSTERIES VOL 3

FRANCES EVESHAM

Boldwood

First published in Great Britain in 2020 by Boldwood Books Ltd.

I

Copyright © Frances Evesham, 2020

Cover Design by Nick Castle Design

Cover Photography: Shutterstock

The characters and events described in the Exham-on-Sea Mysteries are all entirely fictitious. Some landmarks may strike fellow residents of Somerset, and particularly of Burnham on Sea, as familiar, although liberties have been taken with a few locations.

A CIP catalogue record for this book is available from the British Library.

Paperback ISBN: 978-1-80048-567-9

Boldwood Books Ltd.

23 Bowerdean Street, London, SW6 3TN

www.boldwoodbooks.com

To Dave, Chris, Pippa and Nick

MURDER AT THE BRIDGE

AN EXHAM-ON-SEA MYSTERY

1

WEDDING

Libby Forest dropped into a wooden chair, exhausted. She'd spent the afternoon on tenterhooks, half-expecting an unforeseen disaster to ruin the wedding at Wells Cathedral, but the ceremony had passed without a hitch. Now, in a sturdy marquee pitched in a field, the reception was underway. The level of excited chatter rose as guests finished their meals, nibbling cheddar cheese and biscuits, their stomachs full of Somerset beef and local apple pie. The temptation to giggle grew until it was almost irresistible and Libby had to turn it into a sneeze.

Max Ramshore, even more handsome than usual, squeezed her hand. 'Are you coming down with a cold? Or is it an attack of maternal emotion at seeing your son marry?'

'Neither. It's pure relief. I can hardly believe the wedding's over and everything went well. I've been expecting the worst all day.'

'Don't count your chickens. Remember what happened at the Oscars. Nothing's over until it finishes.'

'That sounds very cryptic,' Libby said, 'but at least Bear was on his best behaviour.' Libby let her fingers sink into the warm fur of the huge Carpathian sheepdog by her side. 'He didn't smell the cathedral cat and chase him down the aisle. He thinks cats exist on this earth for his personal entertainment. I hope no one's planned any practical jokes.'

'Don't look at me. I've never found old tin cans tied to cars especially amusing.'

Libby took a moment to gaze round the marquee. The happy couple looked radiant, the service had been touching, and old friends of the bride's family had filled the cathedral. Libby, still new to Somerset, had fewer guests to invite, but the sight of a row of customers from the bakery in the congregation had lifted her heart. Even Mrs Marchant, the old lady who collected stray cats from the streets of Wells, had attended, her dress so old and lace-covered it surely counted as vintage.

Only Ali, Libby's daughter, couldn't be there, to Libby's disappointment. Working on voluntary service in South America, she'd been nursing her boyfriend, Andy, through a nasty bout of pneumonia. He was on the mend now, but the improvement had come too late for Ali to get home, and she'd been forced to talk to her brother through an uncertain Facetime link, promising a visit to England as soon as possible.

Libby shot a glance at Mandy, her apprentice. Dressed in full Gothic splendour, including a tight black bodice and voluminous skirt, Mandy sat beside Reg, Max's basketball-playing American colleague. Libby recognised Steve, Mandy's ex-boyfriend, at the same table, and winced. Would he cause a scene after splitting with Mandy after a row in Wells Cathedral's coffee shop?

Max wagged his finger. 'Stop worrying about Mandy.'

Libby wriggled. 'Did you talk to Reg? You know, about being too old for her?'

'I most certainly did not. I thought we'd agreed she's an adult and can look after herself. She's having a ball with both her admirers in attendance. From the way Steve's looking at her, all big brown puppy eyes, I think he's hoping to get her back. They only broke up because she wouldn't visit him in London.'

'*Couldn't* visit,' Libby corrected. 'She still has a phobia that stops her travelling by train.'

'Well, maybe she could get some help. There are therapists, you know. Anyway, it's not your responsibility. Just relax for once and enjoy your son's wedding reception. The marquee's full of people you don't know, any one of whom may be plotting murder. Look.' He nodded towards a small huddle of Robert's friends. 'Do you think one of those might be a candidate?'

'Don't even think it. I want a perfect day today, with no crises.'

Max wandered away, seeking out old friends, while Libby breathed a happy sigh, slipped her feet out of new, painfully high heels, and watched Sarah's mother approaching. Belinda looked beautiful and voluptuous as always. In a powder blue jacket, navy shoes and wide brimmed hat, she would be every inch the serene mother of the bride, were it not for the tense lines on her forehead and the occasional anxious glance to left and right.

She sank into the chair next to Libby. 'I know this isn't the time...'

Libby suppressed a groan as she recognised the tone of voice. Belinda had a favour to ask. Libby's fame as an investigator had grown locally, and she was approached in the most inappropriate places. At least Belinda hadn't followed her into the ladies.

'How can I help?'

Sarah's mother licked her lips and hesitated. Libby nodded towards Sarah. 'Your daughter looks beautiful; the perfect bride.'

'The thing is...' Belinda swallowed and picked at the skin of her thumb.

Libby took pity. 'Why don't we have a cup of tea? Sarah and Robert are still circulating, so we've got time for a chat.'

Belinda visibly relaxed. 'It's a bit embarrassing. Confidential. I need to know you'll be discreet.' A hint of steel underpinned the words.

'Of course.'

'It's about money, I'm afraid.'

Libby hid a smile. Aside from marital problems, financial embarrassments were the most common reason people asked for private investigations. 'Before you begin, is this an official request or are you asking as a friend?'

Belinda seemed taken aback. 'Oh, I suppose it's official.' She'd probably been hoping for free professional advice, but experience had taught Libby it was best to establish from the outset that a formal private investigation carried a price tag.

The bride's mother coughed and fiddled with an earring as she recovered her dignity. 'I just need to recoup some money. I had a small legacy when my mother died a couple of years ago. I invested it, but the – er – the shares collapsed and I made a loss.' She bit her lower lip. 'I promised Sarah help with the wedding expenses. We don't have much spare cash in the farm, what with the milk prices over the past year, so I didn't want to worry Sarah's dad about it, but soon I'm going to have to stump up the money.'

Libby offered a sympathetic smile, secretly intrigued. It was obvious Belinda was only telling half the story. Did she suspect she'd been cheated? Or perhaps she'd done something foolish. Had she been borrowing money from loan sharks?

Libby glanced over her shoulder. This wasn't a good place for further confidences. 'I'll need as much detail as possible. Perhaps we could meet tomorrow and go through your accounts?'

Belinda chewed harder on her lip. Libby waited, giving her

time. Max, her business partner, would be able to help with the woman's financial problems. He was an expert in international fraud and money laundering, with a history of under-the-radar investigations. He could sort out poor accounting and advise on improved budgeting and wealth management, but Libby suspected Belinda's problems extended further.

'It's a bit complicated...' Belinda's voice wavered as a man wearing a grey linen kaftan approached. Tall and striking, he stood out among the other guests, who mostly wore more conventional wedding clothes. Long grey hair was drawn back into a ponytail, and the man's bushy grey eyebrows framed a strong face characterised by sharp cheekbones and a hooked nose. Belinda stiffened as he approached.

He smiled, but his light grey eyes peered intensely into her face. 'Belinda, my dear. I haven't seen you for a while. Thank you so much for the invitation to your daughter's wedding, but I'm afraid my wife sends her apologies. Her mother is unwell. Nothing serious, but the old lady has a heavy cold and Olivia felt she shouldn't be left alone.'

His words were commonplace, but the man's effect on Belinda was electric. She jumped to her feet, cheeks reddening. 'It's a-a pleasure, Sandy.' In the awkward pause that followed, Libby slipped her feet back into her shoes, stepped forward, and held out a hand. With a little start, as though recollecting her manners, Belinda said, 'Let me introduce Xavier Papadopoulos. He's a sort of distant cousin of mine.'

'And you're the mother of our handsome groom, Mrs Forest.' He pronounced the name slowly, rolling it round his mouth as though tasting each syllable.

The back of Libby's neck prickled with discomfort. 'We're delighted Robert found Sarah. She's a lovely young woman.'

Unblinking, the man watched her face, his smile enigmatic.

'Indeed.' After an unnerving pause, he seemed to lose interest. The snake-like eyes re-focused on Belinda. 'I'm sure we'll have plenty of time to talk this evening, while the young people dance, Belinda.'

She cleared her throat. 'I-I'll look forward to it.' The lie was obvious.

Without another word the grey man left. He strolled through the marquee with slow, measured steps, his back ramrod straight. Heads turned as he passed, as though his personal magnetism sucked in everyone within range. Libby breathed out, suddenly tired. 'Your cousin's a most unusual person.'

Belinda's head turned towards Libby, but her eyes were vague. 'I'm sorry. What did you say?'

Maybe she didn't want to discuss the man. Instead, Libby made a suggestion. 'Would you like an appointment? I'll ask Max to come. He'll help with your money worries. He's something of a financial genius, and very discreet.'

Belinda let out a little gasp, grabbed her bag, and hurried towards the exit. 'N-no thanks. Forget I said anything. It's nothing really. I'll talk to Mike and we'll sort things out.' She threw the words over her shoulder a she hurried away.

Libby's mind seethed with curiosity. Why had the arrival of Xavier Papadopoulos upset Belinda so? Was it just that she was worried about being overheard?

Libby doubted that was the reason for the woman's change of heart. Instinct told her Belinda was frightened of Xavier Papadopoulos.

Next moment, she'd forgotten about Belinda Carmichael. The atmosphere in the marquee had changed, the gentle hubbub of cheerful conversation died away. Libby rose, confused, as an angry voice carried from the far end of the marquee. Libby couldn't make out the words. Then, her son Robert was at Libby's side. 'Sarah's aunt's causing an almighty fuss. She's saying her ring's been stolen. Can you come and help sort it out?'

Libby closed her eyes. Everything had been going too smoothly. She'd known something would go wrong.

2

LADY ANTONIA

Like a ship in full sail, a regal figure in lilac satin bore down on the group of three, wearing a hat apparently constructed entirely of pearls. Libby recognised Lady Antonia Appleby, the widow of Sir John Appleby, one of Somerset's wealthiest farmers. Lady Antonia drew near, face purple, chin vibrating. 'No one's leaving until my ring's been found.'

'One of these *people*...' She spat the word as though swearing, one arm sweeping in a wide gesture that encompassed everyone in the marquee. Ears strained to catch every word of this new entertainment. 'One of these guests has stolen a valuable family heirloom and I insist the police be called immediately.'

Sarah, face pale and pinched, took her great aunt's arm. 'Aunt Antonia, there's no need for that. You must have dropped the ring somewhere. It won't take long for us to find it.'

'Nonsense,' the woman barked. 'I don't drop things. I pride myself on taking care of my possessions. When you have responsibilities like mine, you learn to pay attention to the things that matter. Now, are you going to call the police, or shall I?'

'Please, wait a moment,' Sarah sounded desperate. 'This is Mrs Forest. She's a private investigator—'

The woman interrupted. 'I'm not interested in some kind of amateur sleuth. My diamond ring is worth thousands of pounds and I insist on calling in the professionals.'

Max, who'd been chatting with friends outside the marquee, strolled inside, his smile relaxed as though he remained entirely unaware of any tension in the air. 'Why, Lady Antonia.' He turned the full force of his blue eyes on her and Libby felt a small jolt of pride as he took control of the situation. 'I hadn't seen you here. I wonder if I can help.'

'Maxwell Ramshore. It's been a long time since we last met. I don't believe you've visited for years. Not since my old friend, your mother, died.'

'My loss.'

Libby was constantly meeting friends and acquaintances of Max from all walks of life. Women seemed to melt when they saw him. Libby tried not to be jealous. After all, it was his easy charm that had first attracted her to him. More importantly, though, she'd soon learned to recognise and admire the steel that under-pinned his warm smile and Scandinavian blue eyes.

Max took Antonia Appleby's arm, conjured a comfortable chair from nowhere, and within seconds had seated her in front of a tall glass of champagne. Libby joined them and Max shot a quick glance at her face, followed by the faintest wink. 'Now, Lady Antonia. Tell me about your missing ring. Is it that beautiful diamond cluster I remember you wearing at some of those parties you used to throw? My, those were some evenings.'

The woman nodded and tossed back half a glass of cham-pagne. Perhaps her purple face was not due solely to fury at losing a ring. Several previous glasses of champagne were prob-ably to blame. She beamed at Max. 'Ah, those were the days, when my husband was alive. We used to dance until dawn, and if I remember correctly, you were one of the most eligible bachelors in the room. You and poor William.'

Max murmured in Libby's ear, 'William was their son. He was a merchant banker when I started at my first firm, but he joined the army and died in Bosnia.'

Lady Antonia was still talking. 'When William was a little boy, he used to love that ring. He would make me take it from the safe and let the sun shine through it so he could see rainbows.' Emotion glinted in her eyes.

Max touched her hand. 'I can tell your ring's very precious. Let's see if we can't track it down. First, I think we should make sure it isn't in your bag.' He held up a finger, forestalling any objections. 'I know, we won't find it there, but the police would insist. After all, it could have slipped off your finger when you reached for a handkerchief or pulled out some confetti...'

Mollified, Antonia Appleby clicked open her bag and emptied the contents in a small heap on the pristine white tablecloth. Handkerchief, comb, lipstick, and powder compact, the indispensable accompaniment to a formal occasion for a woman like Lady Antonia. She opened a small silver case and held it out for Max to see. 'See, there's William in his uniform with his father. Both of them gone, now.'

Libby leaned across to catch a glimpse of a tall, tanned man in the uniform of the Coldstream Guards, his arm around an older man. Both men shared similar Roman noses, but the older of the two had an impressive shock of white hair and wore a mayoral chain around his neck. Libby swallowed the lump that had formed in her throat and forgave the lonely widow her need for alcohol.

'Nothing there. I told you so.' Lady Antonia snatched up the handkerchief and touched one corner delicately to her eyes.

Max helped replace the items in her bag. 'Indeed you did. Now, why don't you talk to my business partner, Libby Forest. She works miracles, finding missing treasures.' Max's gaze met Libby's. The last thing Libby had retrieved was a missing cat, but there was no need to tell Lady Antonia. 'If she can't find your ring, of course we'll call the police.'

'Isn't your son, a what-do-you-call-it? Locks people up? A policeman, that's the word. Don't suppose he's of sufficiently high rank to lead an important investigation like this.'

'Joe's a detective sergeant.' Max spoke patiently.

'In that case,' Lady Antonia pronounced, 'I suppose he'll do, if necessary. Still, I'll let this young lady try first. Ask me your questions.' She pushed her face close to Libby's. 'Let's see what you're made of.'

Confused by the elderly lady's sudden mood changes, but happy to be called young, for once, Libby asked, 'I believe you're Sarah's aunt?'

'Exactly so. Great aunt. No, aunt.' The woman frowned, waved a hand in the air, and took another gulp of wine. 'Something like that.'

'What time did you arrive at the cathedral?'

'I was one of the first. It gave me the opportunity to catch up with the man in charge. Wearing one of those red robes. Family friend, you see. We had a good old chat. What was his name, now?' She frowned, but after a moment her brow cleared. 'Oh, never mind. Now, where was I?'

Was Lady Antonia's difficulty with names just due to the alcohol she'd drunk today, or was there a different problem? Libby couldn't tell. With care, she led the old lady through the details of the wedding day. It turned out Lady Antonia always travelled by taxi. 'Did you have the ring on your finger when you arrived at the cathedral?'

'Cathedral? What cathedral? I haven't set foot in the place since they refused to let me bury my husband in the crypt. Ridiculous rules and regulations. A man of my husband's importance should rest in the most prominent position, don't you know?'

She peered at Libby. 'What was I saying? Oh, yes. I talked to the rector at the church.'

Libby let the confusion pass. It hardly mattered if the old lady thought Wells Cathedral was just a church. 'When you arrived here, at the farm, you were wearing the ring?'

'I especially remember because I saw several of the local people glancing at it. I only remove it from the bank for special occasions. Weddings and funerals.' She pointed at Sarah, who was watching proceedings from a distance. 'She's wearing my family pearls, today.'

'Something borrowed,' Libby acknowledged. 'I expect you were looking forward to a family celebration.'

The woman drained the remainder of her champagne and Max replaced it with a full glass. 'I felt an obligation to represent my side of the family, although a wedding reception on farmland seems a little...' Lady Antonia surveyed the marquee from one end to another, 'A little *unusual*.'

With every word, Libby grew more convinced the poor woman was struggling with memory problems. It complicated matters. Had she really been wearing the ring, or had she left it at home? There was no way to tell, unless someone had noticed it on her finger. Perhaps Sarah had seen it.

Leaving Max to entertain his mother's old friend, Libby joined the newly wed couple for a whispered conversation. Sarah confirmed her great aunt had frequent memory lapses. 'I don't remember seeing the ring today, but she would usually wear it. It's her pride and joy, because Uncle Humphrey bought it for their first wedding anniversary. She's lost a lot of weight recently. I don't think she eats properly now she's living alone. The ring was loose and it could easily have slipped from her finger.'

'Could we organise a quick search, in case she just dropped it?'

Robert's eyes sparkled at the idea of gathering their friends, boisterous with champagne, to scour the surroundings. 'Like a treasure hunt.'

Max had overheard. 'I'm sure they'll find it. I'd lay odds the ring just slipped off her finger.'

After an hour, though, Robert and Sarah admitted defeat. The ring was nowhere to be found.

* * *

'Time to call in the police?' Max suggested.

Lady Antonia's enthusiasm for the local constabulary had waned. 'Perhaps we should leave it until tomorrow.' Her words slurred together. 'We don't want to spoil the wedding.'

Libby hunted for Belinda, finally locating her outside the marquee, well away from her aunt. 'Is it the alcohol talking, or is Lady Antonia really having second thoughts about calling the police? Do you know how much the ring's really worth?'

Belinda concentrated on the nail she was nibbling, despite ruining an expensive wedding manicure. 'I think she likes the attention. She's very old and forgetful. Why don't you leave her to me and I'll talk to her tomorrow? After all, we don't want to make a fuss.' With a little wave of her fingers, she disappeared into the melee of wedding guests.

'I don't know what to make of it,' Libby confessed to Max. 'One minute, Belinda has a problem she wants me to solve and her aunt's ring is so valuable we need the police. Then, it turns out both problems were no more than silly mistakes. I'm beginning to think Sarah's mother and great aunt have more in common than it first appears.'

'Both got loose screws, you mean?'

'Hope not. My son's married into that family, don't forget.'

Max gave an exaggerated groan. 'Have you thought about the grandchildren? How are they going to turn out?' Libby just rolled her eyes as he went on, 'What about this missing ring?'

'Just thank our lucky stars Lady Antonia hasn't insisted on the police.'

They walked outside, enjoying the smell of newly mown hay, and the tang of dairy cows, lying in the quiet summer air. 'It's been a strange afternoon.'

'I love the way mystery follows you around.' Max linked his arm with Libby's. 'If you're worried, we could do a little quiet sleuthing to see what's worrying Belinda. What do you know about the rest of the family?'

'There's Sarah's father, Mike. According to Sarah, he spends every waking hour out in the fields or in his office managing the farm.'

'I don't know Mike well,' Max said. 'But he's a member of the skittles team.'

Libby laughed. 'That's a vote of confidence, then.'

'Who's that talking to Sarah?'

'Tim. He's Sarah's older brother, but doesn't live on the farm. Works for a feed company in Minehead, I believe.'

It was almost dark, the clear sky filling with stars. 'Time for the evening entertainment?' Max took Libby's arm as they strolled inside to find a group of young farmers clutching guitars, ukuleles, and an accordion.

The leader counted, 'One, two, three, four...' the guests

cheered, and the band launched into one of the Wurzels' greatest hits.

As the guests roared out a chorus at the top of their lungs, the marquee shuddered and rocked as a heavy weight hit the canvas. A woman screamed. After a moment of stunned silence, the guests rushed outside to find a young man entangled in guy ropes.

He staggered up, cursing. Sarah's brother, Tim, smart wedding suit tight on the legs and arms, fists raised, aimed a punch at the young man's head. 'I know you took it.'

This time, his opponent was ready. He ducked sideways and Tim crashed to the ground. Winded, he gasped, 'Search his pockets. He's got the ring.'

'You lying...'

Robert appeared. 'What's going on? Tim, what's this all about?'

'Liam Weston's got the ring. I saw him pick it up.' Tim stood, brushing grass from his jacket.

The other lad narrowed his eyes. Built like a boxer, he looked capable of giving Tim Carmichael a hammering. 'I dropped a coin, that's all.'

'Prove it.'

Sarah was sobbing. 'Tim, please don't do this. You've had too much to drink.'

'Look here, Sarah.' Liam Weston held out his hands. 'You know I'd never steal from your family. You've known me all your life.'

Sarah gulped.

'Tell you what, I'll turn my pockets out. Prove my innocence.'

He handed his jacket to Sarah. 'Look in the pockets.'

Sarah slid her hand into each pocket, one after another, inside and out. 'There's nothing there.' She held out one hand, showing the stub of a pencil and a few coins. 'That's all he's got.'

Tim's mouth twisted. 'What about his trouser pockets?'

'Oh, really.' Sarah snapped. 'You're going too far.'

Tim thrust his hands into the pockets of Liam's trousers and, with a triumphant flourish, held up the ring. 'See. Here it is.'

3

BRIDGE

'A dose of fresh air is just what we need.' Max turned off the Land Rover's engine and opened all the doors. Bear leapt out and waited, tongue lolling, for Shipley to follow. 'Should we keep Shipley on the lead?'

Libby came round the vehicle and leaned against the door, breathing in the scent of summer on Exmoor. 'I think we should. He's only lived with you a few days. He's always been a bit wild, and he's hard to control when he's over-excited. I wouldn't trust him around sheep.'

Libby had walked Shipley for his former owner when she first arrived in Exham on Sea. It broke her heart when he was abandoned. Tanya, the local vet, had taken him in on a temporary basis, but Libby begged Max to adopt him as a companion to Bear. She wondered if she'd made a mistake. Shipley was a springer spaniel, a breed known for excitability. He'd chased her cat, Fuzzy, into hiding in the airing cupboard on his first visit.

A warm breeze whipped Libby's hair against her face. 'That was some wedding reception.'

'I used to think my job was exciting until you came to Exham.'

Libby giggled. 'The past two years have been like a roller-coaster. I never know what's going to happen next. Good job I like surprises. It was a funny day, yesterday. I mean, apart from that stupid fight. Watching my only son get married made me feel old...' Her voice died away. She avoided mentioning marriage when she was with Max. He'd made it plain he wanted Libby in his life, and he'd mentioned marriage, but he'd never asked her in so many words if she would be his wife. She was glad of that, for she found it impossible to decide how she'd answer. Marriage seemed so final.

Libby's friend, Angela, had suggested Max was scared she might turn him down, but Libby had snorted. The man was so confident, so self-assured. If he wanted something, he'd ask for it. Angela had raised an immaculate eyebrow and given a knowing smile. 'People put on a good front, sometimes, to avoid disappointment. Is Max really as confident as you imagine? Maybe his divorce put him off another wedding.'

Libby grimaced. Her own marriage hadn't worked so well the first time, with Trevor. Her law abiding, insurance agent husband had turned out to be a criminal. If he hadn't died suddenly, he'd probably be in prison right now. As a result, reluctant to make another mistake, she'd reached some kind of impasse with Max. They'd agreed they wanted a relationship, but each kept stepping back from the brink of marriage.

As though following her train of thought, a discomforting knack he possessed, Max asked, 'Have Robert and Ali recovered from the shock of finding out their father was a crook?'

'Ali's seeking solace in fixing the world's problems. She's still in Brazil, volunteering. Robert was close to Trevor, but now he has Sarah.' Libby tugged Shipley's lead, pulling him back from Bear, who'd tracked down an interesting scent. 'I've recovered, too, mainly thanks to you, Max.'

'Stop. You'll make me blush.' As Max laughed, Libby breathed more easily. She'd navigated the awkward moment safely.

They followed a path through a field. Nearby, the hedges rustled with life. The air was filled with the song of blue tits and wrens, and from time to time a sparrow flashed across the path, driving Shipley mad with frustration. Dunster Castle dominated a hill in the distance. By the side of the field trickled one of the rivers that criss-cross Exmoor, its banks wooded with oak and beech. A lark rose, singing its heart-lifting song. Libby stopped and shaded her eyes against the sun, trying to spot the bird as it spiralled high in the air. 'Bear. Come here.' Bear looked over his shoulder, hesitated, finally lumbering back to her side. 'Should we find out more about the ring that caused all the trouble, do you think? Find out if Liam Weston planned to sell it, or if it was just a cruel joke that went too far?'

Max snorted. 'I was waiting for you to suggest it – I knew you couldn't resist the temptation. Of course, we won't get paid – not that you ever charge enough.'

Libby winced. She'd been a successful baker and chocolatier, but the fledgling private investigation service posed a far greater financial challenge. She often undertook inquiries for nothing.

'The really interesting cases are too exciting to resist, even when no one's paying for our services. Like the body in the cathedral library...'

Max threw a stick for Bear. 'I'm glad you said that, because you're right. It's hard to make ends meet on an ad hoc basis. I've been doing a few calculations of my own, and after a lot of negotiation, I've agreed an arrangement with my previous employers.'

'The government. You mean, you haven't entirely given up spying?'

He laughed. 'I think describing my financial audits as spying is going a bit far. Still, I heard from the police head honcho the other day. I did some work with them, if you remember, over a ring of vehicle thieves. The Chief Constable is looking at some kind of consultancy, paying a retainer, so he can call on private investigation services at short notice.'

Libby fell silent.

'What's wrong?' Max frowned into Libby's face. 'Don't you like that idea?'

She wriggled. 'I know it's ridiculous, but I feel a bit like the junior partner in this business. You're paying your way already.'

'You didn't let me finish.' Max stopped walking. 'It's not just my skills the police are interested in, but yours as well, especially since you took that online investigator's course. It shows you mean business. That business at the cathedral—'

'Didn't earn any money from that, did I?'

'But once again, you were ahead of the police. They've reorganised since Chief Inspector Arnold moved on. Joe's been promoted to detective inspector, and he's working for a new guy, Detective Chief Inspector Morrison.'

'And I suppose this Morrison is one of your secret handshake Masonic Brotherhood.'

Max laughed. 'You know I'm not a Mason. Wasn't it Groucho Marx who said he'd never join a society that would have him as a member? I think that applies to me. Anyway, those days are pretty much over. The Chief Constable can't go further than saying they're interested in working with us, but they'd like to,' he put on a pompous, official voice, 'interview us with a view to retaining us both as consultants.'

Libby felt a grin steal across her face. 'Imagine that. It would make me feel like a proper investigator.' She thought aloud. 'Mandy's been doing well with the chocolate business, so I could pass more of that to her. Still, it doesn't help our decision. Are we going to investigate the mystery of why Liam Weston stole the ring?'

'Look on it as a chance to hone your skills,' Max said. 'You know you want to.'

A little knot of excitement formed in Libby's stomach at the thought of working officially with the police. Maybe this private investigator business would work after all.

She jumped as Shipley barked, loudly, and tugged the lead. His nose was close to the ground, following an interesting scent. Libby slid her hand through his collar. He pulled against her, tail wagging, and barked again.

'Come on Shipley. You can't follow every rabbit down its hole.' The dog ignored her.

She hauled on the lead, but the dog resisted, paws planted firmly on the grass. Max looked back. 'What's bothering Shipley?'

'I don't know. Springers are bred as gun dogs. When they catch a scent, they stop and point with their noses. I don't think Shipley's been trained for that, but he's inherited a great sense of smell. He can find things even Bear doesn't notice.'

'Maybe we should let Shipley lead us. He seems very sure there's something interesting ahead. Maybe there are deer nearby.'

Libby let the lead go slack. 'Go on, old fellow. Show us what's bothering you.'

Shipley, no longer restrained, crept forward with legs bent, his belly close to the grass. He led the way down through the trees towards the river, following a muddy path. As they rounded a bend, a small stone bridge appeared in the distance, spanning the water.

'What's that?' A splash of red, ruby bright, caught Libby's attention.

'Not sure.' Max broke into a run. 'Looks like an accident.'

A tractor lay on its side where the bridge met the bank. Libby gasped. 'There's someone underneath.'

Panting, she knelt by the man's side. 'He's not dead, is he?'

'I'm very much afraid so.' Max's fingers searched for a pulse.

Libby's stomach heaved. 'Max, don't you see who it is?'

Max's face was grim. 'I'm afraid I do. It's that lad from the fight.'

'Liam Weston. The farmhand who works for Mike. The one who stole the ring.'

Max had his phone pressed to his ear, speaking to the police. Libby took a step back. The first time she'd found a body in Exham, she'd moved it. She still blushed at the memory. Joe Ramshore had been furious.

Still, it wouldn't hurt to look, as long as she didn't touch. Keeping her distance, she let her eyes run over every inch of Liam's body, from the baseball cap a few inches from his head, to a single battered brown boot. His other leg was twisted under his body.

Blood had trickled from a head wound and soaked into the ground, leaving ominous brown stains on the grass. Liam's eyes, sightless, stared up at the sky, where the lark still sang. Libby shivered.

Dividing the ground into imaginary quadrants, she tried to examine every tuft of grass with her eyes. Here and there, daisies poked cheerful heads above the grass. The ground was dry around Liam's body, since there had been no rain for days. She could see no sign of footprints.

Max called, 'They're on the way.'

Libby didn't reply. Something was glinting in the sunlight, close to Liam's body. She squinted. It was metallic and shiny. 'Max, can you see?' She pointed.

'What is it?'

'I can't tell exactly, but it looks like a key. A tiny, gold key.'

A car pulled up a hundred yards away, decanting the first police arrivals. Libby's fingers itched to pick up the key, but the police sergeant waved her away. In minutes, the area was sealed off with bright yellow tape, officers in white suits bent over the body and tractor. Photographers recorded every inch of the scene.

Libby's head swirled with questions.

* * *

'I'm afraid this has put the cart before the horse.' An air of gloom suffused Detective Chief Inspector Morrison's long face. Sitting opposite Libby and Max at a plain wooden table in the police station, he sucked coffee through a voluminous moustache.

Libby's heart had returned to normal but she couldn't shift the sick feeling inside her stomach. She would never get used to seeing a dead body.

DCI Morrison took a Hobnob from the plate, sighed, bit into it and continued. 'We were planning to meet with you to work out the kind of consultancy contract we need, according to all these rules and regulations we have to abide by for now.' He sighed again. 'It seems events have overtaken us, and you two have got yourselves involved already, so let's work together, see how things go, and use this nasty business as a trial run.' He took another bite of the biscuit, sat back in his chair, and narrowed his eyes, watching Libby's reaction. She hoped her expression conveyed the right amount of interest and gave no sign of her internal wobbles.

Morrison pursed his lips, nodded once, sharply, and continued, 'I'm the Senior Investigating Officer. Joe Ramshore will be leading the inquiry team, so you need to liaise with him. Max, I'm well aware he's your son, which is tricky, but I'll make sure that information goes up the line to the Commissioner, so there's no suspicion of nepotism.'

Max nodded. 'The last thing I want to do is tread on Joe's toes. I'm aware he's newly promoted and he'll want to do things properly.'

Morrison rotated the biscuit in his hand, regarding it intensely, as though wondering whether it was poisoned. Libby debated whether the man was naturally melancholy, or whether his job had driven him to despair. 'Of course. The police will handle all aspects of the investigation. Your role will be providing background checks where necessary. Be aware that at present this is an investigation into an accident.'

Libby said, 'Is there any evidence that it might be more than just an accident?'

The DCI took a long drink, replaced the mug on the table, and grimaced. 'Our minds are open at the moment. Given your past record of finding murder victims even when all the evidence points towards an accident, we're not ruling anything out.'

His eyes were sharp. 'I appreciate the low profile you've kept in the past, and the fact that your name rarely appears in the newspapers. I would very much like that to continue.' The police officer was giving her a warning.

She smiled as innocently as possible. 'What are you expecting us to do?'

'Make use of your local knowledge. Find out whether there's any possibility of foul play. There are one or two points I've asked my team to follow up, even before the pathologist's report arrives. For example, there are several bruises on the body, especially the arms. The bruises match, as though someone grabbed hold of the victim from behind. They could have been made by a thumb and fingers.'

Libby swallowed. 'I suppose you know about yesterday's fight?'

Morrison's faint smile showed he already had that piece of information. Less than two hours since they'd found the body and Morrison was already well on top of things. 'Why don't you fill me in?' he invited.

He was testing Libby's reliability. Joe must have told Morrison about the fight at the wedding. She'd better make sure she remembered accurately, or she'd find herself under suspicion. 'It was a family thing,' she began. 'The bride's brother had an argument with Liam Weston about...' She hesitated, then ploughed on. 'About a missing ring. It looks as though Liam had taken it from a rich aunt.'

DCI Morrison nodded. 'It could be nothing. Fights happen all the time at weddings. Young people pour beer into their stomachs and find any excuse to pick a quarrel. Too much testosterone, some of these lads.'

There was a knock at the door. 'Come in.'

Joe appeared. 'You sent for me, sir?'

Morrison unfolded his body from the chair. 'I'll leave you to talk. Today's other priority, I'm afraid, is my input to the report on traffic violations. More than my job's worth to be late submitting that piece of vital information to my colleagues. Detective Inspector, you're in charge of managing this part of the investigation. He looked at Max and Libby through sad brown eyes. 'Remember what I said. If family business gets in the way it will be the end of our alliance.'

4

DINNER

'Supper tonight at my place.' Max dropped Libby at her cottage. 'We invited people round, remember? I'll pick you up about six?'

Libby groaned. 'I'd forgotten. What was I thinking, planning a supper a couple of days after the wedding? I haven't cooked and there's nothing in the freezer...' Her memory kicked in. 'Oh no. We've invited everyone; Angela, Mandy and Reg. And Claire's coming with Joe. I mean...'

Max laughed. 'Don't look so guilty. I know what you mean. You're a little scared of Joe's wife, aren't you?' Claire was a psychiatric social worker; the kind of organised, professional woman that remembered appointments and made Libby nervous.

'I like Claire. She's very kind and terribly clever, but every time I meet her, I do something embarrassing, like throw up. And you can stop laughing, Max Ramshore.'

'That wasn't your fault. You'd been poisoned, that day on the Levels. I'm sure Claire thinks you're wonderful.'

She doubted that. 'I'd like to show her I can do something properly, but it looks as though we'll be serving beans on toast tonight.'

'Relax,' Max advised. 'We don't meet up to test your cooking. I'll order a take-away: onion dopiaza all round.'

* * *

The friends had meant to spend the evening comparing photos of the wedding, now the happy couple had left for their honeymoon, but Liam Weston's death drove those plans out of everyone's heads and they talked of little else. Claire, tucking a strand of shiny hair behind an ear, held up a warning hand. 'Don't forget, I'm no super sleuth, like the rest of you.'

Mandy swallowed a mouthful of rice. 'Nor me. I mean to keep well away from the Ramshore and Forest private investigations.'

Max scoffed, 'You're Libby's right-hand man, young lady, and don't forget it.' He paused. 'Maybe I should say right-hand woman. Sounds odd, though.'

Libby hardly registered the words. She'd stopped eating, a heaped fork waving, ignored, halfway to her mouth. Was it her imagination, or did Mandy seem unusually subdued? She stole a glance at Reg, Max's American colleague. He'd appeared on the scene a few months ago, investigating thefts of ancient books, and Mandy had fallen for his southern charm. Libby wasn't surprised. The man was well over six feet tall, with a shaven head, enormous, sensitive hands and a honey-toned voice to die for. She was almost sure his work in England, investigating the theft of valuable books on behalf of the International League of Antiquarian Booksellers, was coming to an end. Perhaps Mandy was already pining.

Max whisked away used plates and topped up the wine glasses. 'What do people think? Are we looking at a murder?'

Libby said, 'I know jumping to conclusions is one of my faults, but this time, I'm not so sure. Liam's death could easily be an accident. Tractors turn over far too often on farms.'

Joe agreed. 'All the signs are that Liam was careless. The ground slopes sharply by the river. If he was driving too fast, or misjudged just a little, the tractor wheels could have hit the edge of the bridge hard enough to topple it over.'

'On the other hand,' Max put in, 'Liam was an experienced driver. He's worked on the farm for years. Why would he suddenly make a rookie mistake?'

Libby ran a finger round the top of her wine glass. 'It was the day after that fight at the wedding. No one likes being accused of theft, and it would surely have preyed on Liam's mind. He'd probably had too much to drink at the reception, so he'd be suffering from a hangover as well as a few bruises from the fight, and he'd be worried Lady Antonia, or Tim, might go to the police about the ring, and that he'd lose his job on the farm.'

Max turned to Joe. 'Does he have a record of any sort?'

'A caution once, for being drunk and disorderly in Taunton after a night out. Apart from that, he's clean as a whistle.'

'What about forensics?'

'Nothing yet. Without signs of foul play, the post-mortem isn't high priority, so we'll have to wait a day or two for results. I've asked for an analysis of the stomach contents and blood samples to see if he'd taken anything.'

Libby asked, 'What sort of thing?'

'A few of the young farmers around here take drugs,' Joe pointed out. 'There's a lot of depression in the industry. It's not just low milk prices, though that hasn't helped, but some of the farmers never got back on their feet after foot and mouth wiped out their herds.'

Angela joined the discussion. She'd sat quietly until now, but she'd been born in Somerset and had an encyclopaedic knowledge of everyone in the county. 'Liam didn't have business worries. He'd been working at Handiwater Farm while he saved up enough to start his own herd. Any worries about making a living would sit with Belinda and Mike.'

Max smiled. 'I think that gives us a clue where we need to start looking.'

Libby was keen to visit Belinda after the woman's odd behaviour at the wedding. 'I'll take a trip out to the farm and see how things are.' She said nothing about Belinda's money worries. She'd told Max in confidence, as her business partner, but had no right to spread the information further. Belinda's talk of financial pressures had roused her curiosity and she'd like to know more about the farm. If it was in serious trouble, the farm workers would be worried about their jobs. Perhaps Liam, nervous about the future, had seen the ring in the grass and seized an opportunity to make some easy cash.

Joe sounded enthusiastic. 'Maybe Max could do a little digging into the farm's financial affairs. I can't get a warrant for surrendering them to the police, but there'll be records available. After all, they're a limited company. They have to post accounts at Companies House every year.'

Claire, his wife, sat quietly as the others talked. She looked from one face to another, alert, following the conversation, but her eyes kept returning to Mandy. Libby hid a smile. Mandy wore two eyebrow rings, a stud in the middle of her lower lip, a cross attached to the side of her nose, and earrings that jangled loudly with every movement of the head. No wonder Claire found it hard to tear her eyes away.

The small frown creasing Claire's forehead deepened. Her gaze tracked to Mandy and back to Libby. Was she sending a message? Libby took a closer look at Mandy's face. A light film of sweat showed through the white powder on her nose and fore-head. Libby spoke quietly. 'Are you feeling unwell?'

Mandy stared at the table. 'I'm fine.' Her voice shook, and Claire raised an eyebrow. Libby gave a tiny nod, and as the others tucked into ice cream, they both watched Mandy pushing it around the plate. Hardly a single spoonful reached her mouth.

Finally, even Reg noticed her behaviour. 'Mandy, I'm starting to worry whether it's safe to eat the food. You haven't swallowed anything. I guess you didn't doctor it in some way, when you were out in the kitchen?'

Mandy dropped her spoon, shoved her chair back and rose to her feet, rocking the table. Cutlery rattled and a drop of wine slopped over the rim of Libby's glass. Mandy's cheeks flamed as she gasped, 'I didn't— I can't—' With a sob, she dashed the back of one hand across her eyes and ran from the room.

In the moment of shocked silence, Libby rose to follow, but Claire touched her arm. 'Probably best to let her have a moment alone.'

Concern was written all over Reg's big, kind face. 'I didn't mean to upset her.'

'Have you told her you're going back to the States soon?' Libby asked. 'You know she has a crush on you.'

'Sure, I told her. We had a little thing going for a while, but it kind of fizzled out. Mandy's spent the past few weeks telling me about that ex-boyfriend of hers. What's his name? Steve? I guess I've been something of a father figure. Just as well. I can't stand that music she listens to.'

A knot of worry in Libby's stomach tightened as she remembered a conversation with Mandy about another panic attack she'd suffered on a crowded train, and admitted to sometimes feeling claustrophobic. Despite Libby's pleading, she'd refused to get help, and forbade any further discussion of the matter.

Libby didn't feel she could tell the others about Mandy's private business, but she suspected this evening's problem went deeper than simply feeling unwell. It seemed Mandy's problems had not, as Libby had hoped, disappeared. She whispered, 'Claire, could I have a word?'

She led the way into Max's study. Once there, second thoughts struck her dumb. Claire prompted, 'You know something about Mandy, don't you? Can you give me a hint?'

Libby bit her lip. 'I don't want to break a confidence.'

'It's OK, Mrs F.' Mandy had followed them into the room. 'You're a psychiatric nurse, Claire, aren't you?'

Claire nodded. 'Kind of. Do you want to talk?'

Mandy blew her nose.

Claire beckoned Mandy to an armchair. 'Maybe you'd better start at the beginning. The others can manage without us for a while.'

Libby left them alone. Curiosity ate into her, but she had no business interfering. Neither spoke of their private conversation when they returned to the table. The other guests, with admirable discretion, managed to avoid any reference to Mandy's odd behaviour, instead making a great show of wondering about the tiny key found near Liam's body. Reg spoke for them all when he said, 'What in the world would a big guy like Liam Weston want with a tiny key like that?'

5

FARM VISIT

Libby rose early the next morning, planning to visit Belinda at Handiwater farm. At least the trip would take Libby's mind off Mandy's woes, and maybe answer a few questions about Liam. She planned to take Bear and Shipley for the ride, hoping to borrow Max's Land Rover, for the dogs really wouldn't fit comfortably into her purple Citroen. Bear had often ridden in the back, overflowing the seat and drooling over Libby's headrest, but the notion of shoe-horning Shipley into the little car seemed a step too far.

Max, already seated at his computer, huge coffee cup alongside a substantial slice of Libby's ginger cake, glanced up through steel-rimmed glasses. 'I'm checking the farm's public accounts.' He took a giant bite of cake, gave a vague nod in answer to Libby's suggestion she take the Land Rover, waved an arm in her direction, and returned to his screen.

The road to the farm trailed for more than half a mile through a patch of woodland, winding round fields of sheep, finally ending in a pristine farmyard. Libby wore wellies, expecting to wade through mud, but the stones of the yard were swept clean as a suburban patio. To one side a row of three quad bikes gleamed, chrome polished to a sparkle, paint spotless.

The farmhouse, long and low, was built of local Ham stone. The woodwork sparkled with fresh paint and crystal-clear windows reflected the bright summer sun. There was no sign the place suffered from lack of funds, as Belinda had suggested.

The dogs firmly secured on their leads, Libby rapped on the farmhouse door. No reply. She knocked once more, stepped back and gazed around for inspiration. The house was fronted by a small area devoted to vegetables and flowers and a tiny patch of lawn, but beyond, a metal gate led to a set of outbuildings. Libby tied the dogs to the gate and approached the nearest outbuilding.

She slipped through the door, hearing the gentle hum and rhythmic pumping of a milking parlour, smelling the warm scent of cattle. The black and white cows took no notice of her arrival. They munched hay, apparently untroubled by the pumps attached to their udders. As the milking machinery purred to a halt, the gate at one end of the building clanged open to release the cows, lowing quietly, into a field. The gate closed behind the last animal and its partner at the other end opened to let more enter. Mike appeared at Libby's side. 'Morning, Libby. I guess we're related now the kids have tied the knot.'

'Wells Cathedral was a beautiful place for a wedding, and Sarah looked lovely. You must have been very proud.'

'Ah,' Mike muttered, shifting awkwardly as though uncomfortable with personal conversations.

'See our new robotic milking system? Impressive, isn't it? Hardly any need for me to be here. Not like the old days when we milked by hand.' He seemed far more relaxed talking about the farm.

Libby shook her head. 'It's all most efficient.'

The man grunted. 'You thought I'd be sitting on a three legged stool, my head against the cow's stomach, pulling on the teats by hand?'

Libby laughed. 'I'm ashamed to say you're right. I'm a townie, at heart.'

'Well, I don't suppose you came to watch our latest technology, did you?' Mike narrowed his eyes and wiped his hands on a hank of cloth.

'Take over, Jake, will you?'

An older man in brown overalls grunted as he passed from one cow to another, washing the udders. Mike leaned on the gate, gazing across his fields. 'You found young Liam's body, I hear.' He pulled off his cap, twisting it between calloused fingers. 'A bad business, that. He'd been down that field many a time, and there are plenty of steeper slopes. Can't imagine what the lad was thinking, letting the tractor tip over. Must have been going too fast, I suppose, the young fool.'

'I came to see Belinda, really. You know, see if she's OK, what with that fight at the wedding, and then Liam's death. I thought she might be upset.'

Mike Carmichael led Libby into the house, scratching the back of his head. 'Ah, well now, you've missed Belinda. Gone to town, she has. Shopping therapy, she calls it. Can't think of anything worse, myself, but she reckons it's relaxing. Buying shoes, I reckon. Got a cupboard full, upstairs.'

Mike gestured towards the kettle. 'Tea?' Libby smiled, hiding a sense of unease. It seemed an odd time to go shopping, so soon after Liam Weston's accident. Belinda must be worried sick. Apart from distress at the sudden death of a young man she knew well, there were implications for the farm. The tractor might turn out to be faulty, or badly maintained. Health and safety inspectors would be involved, and the farm could end up in court.

Libby tried to be charitable. Perhaps Belinda needed to get

away from her worries for a few hours. One thing was clear – she wouldn't be talking to Libby this morning.

'Bring the dogs in,' Mike said. 'We're used to muddy paws here.'

Bear sprawled in front of the door while Shipley sniffed every corner of the kitchen, hoping for titbits. He was out of luck. The floor was immaculate and the room smelled of lemon scented polish.

A square scrubbed table dominated the room, an Aga and a deep Belfast sink were ranged along one wall, and an enormous, heavy duty washing machine vibrated quietly nearby. Mike brewed tea, offering a mug of dark liquid and pushing a bowl of sugar across the table. Libby softened the tea with milk from a tall, white jug. 'From your cows?'

Mike winked. 'Raw milk, that is, straight from the cow. The best sort, but we're not allowed to sell it. No, every drop has to be pasteurised and sent off to the supermarkets, to sell for less than it costs to produce.'

He peered at Libby under bushy eyebrows. Two vertical lines appeared on his forehead. 'Now, maybe you've not come to see Belinda after all, Mrs Forest.' His voice hardened. 'Let's get down to brass tacks. You're here to find out about Liam, aren't you?'

Libby didn't bother to deny it. 'I expect the police have visited?'

'Of course. They say there's no reason to suppose Liam's death is anything but an accident. Clumsiness, and too much to drink the day before, poor fellow. Ah. We'll miss the lad. He was a good worker.' Mike's weather-beaten face, wrinkled and leathery from days in the sun, wind, and rain gave no clue to his real feelings.

Libby asked, 'How long did Liam work here?'

'First came on the farm when he was a toddler. His ma used to bring him over to see Belinda. One of the Skinners, she was. Died a few years ago. Cancer or something. It was a bad time for young Liam. His dad went during the foot and mouth.'

'Went? Left home, you mean?'

Mike's voice sounded bitter. 'Not he. Did away with himself. Lost the farm, you see. The whole herd had to be slaughtered. Dumped in one great pit, set on fire, and buried over yonder.' Mike waved an arm towards the window where the rolling landscape stretched to the horizon. Libby shivered. One of those tranquil green pastures hid a grave full of the ashes of a man's livelihood and dreams.

'Liam, though, he still wanted to work on the land. He's been saving up, putting money aside, just about ready to start his own dairy herd, he told me. Not that there's profit to be had in milkers, not these days.'

'I expect you have to diversify.' Was that the right terminology?

Mike heaved a long sigh. 'That's right. Can't make a living from cattle, not these days. We rent out a couple of cottages down in the valley.'

'It's a great place for tourists.'

'That it is. Walking, that's the favourite. Too hilly in this part of Somerset for the cyclists, but camping and riding keep them coming. Then, there's Wimbleball Lake for water sports.' For the first time, Mike grinned. 'We make a good profit off the grockles, that's for sure. Come every year, some of them.'

He lapsed back into silence. Libby prompted, 'Then, there's cheese and yoghurt. I expect they're profitable?'

He shrugged. 'We manage.' His mouth clamped shut, making it clear any further discussion of his finances was off limits.

* * *

As Libby pondered her next question, a vehicle screeched to a halt in the yard. Mike stumbled to his feet without a word, opened the door, and left the kitchen, letting the door bang shut behind him. More surprised than offended, Libby stood by the window, out of sight of the two arrivals emerging from a mud stained four wheel drive vehicle.

One of the newcomers was female, a middle-aged woman in a Barbour jacket, faded hair straggling to her shoulders. It was the sight of her companion that sent a chill down Libby's back.

Xavier Papadopoulos, the grey man she'd met at the wedding reception, wore the loose trousers and kaftan of a would-be guru. A necklace of beads and feathers reached halfway down his chest as he towered above Mike, hovering like an eagle over a mouse. Mike seemed to shrink under the other man's gaze.

Libby leaned close to the window, listening, nerves jangling, butterflies circling her stomach. As the man's eyes slid over the house, she shrank back, hoping he hadn't noticed her peering from the window. Expressionless, he turned away towards the yard and Libby clicked her tongue, annoyed at her own edginess. She knew nothing about the man. He was tall, imposing, and oddly dressed, but that was no reason to fear him. He'd done her no harm.

If only she could hear what they were saying. With a burst of determination, she shoved the door open. Why should she cower in the house as though she had something to hide? Squaring her shoulders, she stepped outside and smiled. 'Hello. I'm Libby Forest.' Her voice was too loud. She tried again, keeping her tone even. 'We met at the wedding.'

Mike turned and looked at her, his eyes so dark in a white face that Libby took an instinctive step back inside the house. Too late, she spotted Bear. Always ready to defend her, he'd crept close to her side and she stumbled against him, saving herself from a humiliating fall with a grab at the fur round his neck. Her right elbow hit the wall with a painful crack.

Regaining her balance, she lifted her chin, trying to retain some dignity. The grey man was openly smirking. Bear growled, the noise rumbling low in his chest, his lips quivering. He snarled, exposing sharp canines. 'It's OK, Bear.' Shipley stood still, alert, every muscle rigid.

Libby spoke to Mike. 'The dogs are nervous.'

The farmer blinked twice before replying, as though he found it hard to focus on Libby. 'Did you hurt your elbow?' he asked at last.

Libby forced a smile, trying not to grimace. Her elbow burned, but she'd be dragged from the yard by wild horses before she'd admit it in front of Xavier Papadopoulos. 'Not at all. I can see you're busy so I won't keep you. I'll come back when Belinda's here.'

Xavier Papadopoulos stretched out his hand. The familiar voice was silky smooth. 'Mrs Forest. It's a pleasure to meet again.' He held Libby's hand a moment too long. Clenching her jaw, refusing to blink, she stared into intense grey eyes, until with a knowing smile the man dropped her hand.

It took an effort to overcome the instinct to wipe her palm on the seat of her jeans. Libby spoke to Mike. 'Say hello to Belinda for me.'

The farmer swallowed, looked at the floor, and muttered something indistinguishable about a quiz that Belinda wouldn't want to miss.

The visitor's companion had watched the brief pantomime without a word. Intrigued by her silence, Libby smiled. 'I'm sorry, I didn't catch your name.'

A nerve twitched in the woman's face. Before she could

answer, Xavier Papadopoulos interrupted. 'This is Olivia. My wife.'

'Pleased to meet you.' The atmosphere crackled with tension, and Bear slipped between Libby and the visitors.

Libby had rarely felt so unwelcome. 'Thank you for the tea, Mike.' She was reluctant to admit defeat. She'd be back. 'Here's my card. Could you ask Belinda to phone me later? I'd like to talk to her about the wedding. There's been no opportunity to have a good gossip.'

Without reading the card, Mike slipped it straight into the pocket of his jacket. Libby felt three sets of eyes boring into her back as she loaded the dogs into the Land Rover, started the engine, and drove away.

She whistled, feeling pent-up strain seep from her body. 'You dogs didn't care for Olivia and Xavier Papadopoulos any more than I did. The man gives me the creeps, and he dominates his wife. I wonder who they are and why Mike was suddenly so nervous when they arrived.' She accelerated up the lane. 'We need to do a little more sleuthing around the area. It's almost lunchtime. Let's find a local pub where dogs are welcome.'

At the end of Mike's long drive, signs pointed in two directions. One was labelled Compton Rival, the other Upper Compton. 'Which do you think?'

Neither dog expressed a preference, so Libby turned left, towards Compton Rival. Less than a mile down the road she passed the first of a small row of cottages. The terrace included half a dozen front doors and separate patches of ground, each defined by its owner's taste: one area packed with bean poles, raspberry canes and strawberries; another covered with Astro-Turf; and another a riot of poppies, cornflowers and hollyhocks.

An elderly man, hard at work in a vegetable garden, raised his head, leaned on a spade, and rubbed his back. Libby slowed the car and called, 'Is there a pub in the village?'

The gardener chuckled and pointed a bony, earth stained finger along the road. 'You're almost there, m'dear, if you're looking for the Red Cow. Go on a bit further and you'll find the Gate Hangs High. Take your pick.'

Libby thanked him and released the handbrake. How could two pubs in the same tiny hamlet make a living? As promised, she arrived at the Red Cow as she rounded the first corner. She drew up in front of the pub. Baskets crammed with cheerful lobelia, petunias and fuchsias hung on the wall, and a vast tin bowl full of water sat beside the door. 'This will do nicely,' Libby told the dogs. 'It seems you're welcome here.'

She unlatched a heavy wooden door and pushed it open, breathing in the country pub smell of real ale, years of wood fires, and floor polish. Cool and dark, in contrast to the blaze of the midday sun outside, the room at first appeared deserted, but as Libby's eyes grew accustomed to the dim light she spotted a woman behind the bar. A little older than Libby, dressed in a tight, low cut pink blouse with copious frills round the neckline, the woman polished the spotless bar with a bright yellow duster. 'Come in, do. What can I get for you?'

At last, someone was pleased to see them. Libby could have hugged the bartender. 'Are you serving lunch yet?'

'Anytime.' The woman pointed to the wall. 'The specials are on the board.'

Libby deliberated, ordered a soft drink and a goat's cheese and red onion tart, and chose a seat at a small round table. Situated in the bay window, she could watch the road. Any sign of the Papadopoulos couple and she'd be out of the place in a second.

The woman bustled round with knives and forks, glasses and napkins. 'You're not from round here, are you?' Her voice was cheerful. 'On your holidays?'

Libby smothered a sigh. Holidays were a thing of the distant past. 'I live in Exham,' she confessed. 'I'm just enjoying the countryside today. It's my day off.' If only that were true. 'Lovely out here, isn't it?'

The woman leaned on the bar, ready to chat. 'Full of summer visitors at the moment. This place will be heaving in half an hour. You've arrived just in time to beat the rush.'

'I've been visiting Handiwater Farm. I expect Belinda and Mike come in here quite often?'

The woman shook her head. 'Not them. They go to Upper Compton.'

'The two villages are very separate, then?'

The woman gave a fruity chuckle and settled her blouse more comfortably on her shoulders. 'I should say so. Them at Upper Compton think themselves a cut above those of us down here in Compton Rival. They wouldn't be seen dead in this old pub.'

Libby looked around. 'But it's lovely. They're missing a treat.'

'Nice of you to say so.' A bell pinged behind the bar. 'That's your dinner ready.'

Libby tucked into her tart, enjoying the raspberry dressing on the salad and making a mental note to make something similar at home. A group of three walkers arrived, equipped with boots and rucksacks, and sat at a nearby table. The barmaid organised their drinks and food, and Libby was left to wonder, in silence, why the two villages didn't get on.

Bear and Shipley had emptied the water bowl at the door and now sat at her feet, watching with unblinking eyes as the newly arrived humans tucked in to plates of steak, alert for any food that might fall on the floor. Libby finished her meal and returned to the bar. 'Is there anything I can give the dogs? I've been out longer than I intended and they're hungry.'

'Of course, my dear.' She pattered behind the bar, returning with a dish of beef scraps. 'There, that should do. Nice dogs.' She sniffed. 'They'll not be welcome in Upper Compton, you know. That Zavvy Papadopoulos and his wife will see to that.'

Libby kept her tone light, keeping up the pretence of a general chat, as she paid the bill 'I met them earlier today.'

The barmaid puffed air between her lips in a show of disgust. 'You don't want to have much to do with them. Think they own the county, they do, living in that old house. That Olivia comes from one of the oldest families round here, and Coombe House belongs to her. She was a pretty girl back in the day. You wouldn't know it from the look of her now, but they say you grow to look like your husband, don't they? Or is it your dogs?' She looked from Libby to Bear and chuckled. 'Olivia used to get on all right with the rest of us until she met that Zavvy and had her head turned.'

'Unusual name for this part of the world, Papadopoulos.'

The bartender polished knives with a bright yellow tea towel. 'Olivia met him on a Greek island. Had a holiday in one of those retreats, where you go to lose weight, or stop smoking, or some such. I don't hold with that sort of nonsense, myself. People with too much money and not enough sense or willpower to sort out their own lives, if you ask me.'

She leaned across the bar and dropped her voice to a whisper. 'I heard Olivia had a problem.' She glanced round the room, leaned closer, and hissed, 'Drugs, you know.'

She dipped glasses in a bowl of frothy water, dried them on her towel until they squeaked, and hung them in a wooden rack over the bar. 'That's why her family sent her out there. They got more than they bargained for when she came back from Greece with Zavvy. Nasty piece of work, he is. Wouldn't be surprised if he was behind Liam Weston's accident.'

'You've heard about that, then.'

'All round the village. We don't keep no secrets out here. Poor young fellow, Liam. Nothing but bad luck in that family.'

'His parents' farm went bust in the foot and mouth, or so I heard...'

The barmaid took a long look at Libby. The friendly smile had evaporated. She sucked her teeth. 'You heard that, did you? Got a good grapevine?' She turned away to polish the Exmoor

Ale beer pump with a vigour that signalled the end of the conversation. Libby called the dogs and made her way out. She'd asked one question too many. The barmaid showed every sign of regretting her earlier gossip.

As Libby reached the door, the woman coughed, glanced round at the walkers and muttered. 'Liam's dad's farm was a mile down the road in that direction.' She flicked her head to the right. 'Just the farmhouse left now, on the edge of Upper Compton. If you go down there, you watch your step. Make sure those dogs are with you. You can't be too careful.'

Libby drove back the way she'd come, passing the lane leading to Mike's farm. Half a mile later she came to a tumbledown brick building set back from the road on the edge of the next village. Curious, she stopped the Land Rover and walked across, peering through cracked windows into desolate, neglected rooms.

There was nothing else to see, and certainly no evidence to suggest she needed the dogs' protection. What had the barmaid meant by her warning? Was she talking about Liam's dilapidated old family home, or was there danger in Upper Compton, where the unpleasant Papadopoulos couple ruled the roost?

7

MANDY

Still unsettled by the unpleasant episode with Mike and his visitors, Libby was glad to spend the next morning in the Exham bakery with Mandy. Frank, the baker, was on his day off, and he'd rearranged their schedule so Libby and Mandy spent one day a week working together. Delighted with the recent improvement in the fortunes of the bakery, mostly as a result of the popularity of Libby's cake recipes and luxury chocolates, Frank was keen to encourage Mandy in her training.

This afternoon, the supervisor from the local further education college was planning a visit. In a couple of weeks, Mandy would be taking her first exam on the route to a qualification in catering. Libby offered to rearrange the meeting, to give Mandy a chance to recover from her distress during supper, but her apprentice turned down the offer. 'I'm fine, Mrs F. I don't know what came over me.'

'Don't worry. If you need anything from me, just ask. Otherwise we'll carry on as normal.' Mandy hadn't confided in Libby about her talk with Claire, and Libby knew her apprentice better than to ask too many questions.

Mandy moved around the kitchen, as though unable to keep still. 'To tell you the truth, Mrs F, I'm nervous about this afternoon.'

'Well, there's no need to worry. You're doing a great job in the business. I'm sure you'll sail through the supervisor's questions with no difficulty.'

Mandy's laugh sounded shaky. 'I'd rather be selling chocs to shops like Jumbles than answering questions. I know I can do that, but I was hopeless at school. Not a single qualification.'

'Well, this is your chance to shine, because I'll be writing a great report on your progress. You've been a real asset.'

Mandy's cheeks turned pink. 'Thanks, Mrs F.' She took a very deep breath. Libby kept busy, stacking chocolate boxes on shelves, saying nothing, sensing Mandy had something to say. 'That Claire,' Mandy ventured, 'she says I could talk to one of her therapist friends about this claustrophobia problem of mine.' She pronounced the word with care. 'Claire says it's more common than people imagine. She reckons it's easy to deal with in just a few sessions.'

Libby nodded, wishing Mandy had taken her advice months ago and asked for professional help. She'd been more distressed by Mandy's panic attack the other evening than she'd admitted. Now, it looked as though it was a blessing in disguise. 'I think that's a great idea. Claire knows what she's talking about.'

'She says I don't need to worry about seeing a psychiatrist every week for a year, like I thought. She says I'm not mad. I just got into bad habits.'

'Sounds very positive. Have you got an appointment?'

'That's the trouble. I'm going to have to pay for the sessions or go to my GP and wait months for an appointment.' Mandy glared at Libby. 'And don't you even think of offering to pay. You've done more than enough for me already and I can just about afford the first few sessions.'

Recognising the challenge in Mandy's over-bright eyes, Libby bit her tongue. 'Who's the therapist? Anyone in Exham?'

'Someone called Julia Enders.' The bakery bell clanged as the door swung open. Mandy hissed, 'Lives in Bath. I'll go after my next visit to Jumbles. They want to see some more chocolate samples this week.'

The new arrival in the shop, an unfamiliar young man, interrupted. 'Julia Enders, did you say? Why, I know her very well.'

Libby stitched a cool smile on her face. 'Can I get you something?' she asked.

The man ignored her, focusing on Mandy. 'Well, you're a sight for sore eyes. Haven't seen a proper Goth for ages. Didn't know they still existed in this backwater.'

Libby, offended by the sneer in his voice, shot a glance at Mandy, praying the young woman would hold on to her temper. Mandy, though, wore a broad smile. 'Hello, Peter. Long-time no see.'

Libby said, 'You two know each other? Don't tell me, you were at school together.' There was only one secondary school in Exham, and most local people knew each other. When Libby first arrived in town, she'd felt like a stranded goldfish in the close community. Many still regarded her as an outsider.

Mandy giggled. 'This is Peter.'

'And you must be the famous Mrs Forest.' The young man's feet were set wide apart, his hands in his pockets; he seemed altogether too self-assured for Libby's taste.

Mandy, though, had brightened up at his appearance. 'How do you know Julia Enders?'

'Friend of my uncle.' He winked. 'A very good friend, if you know what I mean. What do you know about her?'

Mandy hesitated. 'I suppose there's no reason to keep it a secret. I'm going to see her about my phobia.' The defiant gleam in her eyes sent a warm glow of almost maternal pride through Libby.

Peter looked Mandy up and down. 'You're the last person I'd expect to have a phobia. You beat me up in the school playground, just because I called you a stupid Goth, remember? What's this phobia then? Spiders?'

Libby hated the sarcasm in his voice, but Mandy laughed. 'Claustrophobia actually. Can't travel in trains and coaches. Nothing mega.'

'Well, Julia deals with all kinds of phobias. She reckons to shift 'em in one session.'

He lounged against the counter, munching a doughnut. 'Julia says she can re-programme your brain to help you overcome learned anxieties, or some such palaver. Works for all sorts of mental problems, apparently—' He broke off, wiping sugar from his chin, as the door swung open again with a jaunty jangle, and the owner of the flower shop appeared.

Libby stifled a sigh. Gladys Evans was one of the worst gossips in town, and from the look on her face she'd caught the end of Peter's sentence. A busy shop was really the worst place to talk about serious subjects. 'Phobias? If you're talking about alternative remedies,' the florist began, 'I can tell you what to do. My sister had a dreadful fear of lifts, because she was shut in a cupboard by mistake when she was a child. The hinges were on the inside, and she couldn't get out for an hour. Our mother broke the door down with a hammer in the end...' Mandy's mouth hung open. Her eyes opened wide as the woman went on, 'My sister went to a fortune teller at the County Show and the woman picked up on the problem. She saw my sister a few times...'

Mandy sounded breathless. 'What did she say?'

The florist shook her head. 'Can't remember what it was exactly. Something to do with eggs. Or was it candles? Anyway, she was cured in the shake of a rat's tail.'

Libby began, 'I really don't think we need a fortune teller,' but Mandy's eyes gleamed. 'I've always wanted to have my fortune told. Who was it at the fair? Was it a local person?'

'She lives over Dunster way, I think,' Gladys replied. 'I can let you have her address, if you like. She's not usually a fortune teller, of course. That's just for the shows. She's what they call an alternative therapist.'

'Mandy, I really think you should stick to this Julia, if Claire recommended her. You know she's properly trained, and...'

Mandy was too busy making a note of the alternative therapist's address to listen. Libby's heart sank. Her young friend was grabbing any idea that came her way. Maybe it was best to end the conversation here, before another customer arrived with an even more ridiculous suggestion. She served Gladys. 'Your usual sandwich?'

Peter, Mandy's old school friend, watched with a superior half smile playing on his lips. Libby's hand itched to slap the smug face. Instead, she said, 'I take it you've just arrived back in Exham, if Mandy hasn't seen you before today.'

Peter grinned. 'I'm sizing up the opposition.'

'I'm sorry? What opposition?'

'I work for Terence Marchant. We're opening a new patisserie in Exham and Terry asked me to look at the local cafés and sandwich shops. Of course, our place will be rather different. More focused on croissants and macaroons than cheese and pickle sandwiches. I don't think you've got anything to fear.'

Mandy's face turned pink. 'You mean, you're a spy? Then you can get out of here, Peter Morris. I never liked you when we were at school and I was right. And I won't be visiting any therapist you know.'

Peter smirked harder. 'No need to get in a tizz. We don't want to make your phobias worse, do we?'

Libby's heart hammered. Her instincts had been right. She'd known the lad was bad news as soon as he came in. His trousers were shiny and much too tight and his hair slick with grease. She held the door open. 'Thank you for coming in, Mr Morris. You can tell your boss we're managing very well, and there's plenty of room for all kinds of shops in Exham.'

Peter used his elbow to shove himself off the counter, swallowed the last of his doughnut, and snorted. 'You can go on selling your buns, Mrs Forest, and your home made chocolates. Terry thinks there might be a place for them in the patisserie. Of course, they'll need to be of professional quality. I expect he'll pop in one of these days for a sample, and you'd do well to offer your best products. He's quite the businessman. You'd best stay on the right side of him.'

As the door closed, Libby let out an angry whistle. 'So, Terence Marchant thinks he might possibly be interested in my chocolates.' Her voice was heavy with sarcasm. 'How very kind of him. I think we'd better tell Frank what's going on. Between you and me, and despite what I said, I think Exham has just about as many food outlets as it can manage. Do you think we should be worried?'

Mandy gave a short, unconvincing laugh. 'I'm sure this place is popular enough to beat off Peter Morris and his boss. Is Terence Marchant anything to do with the cat lady in Wells?'

'He's the rich son. I was worried about her, and I visited him to discuss all those cats she keeps. He told me he might start a rival business in Exham. I thought he was just winding me up, but it seems I was wrong.'

More customers arrived. As Libby served, she watched Mandy from the corner of her eye. The young woman kept staring at the address and phone number of the alternative therapist. If only there was something Libby could do. An unqualified therapist could lead to trouble, but she knew better than to try to stop Mandy. Opposition would only make her more determined. Libby added it to the mental list of things to worry about in the middle of the night when she couldn't sleep. The list seemed to be growing fast. 'Can you manage here for an hour or so, Mandy? I'd like to call round to see Frank. I know it's his day off, but he needs to know about Terence Marchant's patisserie as soon as possible.'

* * *

Libby was disappointed to find Frank away from home. She rang his mobile number, but he didn't answer. It was no surprise. He'd never come to terms with mobile technology. Libby shrugged. He'd taken a few days off. He rarely spent more than twenty-four hours away from his beloved bakery, but it was fully staffed for the next few days and he'd be back soon enough. Terence Marchant's new shop wouldn't be opening for a week or two.

Libby slipped a note through the door, asking Frank to get in touch when he returned home, and spent the rest of the day with Mandy in the bakery. The college catering supervisor arrived, questioning Mandy about food hygiene and health and safety. Pleased with the apprentice's progress, she left clutching a bag of Belgian buns left over from the lunchtime rush.

Mandy beamed. 'She says I'm doing really well.' She'd removed the rings from her face and ears in honour of the supervisor's visit, and apart from purple lipstick could pass for any attractive young woman, so long as she stayed behind the counter. The Doc Martens on her feet gave the game away, though. Libby wondered if the supervisor had noticed them.

At the end of the day, when the shop was clean and shiny, Libby and Mandy took off their overalls and prepared to lock up. 'My feet are killing me,' Libby muttered. 'It's these stupid kitten heels. Maybe I should get some boots, like yours.'

'You could do worse, Mrs F. Lots of space for the toes.'

As Mandy dug into the pocket of her overall and dropped the little pile of pencil, paper, and handkerchief on the counter, Libby peeked at the address of the alternative therapist.

Abbott House, near Upper Compton, she read, and a shiver crept down her spine. That was the village the barmaid had mentioned, where Mike's creepy visitors, Olivia and Xavier Papadopoulos, lived. Libby didn't want them anywhere near Mandy. Despite her determination to stay out of her apprentice's private life, she had to say something. 'That address...'

Mandy raised an eyebrow. 'Yes?' Her tone was belligerent.

Libby opened and closed her mouth several times. The urge to stop Mandy was almost overwhelming, but she knew it would be a mistake. Already, Mandy's eyes glowed with the light of battle. 'Are you planning to visit?'

Mandy shrugged. 'Yes, but I don't know how I'm going to get there.'

The cold hand of fear grabbed hold of Libby's insides. She didn't want Mandy getting involved with this therapist and she hated the thought of her visiting Upper Compton on her own.

She thought quickly. 'You know, we haven't taken delivery of that vehicle I ordered. Remember, I said I'd get another car for the business.' Thank goodness it would be tax-deductible.

'You did well to pass your driving test first time, and you can drive it when it arrives, but in the meantime, if you really want to go over to see this woman, I'd like to come with you. We can go in the Citroen and take Bear. I always feel better in a strange place when he's around.'

Mandy's face was difficult to read, but she was fond of the dog, so Libby ploughed on. 'I think we should leave Shipley behind. He's still a bit wild. In fact, the vet's running some obedience classes for talented but crazy dogs, and I'm planning to take him, soon. Meanwhile, if you really insist on visiting this woman in Upper Compton, I'll take you.' That way, she could keep an eye on her apprentice. Keep her out of harm's way. They'd both be fine, with Bear in tow.

Mandy picked up her phone. 'Thanks, I'll ring and see if I can make an appointment.' She hesitated a second. 'Would you come in with me? You know, like, for moral support?'

8

Mandy's appointment with the alternative therapist was set for three the next afternoon. She spent the morning on the telephone at the bakery, cold calling likely distributors of Mrs Forest's Chocolates. Libby was impressed. She hated trying to sell things to strangers. 'They can always say no,' Mandy pointed out. 'Anyway, your chocs are so scrummy, I know they'll love them.'

'Well, if you don't need me to help, I'll leave you to it. I've arranged a meeting with the vet to talk about Shipley.'

'The obedience classes?'

'Exactly. Shipley's a beautiful dog, and he's won prizes for best in breed at the local show, but he wouldn't win anything for his behaviour.'

As though to prove her right, Shipley darted round her feet, yapping and whining, wildly over-excited, when she collected him from Max's house. Once inside her little purple car, he sniffed every corner.

Max held the car door as Libby calmed the dog, offering a chew. 'That animal has an over-developed sense of smell,' he said.

The vet was delighted to see Shipley, and he responded by

leaping wildly around, despite Libby's stern commands. Tanya turned her back on the dog. 'I won't encourage him,' she said. 'Now, you wanted to talk about obedience classes. Let's go inside. Come on, Shipley, walk to heel.' To Libby's astonishment, the dog stopped leaping and barking and walked sedately, close to the vet's ankles.

'How did you do that?'

'He likes authority. The advanced training classes start tomorrow. I don't run them, I get an ex-police dog trainer to do that. He's like the dog whisperer and he'll soon sort Shipley out.'

Libby said, 'I rather suspect I need as much help as Shipley. Bear was well trained before I met him and the only other animal I've ever owned is Fuzzy. My cat. And she does exactly what she likes.'

The vet laughed. 'You mean your delightful marmalade. The one who broke her leg? How does she feel about Shipley?'

'When he's around, she hides in the airing cupboard. If he gets too near, she makes a swipe at his nose, but she only comes out to see Bear, these days. She worships that dog.'

'Poor cat. The sooner Shipley falls into line, the better. Can you make the class tomorrow morning?'

'I wouldn't miss it for the world. Officially, Max has adopted Shipley as well as Bear, but I think he'll be delighted if I take the training off his hands.' *And it will buy me a little more time to decide what I really want.*

* * *

Even Bear seemed subdued as Libby and Mandy arrived in Upper Compton. The village was bigger and less cosy than its smaller relative down the road. There was no welcoming pub, bright with summer flowers, just a featureless brick building close to the road, with no room for outside tables and chairs. Libby felt no temptation to eat there.

Her heart sank lower with every yard they covered, until the car crawled round the increasingly twisty lanes leading to Abbott House. Mandy's hands were clasped tight in her lap. She was as nervous as Libby.

'Are you sure about this?'

Libby wished her young friend would change her mind, but Mandy shook her head. 'I'm going to beat this phobia.'

Libby fell silent, determined not to keep recommending Claire's therapist friend, but she felt heavy with trepidation. *This is a mistake.* At least she could keep an eye on the meeting.

They followed the directions of the Satnav, enunciated in perfect Received Pronunciation by the invisible female. Libby imagined her as Charlotte, a wealthy woman lying on a chaise longue, sipping champagne between announcements.

As they drew nearer to Abbott House, even Charlotte sounded unsure, describing the road as an Unnamed Lane. The hedges grew closer until Libby's Citroen touched vegetation on both sides. Brambles scraped along the paintwork, setting Libby's teeth on edge, as the ground dipped sharply down into a valley.

'I hope we don't meet a horsebox.' Mandy's voice trembled.

Just as Libby began to suspect the house they sought was some kind of joke perpetrated by the Exham flower shop woman, she saw a building. Tiny, half-hidden by overhanging elm trees whose dense canopy of leaves shut out all but the most persistent rays of the sun, it was nothing like the grand mansion she'd expected. 'I suppose this must be it?'

Mandy peered out of the window. 'The name's on the gate.'

Neither she nor Mandy were in a hurry to leave the familiar safety of the car, but Bear was restive, never content to sit quietly in a stationary vehicle. Libby climbed out and reluctantly led the way to the house.

The door flew open. 'Ah, Mandy. There you are.' Once more, Libby's expectations were confounded. She'd imagined a fairground fortune teller in tasselled shawls, gold bracelets, and a beaded head-dress. Kate Stephenson was a tiny, energetic woman in denim dungarees over a white t-shirt, with a blue square tied round her head. Fair curls escaped, framing delicate features. She wore no jewellery at all. 'Sorry about the clothes.' She laughed. 'I've been trying to clean the house while the kids are at school.' She bent over Bear, and he allowed her to stroke his head.

The tension ache at the back of Libby's neck subsided. She shot a sideways glance at Mandy, who returned a sheepish grin. They'd both let their imagination run away with them.

Instead of taking them inside, Kate Stephenson led the way round the corner of the house, under a wooden arch in the even deeper shade of a sturdy yew. The tree's wide trunk spoke of great age. There was something about yew trees. What was it, now?

As they reached the back of the house, Libby remembered. Yew trees were traditionally planted at the entrance to cemeteries. The wooden entrance was the lychgate. Sure enough, rows of discoloured gravestones marched down the garden. The quiet of the surrounding woods was broken by rooks rising up, cawing and flapping. Under the noise, water babbled gently.

They followed a path between the graves, towards a corner of the garden where a summer house stood, doors flung wide, offering a glimpse of a white painted interior. 'I hope you're not bothered by the old gravestones,' Kate said. 'Some of them date back to the seventeenth century. The cottage used to belong to the sexton who dug the graves. My boys and I love it here, living among the departed. My husband died a couple of years ago. He's over there,' she pointed to a nearby, newer headstone, with a vase of flowers in front of it. 'We still feel so close to him.'

Libby gulped and followed her into the summer house. White walls reflected the daylight streaming through enormous windows. A small round table stood in the centre of the room, with four comfortable looking chairs pulled close. A pink sofa and a second, rectangular table against the far wall completed the furnishings.

'Have a seat.' Kate smiled, showing a set of perfect white teeth. 'Don't worry, I'm not a witch, by the way. I only do fairground work for fun.' Her bright green eyes sparkled as though she sensed Libby's antagonism and found it amusing. Bear settled next to the pink sofa, his gaze following every one of Kate Stephenson's moves. Libby slipped a finger through his collar and sat close, glad he was there.

Kate turned her attention to Mandy. 'Of course, you're the one needing my help. I can tell by your aura.'

'My aura?' Mandy's brows met over her nose.

Kate laughed, the sound as musical as the murmur from the nearby stream. 'Nothing scary. Everyone has their own aura and it changes according to mood. Yours is a little orange today. You're anxious, of course.'

She bustled around the room, brewing something in a small pot with a bamboo handle. 'Don't you love the way the Japanese make tea? I've been to Japan and seen the tea ceremony. They're completely mindful through the whole process.'

Mandy nodded, eyes dark, face serious, but Libby stifled a groan. Max had once described mindfulness as a pseudo-scientific way of justifying the art of doing nothing. She'd argued at the time, but Kate's mention of auras and tea ceremonies within five minutes of their arrival left Libby cold. She subsided into the comfy cushions of the sofa and drank green tea.

Kate sipped from her cup in silence. Birds chattered outside. Somewhere, a clock ticked. Libby tried not to make slurping noises.

At last, Kate said, 'Now, Mandy, let me help you.'

Mandy peered around the room. 'Don't you use a crystal ball, or tarot cards, or something?'

'No need. I can already sense your troubles, Mandy. You've had a difficult life. A broken home.'

'Well, only recently. It was fine when I was a kid.'

'Of course, it seemed fine to you. Both your parents were at home and you thought they were happy. Children always make the best of things. But, underneath, you knew something was wrong.'

Kate paused. Mandy stammered, 'W-well, I suppose I knew Mum was nervous around my dad. But I never saw him lay a hand on her. Not then. Not when I was small.'

'She hid it from you, to protect you. Then, there was the thing you were scared of...'

Mandy's head jerked up.

'What was it, now? Something in the house...'

This time, the pause dragged on until Mandy broke into the quiet, her voice small and scared. 'The attic.' She chewed on her lower lip. 'There was a ladder that led up to the loft. Mum and Dad kept old curtains and bits of carpet there. I wasn't supposed to go up on my own.'

'Your father stopped you, didn't he?'

'He told me I'd fall through the floorboards.'

'But you wanted to see it?'

'That's right. So, one day, I went up there, and he caught me, and he was so mad.'

Kate laid her hands on Mandy's, tightly clasped on the table. 'I expect you thought it was your fault.'

'It was. You see, there were boxes up there. It was dark, up in the attic. It smelled musty, from the old curtains, I suppose, and there were boxes I'd never seen before. Some were just old clothes. You know, my baby clothes. Mum must have kept them. At the back of all the other boxes, I found a small one. It was different from the others – smaller, made out of painted wood.'

Mandy's lip trembled as she continued, 'I had this awful feeling before I opened it. I don't know what I expected to find, but I had to look. They were photos. Horrible pictures. Dad had been in Bosnia, you see, with the army in 1995, just before I was born. The photos were terrible – pictures of dead people. Some were soldiers, but others were just ordinary people. Women and children too. Covered in blood, a-and lying in heaps.'

Libby closed her eyes. Mandy's father, Bert, was a bully. Once, when Mandy was lodging with Libby, he'd got drunk and tried to break into the house to find his daughter. Libby had no idea he'd once been a soldier. A bad time in Bosnia could explain his violent moods.

Kate said, 'Did your father know you found his photos?'

Mandy nodded. 'He caught me looking at them, and he was furious. He shouted, and then he started to cry.' Her voice shook. Kate offered her a box of tissues. 'Is that why I don't like small spaces? Because of the attic?'

Kate replaced the tissues on the table, near Mandy. 'We can't be sure, at the moment, but it made a big impression on you. We need to talk more, another time, but if that experience started your fears, you'll begin to feel different, already.'

Mandy was nodding. 'I never thought about it like that before.' She screwed the tissue into a ball. 'Do you think that might be why Dad... Why he...' Her voice faded away.

'You can say it here. You're safe.'

Mandy took a deep, shuddering breath. 'That's why Dad

used to hit Mum, isn't it? He was angry all the time and he took it out on her.' She spoke slowly, as though thinking it through, her voice growing in confidence. 'It wasn't my fault at all, was it?'

Kate smiled. 'No. Not your fault.'

Libby was astonished. She knew about Mandy's claustrophobia, and she'd seen her father's anger, but she'd never imagined there could be a link. She'd heard of soldiers suffering from mental health problems, even years after they left the army. Posttraumatic stress disorder. That's what it was called.

Kate sat back. 'That's enough for now, Mandy. We'll talk some more, another time. There are bad things in your family's past, and we need to uncover them. It will take careful thought. I'll consider how best to handle it. You come back in a few days. I'm sure I can help you.'

She led them through the cemetery garden. 'Perhaps you'll be able to come alone, next time?' she suggested. Libby narrowed her eyes, searching Kate's face, suddenly uneasy, but the warm smile was still in place and the woman's green eyes were wide. 'You can bring a friend if you wish, but sometimes it's easier to talk when it's just the two of us.'

She turned to Libby. 'Give my regards to Max, when you see him. I knew him once, many years ago.'

Libby started. Max had never mentioned Kate. Well, she couldn't expect to know everything about him. That was part of his charm, wasn't it?

Anyway, Kate was still talking. 'I heard about Debbie. That she died. If you like, you can tell Max how sorry I am. I'll understand if you'd rather not.'

* * *

As Libby and Mandy climbed back into the Citroen, Bear scrambling into the back seat, Libby broke the silence. 'Are you OK?'

Mandy nodded, but still said nothing. The silence continued as Libby started the car, the engine juddering in protest. The steep slope and muddy ground were almost too much for the aging vehicle.

Mandy pulled out a tube of mints. 'Want one?' Libby shook her head. Mandy sucked noisily. 'Who's Debbie?'

Libby hesitated. Max had trusted her with the story of his daughter's death in a horse riding accident. In a town like Exham, where everyone knew their neighbour's business, Libby was amazed no one had ever mentioned it to her. She supposed Max had worked hard to keep it private; Joe, as well, for Debbie had been his sister. Libby struggled for the right words. Although she often listened to gossip in her work, she tried not to fall into the trap of spreading it herself.

The car lurched as a stray branch scraped along the driver's side, and Libby made up her mind. 'I can't share it with you, Mandy. It's something that happened to Max many years ago. He would have to tell you himself.'

'OK, no problem.'

Libby shot a sideways glance at the set of her companion's jaw. Mandy didn't usually give in so easily. Probably, she was still thinking about today's session with Kate Stephenson. It had certainly left Libby confused. Set to distrust the so-called alternative therapist, she'd been astonished by the ease with which the woman uncovered some of Mandy's fears. Perhaps she'd been too hasty.

As Libby persuaded the car round a dog-leg bend, she came face to face with a heavy Range Rover. Both vehicles drew to a halt, the lane too narrow to allow them to pass.

Xavier Papadopoulos watched, stony faced, from behind the

wheel. The nearest passing place was ten yards or so behind his vehicle. For a long moment, Libby's eyes locked with his in a silent battle. It was his responsibility to reverse and she wasn't going to let the man intimidate her into giving way. She'd have to travel backwards and negotiate the tricky bend. She waited, jaw set, stomach churning.

The stand off seemed to last for hours. At last, the Range Rover scraped into reverse gear. With a glare that sent shivers down Libby's spine, Xavier Papadopoulos crunched his gears into reverse and shot backwards with wheels squealing. Swerving just far enough inside the passing place, he let Libby's Citroen squeeze through the gap. Bear barked, loudly, as Libby waved her thanks.

Mandy giggled. 'Well, Mrs F. I wouldn't want to argue with you when you have that look on your face.'

9

ST MARY'S

Next day, Max and Libby left the Land Rover under a tree in a pretty Exmoor village. 'Why are we here?' Libby asked. 'Upper Compton is still a few miles away.' Max linked his arm with hers. 'I want you to meet someone. First, though, tell me about your adventures with the alternative therapist.'

They strolled down the lane, Bear and Shipley snuffling for rabbits in the hedgerow. Libby grunted. 'I can't decide whether Kate Stephenson has some sort of psychic gift, or is playing tricks. The session with Mandy wasn't at all as I expected. I thought there'd be more jingling silver bracelets and patchouli oil, but instead, we sat very sedately and drank tea. It seemed to help Mandy, which I suppose is a good thing, but Kate made me nervous. She seemed to know everything.'

Max gazed across the hedges towards empty green fields leading down into the valley. 'Don't let your imagination run riot. She knew Mandy's name. It would be the easiest thing in the world for her to find out about Mandy's father. He's been in court. That would be reported in the papers and you'd be able to find reports on the internet. Given that knowledge, it wouldn't take too much work to uncover his background in the army and come up with a convincing story for Mandy.'

'Maybe.' Libby had learned to trust the knot of anxiety that formed in her stomach. It nearly always meant something was wrong. When she ignored that tiny ache, bad things often followed. 'Kate, the therapist, or whatever she's called, said something odd, by the way. She sent you her best wishes.' Libby kept her eyes steadily on the road ahead. 'You didn't mention knowing her.'

'I don't know her.' Max sounded perfectly calm. They walked on a few paces. 'What was her last name?'

'Stephenson.'

He shrugged. 'No, doesn't mean anything to me.'

'But she knows you. She mentioned Debbie.'

'What?' Max swung to face Libby, his eyes wide. Libby twirled a leaf in her fingers, trying to appear casual. Max rubbed a hand over his face. 'Let me think. Is Stephenson her married name?'

'Oh. Of course.' She hadn't thought of that. Max probably knew Kate before she was married. Such a silly system, changing your name when you married. It made it so tricky to trace people.

Max walked faster. 'I wonder... I knew a Kate when I worked in the bank in Bristol, just after I left university. Kate Mitchell was her name.'

'Did you know her well?' Libby made an effort to sound relaxed.

'We went around together for a while. Nothing intense. It all fizzled out when I met my wife and we lost touch over the years. I haven't seen her since then.'

'Well, she seems to know a lot about you.' Libby caught her lower lip between her teeth, annoyed at the edge in her voice.

Max, deep in his own thoughts, seemed not to notice. He murmured, almost to himself, 'I suppose my divorce is common knowledge, but how did she know about Debbie? We lived in London when she died.'

Max had told Libby the sad story: he'd had a row with his teenage daughter, she'd flounced away, ridden her horse without a helmet, fallen and suffered a fatal head injury. At the time he'd been focused on making big money as a banker, and he'd let family relationships slip. After Debbie's death, he'd blamed himself and hit the whisky bottle, hard. A messy divorce soon followed.

The knot in Libby's stomach tightened its grip. Kate Stephenson had certainly done her homework. Libby straightened her shoulders, tossed aside the leaf, and took Max's hand. 'I imagine Kate's the kind of person who has her ear to the ground. Let's not worry about it. There's no need for you to do anything.'

'I suppose not.' Max sounded less than convinced.

Libby tried a change of subject. 'Anyway, I want to concentrate on Liam Weston's death. We still know so little about him.'

'That's why I brought you out here, today, to St Mary's church. I'm hoping the local rector will be able to tell us more.' Max squeezed Libby's hand. 'He's been at St Mary's for ten years or so. That's long enough to find out all about the local population.'

'What did you say his name was?'

'John Canterbury.'

Libby laughed. 'That's a good name for a rector, especially one with ambition.'

'The couple of times I've run into John, playing skittles in one of the local pubs, he's struck me as someone completely uninterested in moving up the hierarchy. We won't be seeing him inducted as Bishop of Bath and Wells any time soon. Oh, and here we are...'

The tiny church, attached by a stone wall to a couple of small thatched cottages, was distinguished by a spire that pointed heavenward. Libby glanced around. Another churchyard; her second in a couple of days. They walked the short distance to the heavy wooden door of the church and left the dogs outside, lying happily in the shade. Even Shipley seemed content to rest quietly, for once.

Max and Libby entered the cool, dark interior of the church. Tacked to a cork board on Libby's right were a dozen or so notices, some printed, several handwritten. A quick scan showed they were notices of events about to take place in the village. The local playgroup was due to meet on Tuesday mornings and Thursday afternoons. The cricket team was playing away next week in Devon, a bring-and-buy sale was due in a few days, and a Grand Summer Quiz was advertised for this evening, to be held in the church hall. An entry ticket entitled the holder to a free glass of wine or a soft drink.

Everything on the board suggested a calm, peaceful community, crime free, where organising an evening without falling foul of the licensing laws was a main concern. Libby began to doubt there was anything odd about Liam Weston's death. Perhaps she'd been reading too much into a careless accident. She'd let the strange Papadopoulos couple spook her, and that unnerving experience in Kate Stephenson's house had left her nerves jangling. A dose of uncomplicated low-key Anglican religion would calm her twitchy nerves.

They walked into the body of the church to be greeted by a small, round, smiling man wearing enormous glasses. The spectacles were held in place by two very large ears that stood out almost at right angles from his head. With an effort to avoid staring at these twin excrescences, Libby kept her eyes on the centre of the man's face as Max introduced her. 'Libby, this is John Canterbury, the rector of this parish, and several others in the area.'

The rector, exactly the kind of welcoming vicar Libby had hoped for, beamed. 'How lovely to see you again, Max, though I haven't forgiven you for your part in that last skittles match. My team will be taking vengeance very soon. Now, I hope you didn't mind meeting me here. I just popped into the church to make sure everything was ready for the funeral later today. Mrs Banks, one of the most stalwart members of my congregation, I'm afraid, passed away last week. Almost ninety, so the event was not unexpected, but the loss will weaken our Sunday singing even more.'

His mouth drooped comically, but the twinkle in his eyes remained. 'I suppose you don't live around here, Mrs Forest, and better yet, sing?'

'Sorry. I'm from Exham. And not really a churchgoer, I'm afraid.'

'Ah well, not to worry.' The good humour was infectious. 'We'll have to make do with our choir of six, and hope no more are called away to higher things. We could use some young boys and girls, really. Anthony Palmer's the only choir member still at school, and he's obliged to attend because his father's our church-warden. Lovely voice, the child has. Quite beautiful, but only a few months left before it breaks.' He heaved a sigh. 'Still, you didn't come here to talk about church music, I'm sure.'

He straightened a pile of leaflets, handing one to Libby. 'Here's a short history of the parish. You may find it interesting.'

She tucked the leaflet into her bag and followed the rector out of the dim light in the church into bright June sunshine.

'Now, Max.' The smiling rector leaned against the ancient honey coloured wall of the nearest cottage. 'I live just up the lane. Not in this charming cottage, sadly. Mrs Banks' daughter has that pleasure. But if you come with me, I'm sure I can rustle up a can of tomato soup and some bread. Not much to offer a famous cook such as yourself, Mrs Forest, but perhaps it will stave off the worst of the afternoon's hunger pangs.'

* * *

The rector lived in a small, modern bungalow on the edge of the village. He led Libby and Max inside. 'My wife's at work, so you'll have to put up with me, I'm afraid. She's a pharmacist at the local hospital. Let's see what she's left for lunch.'

Instead of the promised can of Heinz soup, John's wife had left plates of salmon and cucumber sandwiches and an apple pie, all tightly covered in cling film. The kitchen was clean and tidy, almost as neat as Libby's own, though without the industrial-scale oven and sink units. The rector removed a pile of books and papers from the scrubbed table in the dining room: a Bible, leaflets, and a couple of heavy reference books.

The rector noticed her interest. 'Some fascinating information about old Somerset in these books. Glastonbury, of course, is so old it was mentioned in William the Conqueror's Doomsday Book, as well as in this one about old religions.'

Libby peered more closely: *A History of Ancient Somerset* and *The Golden Bough*. 'There's so much to find out about the county's history,' she said. 'I've only been here a year or two, and I'm still learning.'

Max chuckled. 'All the old places seem to have present-day mysteries, as well as the old ones. Did you hear about the body on Glastonbury Tor, and the murder in Wells Cathedral library?'

'Oh, yes. I've been following your adventures with admiration,' the rector said. 'So I'm not surprised you're interested in young Liam's story, Mrs Forest. I expect that's what you wanted to ask me about?'

Libby nodded and the rector continued, 'Poor lad. I knew him well, of course. At least his parents went before him. There's nothing worse than burying your own child. Those are the worst funerals for the clergy, you know, because it's so hard to find the smallest crumb of comfort for the parents. It seems against the natural order of things for a child to go before his parents. Older people, now, they're another matter. When they've lived a happy life, they're often ready to pass on.'

His round face beamed with goodwill that hinted he'd find just the right words to say to grieving relatives. He went on, 'Liam was well liked around these parts, despite his hot temper, and he was a hard worker, I believe. Wanted to set up his own herd of cattle, learning everything he could from Mike Carmichael. He was like one of the family to Mike and Belinda, you know. There are only a couple of years in age between Liam and Tim, their son.'

He offered Libby another sandwich. 'To tell you the truth, I think Mike would almost rather have had Liam as his heir. Tim's always been a little…' He laid a finger on his mouth, as though trying to stop criticism pass his lips. 'How can I put it, now? Young Tim can be a little too fond of going out with his mates and having a good time. I'm sure he'll settle down in time. Most do.'

Libby drained a coffee cup. 'My son just married Sarah, Tim's sister.'

The rector beamed, revealing large white teeth, so crowded they crossed one another, lending a certain goofy charm to his smile. 'Now, she's a lovely girl, is Sarah. I always thought she'd end up with a local boy like Liam.' He raised both hands in the air in an apologetic gesture. 'So sorry, that came out wrong. No offence intended.'

'None taken. I suppose most people round here end up marrying people they've grown up with?'

The rector smiled at Libby. 'Ah, now, that used to happen a great deal. Of course, it's not just marrying relatives that makes folk behave oddly. Dementia, now, is a big problem, these days. Old people lose their memories. Look what happened at your son's wedding, for example, about Lady Antonia's ring.' He shook his head. 'The poor woman's having a few problems, I'm afraid. We can't all keep as sharp as our recently departed Mrs Banks. She was on the ball, terrorising choirboys for every wrong note, until the day she died.'

He chuckled. 'Still, now, I've been rambling on. What was I saying?' He glanced around, eyes narrowed, as though searching for inspiration. 'Oh yes. Children don't stay around here, like they used to. Wages are low, and it's easier to find work in the cities.' He poured more coffee. 'It's good to have new life in the area.' He looked from Max to Libby, and she felt a blush start on her neck.

Max stepped in, bringing the conversation firmly back to Liam. 'What can you tell us about the lad who died?'

The rector steepled his fingers and closed his eyes. 'Not a churchgoer, I'm sorry to say. At least, only at Christmas and Easter, along with most people here.' The grin returned. 'Best attendance I ever have is when we bless the animals. Church is full of folk, those days, apart from the goats, sheep, and donkeys. Once, we even had a llama up from Barrow Farm over in that direction.'

Libby asked, 'How well did Tim and Liam get on? Were they friends?'

The rector let out a sharp bark of laughter. 'Not them. Jealousy, you know.'

Libby leaned forward. 'Which way? Was Liam jealous of Tim, or the other way round?'

The rector leaned back, arms folded. 'Tim resented the way his father relied on Liam. Now, don't get me wrong. A little bit of jealousy doesn't mean Tim would want to hurt Liam, but since Liam became Mike's right-hand man, Tim refused to have anything to do with farm business. He works in Minehead, these days, with a feed supplier.'

He rose, his chair scraping awkwardly on the laminated floor, and began to stack dishes in the dishwasher. 'Now, I'm afraid I have to get away and finish preparations for old Mrs Banks. Come and see me again soon, won't you? I'd love to hear about your adventures as our local sleuth.'

10

SULTANA CAKE

Libby spent the drive back to Exham thinking about the rector's words. No one yet knew if Liam was the victim of foul play or an accident. Suicide seemed unlikely, given the manner of his death, but she would rule nothing out.

There was no evidence of foul play, but Libby was learning to trust her instincts. While the police checked for giveaway fibres from clothes and tested blood samples, Libby kept wondering if anyone might want Liam dead, and why.

So far, he seemed to be an ordinary, hard working farm hand with no family and no obvious girlfriend. There had been no sign of a 'plus one' at the wedding. No one gained from his death.

What about hatred? 'Max, what was it the rector said about Tim and Liam?'

'Tim resented the way his father relied on Liam. That's what I remember.' Max chuckled. 'Are you thinking what I'm thinking? Maybe Tim hated Liam more than others realised. He'd even walked away from the family business out of jealousy.'

Libby groaned. 'And that fight over the ring at the wedding. Tim could easily have set that up to incriminate Liam. Then, as that turned out to be a damp squib, he might have caused the accident.'

'Wait a moment. Let's not get too far ahead. How could Tim arrange Liam's death?'

'In any number of ways.' Libby counted ideas on her fingers. 'Brake failure or tyre pressure, or some other damage to the tractor...'

'The police would notice that...'

'Poison?'

'Some unnoticeable poison from the Amazon rain forest? Come on, Libby, how likely is that.'

She shrugged. He wasn't taking her seriously. 'There are other untraceable poisons, you know.' She let the silence hang a moment. 'Anyway, my point is, Tim is definitely a suspect.'

'I'll give you that,' Max's hands gripped the wheel firmly, 'but we need to keep open minds. We don't know of any other motive, yet, so let's keep looking. Meanwhile, is this afternoon the first of Shipley's retraining classes? Are you willing to take him? I know I'm his official owner, but he's your dog, really.'

He sounded distant. Libby shifted in her seat. If it wasn't her imagination, a rift was growing between them. Max had been different this morning; unusually polite and thoughtful, letting Libby do most of the talking. Libby missed the robust teasing she'd grown used to.

His attitude to Shipley had changed, too. Perhaps he was mentally sorting things into piles: deciding which possession were his and which belonged to Libby. Her fingers tightened on the seat belt. Those were not the thought processes of someone contemplating marriage. Maybe Max was having second thoughts.

Libby stuck her jaw out. She wasn't going to lay herself open to rejection. If Max was losing interest in her, it was a good thing they'd never made any real commitment. They could carry on as business partners. Maybe Max would let Shipley move to live with Libby and Mandy, who was still Libby's lodger at Hope Cottage.

She blinked hard and took a deep breath, forcing herself to concentrate on events in the Exmoor villages. She had a bad feeling about the people she'd met recently. Instinct again? Well, this time she wouldn't tell Max. She was perfectly capable of visiting the Papadopoulos couple alone. Shipley would protect her.

* * *

Shipley's snores reverberated in Libby's ears on the drive back to Exmoor. The hour long obedience training had exhausted the poor animal, and he wasn't the only one. Libby's head spun from the effort of remembering the commands. It wasn't just the words that mattered, she'd learned. It was all about tone of voice and gesture. 'We've both been back to school this afternoon, Shipley.'

Shipley paused on his way into the Citroen, sniffing round the boot of the car. Inside, safe in a tin wrapped in layers of cardboard was a cake Libby had picked up from home. She had a plan to gain entry to the Papadopoulos house, and the cake was an important element. Who could resist sultana cake? 'You can smell it, can't you?'

The dog's ability was amazing. No wonder the ex-policeman who ran the session was impressed. 'That dog would have made a brilliant drug sniffer,' he'd said.

Tanya had laughed. 'Or mortuary dog. Isn't that what they call them? Dogs that can pick out a dead body from miles away?' She grinned at Libby. 'You could do with one of those in your line of work, Libby.'

'I'm hoping it won't be necessary for a while. There have been too many deaths in the area already.'

The dog slept in the back of the car while Libby enjoyed a little peace and quiet. As she passed the pub in the next village, she waved at the barmaid rearranging chairs in the sunshine, but her mood slipped as she drew nearer to Upper Compton.

Shipley woke, looked out of the window, lost interest, and scratched the back seat, as though trying to dig through to the boot of the car. Libby, suddenly nervous, wished she'd left the cake at home. The excuse she'd dreamed up for her visit seemed wafer-thin. Well, it was too late now. She'd have to go through with it.

Her skin tingled as she drew up on the gravel outside the Papadopoulos's house. Solidly built, it boasted a central front door and symmetrical windows that gazed out like blank eyes. Libby retrieved the cake and rehearsed the story she'd planned during the drive. It sounded ridiculous, now, but it was too late to turn back. The occupants must have heard her arrival.

Trying to look more confident than she felt, she strode up the path leading between overgrown beech hedges to the front door, Shipley following close at heel, just as he'd been taught today. Usually, he'd bound ahead, barking wildly and running rings around Libby. This dog training business had already made a difference.

At the front door, Libby swallowed hard and leaned on the bell push, listening to the distant jangle echo through the house. She pasted a warm smile on her face as Olivia Papadopoulos opened the door and spoke as cheerily as possible. 'Hello. I don't know if you remember me.'

The woman's eyebrows twitched and a tight smile dissected her face. 'Of course, I remember you, Mrs Forest.'

Libby moistened her lips, straightened her shoulders, and

embarked on her story. 'I know you're friendly with Belinda at the farm. You see, I made this cake for her. It's meant to be a surprise, but when I took it to the house just now there was no one there. I don't want to transport it all the way back to Exham, and I remembered the quiz this evening in St Mary's church hall. Mike had mentioned it to me, and the rector said everyone attended, so I thought I'd take a chance you were going and ask if I could possibly leave the cake with you, to pass on to Belinda tonight.'

She came to a sudden halt. The gabbled story sounded hopelessly contrived.

'Then you'd better come in.' Mrs Papadopoulos smiled. 'Why, I'd be delighted to pass on your cake. Belinda's told me how brilliantly you cook. Mind you,' she led Libby down a long, gloomy corridor, turning left into a conservatory, 'I might be tempted to eat it myself. What kind of cake is it?'

This was going better than Libby had dreamed. The woman was so welcoming she'd even waved Shipley into the house too. Perhaps Libby had been too quick to judge. Just because her husband was weird, with strange, hippie clothes and cold eyes, it didn't mean Olivia was scary. Libby had been imagining things at the farm. Mike and Xavier had business to discuss, that was why they'd wanted Libby gone. She relaxed, cheered by her internal pep talk. 'Sultana.'

'Oh my. My favourite.' The woman heaved a loud sigh. 'Never mind, I'll wait until the quiz. Perhaps Belinda will share.'

The woman seemed inclined to chat. Libby gestured towards the woodland visible through the conservatory glass. 'What a wonderful setting for your house.'

'Yes, we're very lucky. It's just the place for our little meetings.'

'Meetings?'

Olivia's eyebrow twitched. 'Just a few friends, you know. We get together from time to time to share memories.'

In the distance, music played. Olivia wore an odd expression. 'That's my husband. We have a grand piano in the music room.'

'How wonderful,' Libby heard herself gush. 'I recognise the music. Rachmaninov, isn't it?'

Olivia's smile grew broader. 'So, you're a musician, Mrs Forest?'

'Not really...'

'Come, he won't mind us listening. This way.'

Libby followed the woman up the curved staircase. It led in a perfect spiral to an upstairs landing. Mrs Papadopoulos took Libby's arm. 'Come in. He'll be so pleased to play for you.'

Her fingers were tight against Libby's flesh. 'I need to go,' Libby said, suddenly nervous. She stepped aside, shaking off the woman's fingers.

'Nonsense, my dear, you can spare a minute or two to enjoy the music.' Olivia pushed open the heavy door to reveal her husband, half hidden by a beautifully polished grand piano. 'Look, dear,' she said. 'Remember Mrs Forest? She's enjoying your music.'

Xavier Papadopoulos stopped, hands resting motionless above the keys, and smiled at Libby. 'I knew we would be seeing more of you, Mrs Forest. I'm never mistaken about people. Now, what can we do for you?'

'I was just – er – bringing a cake. To pass on to Belinda Carmichael. She's not at home.' Libby's voice sounded thin in the large room. She spoke louder. 'I hope you don't mind my dog being in here. He's rather excitable.'

Giving the lie to her words, Shipley remained motionless, nose in the air as if he smelled something no human could detect.

Olivia Papadopoulos laughed. 'Dogs always behave beautifully around my husband. He has a gift for animals, you know. One of many.'

Libby forced a smile. 'Well, the music was certainly beautiful, but I need to be getting back now.'

Olivia Papadopoulos took her arm again. Once more, the bony fingers gripped just a fraction too tightly. 'It's been such a pleasure to have you with us. If you're free this evening, why not come to our quiz too, and give Belinda her cake in person. We could use another team member. Liam Weston was in our team, poor boy, and we miss him dreadfully. Such a sad death.'

Libby's rapid increase in heart rate warned her to refuse the invitation. This pair gave her the creeps. She wanted to get out of the house, drive away, and never come back, but the possibility of finding out more about Liam was too good to turn down. That was, after all, why she'd trekked out to Exmoor in the first place.

At least she'd be able to spend a minute or two alone with Belinda. The two of them hadn't met since the wedding, although they'd chatted regularly about preparations during the run-up to the big event. Belinda had recommended the venue near Wells for the reception, but lately, she never seemed to answer a phone. It seemed odd, but maybe she'd taken offence when she asked Libby for free help with her finances.

The quiz tonight would be a great opportunity for Libby to get to the bottom of Belinda's problem.

* * *

Libby hoped to spend a few moments alone with Belinda before the evening's entertainment began, but Mike was already seated with the Papadopoulos couple and, to Libby's dismay, there was no sign of Belinda.

Olivia rose and approached Libby. 'Such a shame.' She sounded breathless. 'Belinda came home from her shopping trip today with a dreadful cold, so Mike sent her to bed. Such good luck you've joined us. Mike can take your cake home later.'

Libby couldn't care less about the wretched cake. She wanted to see Belinda. Hadn't the woman been on a shopping trip when Libby visited the farm? Did the woman do nothing but shop?

Thinking hard, Libby subsided into her seat next to Mike at the table spread with sheets of paper and a pile of pens. She nibbled squares of cheese. Perhaps Belinda regretted mentioning her money worries when they spoke at the wedding. She'd been avoiding Libby ever since.

The rector scurried round, settling people in their seats, sorting lone arrivals into teams, and pouring wine. There were empty chairs at Libby's table, but when someone from the next table claimed them, Xavier Papadopoulos shook his head. 'So sorry, we're waiting for the rest of our team.'

Libby watched the door. At the last moment, just as the rector tapped a spoon against a glass to call for quiet, the latecomers arrived. As Max entered, Kate Stephenson leaning on his arm, Libby's breath stuck in her throat. 'What are you doing here?' she hissed as he slipped into the next chair, Kate on his other side. 'You might have told me.'

Kate and Libby exchanged waves as Max murmured, 'You didn't tell me you were coming, either.'

Libby bit back angry words. He was right. Under cover of the rector's voice, as he gave instructions for the quiz, she muttered, 'OK. But why are you here?'

'Kate invited me. Remember? We knew each other years ago.' Libby had carried Kate's message herself.

'Give my regards to Max,' Kate had said, pearly teeth gleaming.

There was no time for further talk for the quiz had begun. As the evening progressed, Libby grew hotter and more annoyed, while Max spent the evening ignoring her, leaning much too close to Kate Stephenson. The alternative therapist knew almost all the answers, from the names of obscure capital cities to the top forty pop tunes of the 1980s.

For some reason, Libby could hardly remember her own name, never mind the names of five chemical elements beginning with vowels. The more she tried to think, the less she remembered. She thought she might explode when she caught sight of Xavier Papadopoulos watching her, a patronising smile across his face, as she gave yet another wrong answer to a geography question. How was she supposed to know the names of land locked African countries, anyway?

The final straw came at the end of the evening. Their team came second, but Kate won a prize for the best individual performance.

As she drove home, Libby tried to think objectively. Was she unfair in expecting Max to have nothing to do with other women? She hadn't agreed to marry him, had she?

Her disappointment was unreasonable. He was a free agent.

No matter how severely she spoke to herself, there was no resisting the truth; she was jealous.

11

CROISSANTS

Libby was first to arrive at the bakery next morning, determined to put Belinda and the Papadopoulos couple out of her mind. She wished she could so easily forget the way Max had looked at Kate. As she unlocked the shop, switched on the oven and mixed flour with yeast and water, her head swam with images of the alternative therapist, all smiles, head close to Max's as they argued whether or not Botswana was on the coast of Africa. Libby took out her feelings on a mound of dough.

The front-door bell jangled and Mandy burst into the shop. 'Have you seen it?'

'Seen what?' Libby thumped harder.

'They've started work on the new shop. You know, like, where Leather Heaven used to be? Guess who's bought it?' The small independent shoe shop had been forced out of business during the recession and the premises had passed through several pairs of hands since.

An invisible cloud of doom seemed to gather over Libby's head. 'Terence Marchant?'

Mandy nodded. 'I just saw Peter. He couldn't wait to give me the news. Smug little...' With a show of huge self-control, she fell silent.

'Quite.' Libby squeezed dough between her fingers. 'I suppose we knew it would happen sometime.' Viciously, she chopped the dough into equal portions and tossed each into an oiled metal bowl.

'What can we do? If Frank's bakery closes, I'll be out of work and I won't get a chance to finish my apprenticeship.' Mandy was breathing hard.

Libby forced a smile. 'Don't worry. We have plenty of outlets for the chocolates, thanks mainly to your business flair, so we'll keep going even if the worst happens. Poor Frank, though. The new shop's likely to dent his profits, and he hasn't seemed really well since that business with the poisoned cyclists.'

Mandy said, 'That's an idea. I suppose poisoning the competition is out of the question?'

Before Libby could answer, the morning's first customers arrived, full of gossip about the new shop. 'I hear they'll be serving those French crossings,' old Mrs Blandish announced, handing over a pile of coppers in payment for her weekly order of a small split tin and half a dozen currant buns.

'Croissants?' Mandy suggested.

The old lady shrugged. 'Some such. Can't get my tongue round these foreign words.' She winked at Libby. 'You'd better check that money. Never was much good at sums,' she said, as she did every time.

Libby counted the coins into the till, sucking in her cheeks to keep her face straight. 'Perfect as always.' She avoided Mandy's eye. Like many of the town's oldest citizens, widowed Mrs Blandish rarely left Exham on Sea except for an annual trip to Birmingham to stay with her daughter. A farmer's wife all her married life, she'd never had the leisure time to cross the Channel for a taste of real French croissants.

A small ray of hope – perhaps Terence Marchant's raid on Frank's customers would fail, and they would stick to their old ways.

* * *

Later that day, Libby's kitchen rang with the noise of chocolate grinders and food processors. She emptied smooth, tempered chocolate into piping bags and began to fill paper cases. Mandy sat on the other side of the room, fingers flying over a computer keyboard as she recorded weights, volumes, and notes about the ingredients.

'I gave this batch an extra two minutes,' Libby called. 'I think perhaps the beans were less ripe than the last ones. Fingers crossed I got it right.'

Mandy tapped into the machine. 'Me too, Mrs F. That was one expensive batch.'

'It puts the unit price up quite a bit,' Libby admitted, 'but with luck, it'll improve the quality.'

'Enough for us to call it a premier range?'

Libby looked up again, surprised. 'Good idea. I hadn't thought of that.' She paused in her work, impatient to reveal the surprise she had in store for her apprentice.

'Mandy, I've got something for you.' She peeled off her gloves, opened a drawer, and took out a set of keys, dangling them in front of Mandy. 'Here.'

Mandy leapt to her feet. 'You mean...'

'Don't get too excited. It's just an old banger, but it should get you around the countryside.'

Mandy grabbed the keys and dashed outside. 'Where is it?'

Libby giggled. 'It's hidden round the corner. I wanted it to be a surprise.'

She followed Mandy down the street. 'There.' She pointed at a bright yellow car. 'It's five years old, but it's only done 20,000 miles. Go on, try it out. It belongs to the business, officially, but you can hang onto it.'

Mandy, breathless with excitement, drove away with a flourish. The house seemed suddenly quiet. Libby piled used bowls in the dishwasher, suddenly lonely. There was plenty more work to do, but she'd lost her enthusiasm.

She trudged upstairs to the bathroom, where the airing cupboard door was ajar. A pair of green eyes gleamed in the depths of the cupboard. Libby addressed her marmalade cat. 'At least you're still here with me, Fuzzy.' The cat opened her eyes wider, glanced at her mistress, and turned her back. Libby sighed. 'You're such good company.'

Shipley appeared from behind her back and Fuzzy hissed. Libby diverted the dog down the stairs and out into the garden.

Back in the kitchen, she settled in Mandy's chair and looked at the business records. An hour later, she raised her head and rubbed her eyes. The business was fine. She should be excited, but despite her best attempts she couldn't raise more than a small smile. The records showed increased sales, not only to Jumbles, their main outlet in Bath, but also to other department stores in Bristol and even Exeter. Three small shops in Taunton were now stocking Mrs Forest's Chocolates.

Libby had to face it. Mandy was a far better businesswoman than she would ever be. She'd earned the car.

As Libby finished adding columns of figures, her phone rang. Her heart lurched as she glanced at the display screen. Why was Robert phoning from his honeymoon?

'Mum?' The panicked voice was almost unrecognisable. 'It's Sarah. She's gone.'

12

SARAH

'Where are you?' Libby managed to keep her voice calm.

'I'm in the hotel. Mum, I don't know what to do.'

Libby guessed he was pacing, unable to settle. 'Sit down, breathe out, and tell me what happened.'

'Sarah and I had a row, yesterday. It wasn't anything really, just one of those stupid arguments about which restaurant to choose. I wanted to eat in the hotel and she wanted to go somewhere new.'

'That doesn't sound too serious. Did she drive off in a huff, or something?'

'No, nothing like that. We made it up. I took her out to the restaurant she wanted, though I don't know why she was so keen to go there. It wasn't as nice as this place.'

Libby forced herself to be patient. 'So when did she disappear?'

'We finished our steaks and the waitress brought the dessert menu. Sarah can't resist a dessert. She's a Pavlova and chocolate tart kind of a girl, but before she'd even ordered, she went to the ladies and didn't come back.'

'You mean, she left the restaurant?'

'She took the car. I had to get a taxi.'

At least, if she'd taken the car, it was Sarah's choice to leave. She hadn't been abducted. Libby had been letting her imagination run away. She opened her mouth to ask questions, but closed it again. She'd never discoverthe truth over the telephone. Instead, she said, 'I'm on my way. Don't move until I arrive.'

* * *

The hotel was a large, five star affair on the Devon and Somerset border overlooking the sea. Robert and Sarah had decided, to Libby's surprise, to honeymoon in the West Country. 'We'll go abroad another time. For now, we want to walk in the countryside and enjoy a spot of luxury in the hotel. No need to clock up a huge carbon footprint.'

The hotel was situated hardly any distance from Exham as the crow flew, but the winding roads of rural Somerset tripled the length of the journey. Stuck behind a tractor on the steep incline from Porlock, Libby gripped the wheel with white knuckles.

She should have asked Max to lend her the Land Rover, but they hadn't spoken since the quiz. She'd been too annoyed about Kate Stephenson. The car chugged slowly up the hill and she feared the engine was about to give up the attempt. 'Hurry up,' she muttered through clenched teeth.

As the vehicle coughed its way between the tall ivy covered walls leading to the hotel, Libby's stomach turned over as she caught sight of her son, waving from the imposing entrance. She left the car on the gravel drive. She'd argue with the hotel management later, if necessary.

Robert's face was puffy and pink. He'd looked like that as a little boy, falling over, scraping his hands and knees, and then trying not to cry. Usually undemonstrative, he wrapped his arms round his mother in a giant bear hug. 'I'm so glad you're here. I just didn't know what to do.'

Libby led him into the lounge and ordered cups of tea, judging that to be more calming than coffee. He was already hyped up.

At last, stammering and hiccupping, he told Libby the story. He'd waited in the restaurant, choosing dessert, relieved Sarah had forgotten their quarrel. He'd topped up her glass and settled back, looking round the room.

'After she'd been gone about a quarter of an hour, I thought it was part of some practical joke,' he said. 'You know how the lads were teasing, saying they knew where we were going for the honeymoon. I thought they might have set me up, but the place was full of couples and I didn't recognise anyone.'

He tried to laugh and Libby thought her heart would break as he screwed his knuckles into his eyes. 'Eventually, I asked one of the waitresses to go into the ladies to check for Sarah.'

'But she wasn't there?'

'She'd disappeared.'

Libby said, 'Did you call the police?'

'They'll say she left of her own accord. After all, she is an adult, but she isn't answering her phone, and she always has it with her.'

'Maybe the battery's run out?'

Robert gave a painful laugh. 'You know Sarah. She's too efficient to let that happen.'

It was true. Libby had often envied Sarah's organisational abilities. 'It's probably time to contact the police, now she's been away all night.'

Robert shrugged. 'They won't do anything.'

'Not at first.' Libby bit off the words. She'd been about to point out the police would be interested once Sarah had been missing for a few days. 'Let's get home to Exham. You should go to the farm and tell Sarah's parents while I talk to Max.'

* * *

Max looked less than welcoming when Libby drew up in his drive. She'd called him on the phone, and told him what had happened.

Now, his first words took her by surprise. 'Why did you go rushing off to Devon without telling me? Maybe I could have helped if you'd asked me along.'

She clicked her tongue. 'I can look after myself, you know.' She had no time to worry about his feelings. 'Robert's beside himself with worry, and I need to concentrate. What could Sarah have been doing, running away without telling him? They haven't been married a week, yet.'

Max sighed. 'Honeymoon quarrels? They're common enough. The happy couple spend a fortune on the ideal wedding, with so many details they're exhausted by the time it happens. They imagine a perfect day, a honeymoon like a holiday advertisement and never a cross word, until reality kicks in. Thousands of couples split up in the first year of marriage.'

Libby frowned. 'Even if that's true, this is more than a honeymoon spat. Sarah knows Robert will be beside himself with worry and she'd contact him if she could. I think we should talk to Joe, even if we keep it unofficial, to see what he thinks. After all, having a police officer in the family should give us a few advantages, don't you think?'

Libby winced at Max's mixed expression of amusement and irritation. She was giving out mixed messages which was unfair, although they accurately represented the confusion in her head.

She still couldn't decide whether or not she wanted to be part of Max's family. 'Please talk to Joe.'

Max held up his hands. 'I give in. I'll text him, see if he can come round once he's off duty. He's busy on Liam's case at the moment, and that's more important than Sarah driving off in a huff. At the moment, at least.'

As he texted, Libby pondered aloud. 'It's out of character for Sarah. She's always so sensible and thoughtful. She's brought Robert right out of his shell. Since she came into his life, he's sent me lovely presents on Mother's Day and hasn't forgotten my birthday once. She's too kind to let Robert worry, even if she's angry with him.' She touched Max's hand. 'You don't think something dreadful could have happened to her, do you?'

Max smiled and the tension between them dissolved. 'Let's not rush ahead, imagining the worst. One step at a time. Logic and good sense are your specialties, Lib, so keep a cool head. We'll work it out.'

BELINDA

While Max phoned his son, Libby watched Shipley exploring every inch of the garden, snuffling behind shrubs and following the trail of night visitors from the kitchen window. Bear leaned against her legs, his eyes on the younger dog, like a wise teacher minding an overexcited pupil.

Max followed them outside, dropping the phone in his pocket. 'Joe agrees there's little the police can do until Sarah's been missing a while. Do her parents know she's missing?'

'Robert's already at the farm. He dropped me off at home and took my car.' Her son's lanky body hunched over the steering wheel of Libby's tiny car would have made her laugh under less tense circumstances.

'Let's get over there.' Max ushered the dogs into the Land Rover, brushing dried mud from the seats. 'If Shipley's as clever as you say, maybe we could teach him to work a vacuum cleaner.'

Normally, it would have been a joy to ride through the countryside on such a day, with the July sun shining, but not yet hot enough to bake the soil or dull the green of the grass verges. As they drew near Handiwater, the Carmichaels' farm, Libby's spirits plummeted further. Last time she'd visited, Mike's strange behaviour had unnerved her, and the Papadopoulos couple had set her teeth on edge, but those minor irritations paled to nothing compared to her dread of what she might find today. Belinda, Sarah's mother, must be beside herself with worry.

Mike was at the table, sitting beside Robert, rocking gently and staring into space. A slice of toast lay, neglected, on a plate. Bear, as though sensing the atmosphere, leaned against Mike, gazing at him through big eyes, but for once the farmer took no notice.

Shipley snuffled into every corner of the kitchen, finally subsiding under the table.

Robert whispered, 'I can't get any sense out of him since I told him Sarah's missing. He's hardly hearing me.'

Max laid a hand on Mike's shoulder. 'Mike. Come on, man. Let's find out what's going on.'

Mike's eyes seemed out of focus. 'What? What did you say?'

Libby sat on the opposite side of the table, leaning across to touch Mike's hand. 'Where's Belinda?'

He heaved a long, heavy sigh. 'Gone.'

'Gone? Gone where? When?'

'A few days ago.'

Libby and Max shared a startled look. Max said, 'You mean, she was already missing when you were at the quiz?'

The farmer shrugged. 'I thought she'd be back by now. But if Sarah's gone, too...' He left the end of the sentence hanging in the air.

Max walked round the table, pulled up a chair, and sat next to Libby. 'I think you'd better tell us what's going on.'

Mike was silent for a long time, until Libby's urge to give him a good shake became almost overwhelming. At last, he seemed to rouse himself from his thoughts. 'She's been acting funny lately.

We've always had the odd argument. Well, you do when you've been married awhile. She has a temper on her, does Belinda. A firecracker, that's what Sarah calls her.'

Libby felt Robert stiffen at the mention of his new wife's name, but Mike kept talking. 'She's often walked out the door, saying she won't return. Always comes back, though.'

Libby put in, 'How long does she stay away for?'

'That's the thing, you see. Never more than twenty-four hours before, no matter how angry she's been.'

Robert stood up, his face pale. 'But now, she and Sarah are both missing.' He pressed a hand to his mouth as if to stop his lips trembling. 'Something terrible must have happened.'

He looked from Max to Libby, eyes wide, his breathing ragged. 'What are we going to do? How are we going to find them?' He took a step towards the door.

'Wait.' Max's voice cut in. 'We'll find them, for sure, but we need a plan, or else we'll rush around like headless chickens.'

At that moment, the door flew open and Sarah's brother, Tim, burst in, causing Shipley to bark wildly and Bear to raise his head from his paws and sigh.

'I came as fast as I could.'

* * *

Tim's appearance in the farmhouse, looking as pale and distraught as his father, sent the tension levels in the room sky high. Libby put aside her suspicions over Tim's involvement in Liam's death, making a mental note to follow that up later. Meanwhile, his concern for his sister and mother was obvious in his strained face and staring eyes.

Determined to be practical, Libby said, 'The first thing is to go through Belinda's papers. See if there are any clues – letters, or...'

She stopped abruptly. Presumably, Mike didn't know about Belinda's money worries.

Robert, arms folded, his face like stone, said, 'Do you know anything about this, Tim?'

Tim squared up to him, his face only inches away. 'Are you accusing me of something?'

Robert's chin jutted and he breathed hard. 'Seems to me, whenever you're around, there's trouble.'

Tim, face brick-red, clenched both fists. 'At least I haven't lost my wife less than a week after the wedding.'

Robert, clearly no longer able to manage his feelings, made a strangled sound and released his tension by swinging a right at Tim's face.

In a flash, Max was out of his seat, closely followed by Shipley and Bear. He grabbed Robert's wrist and twisted it behind his back. Mike, roused from his turpitude by the fight, jumped up, snatched at Tim and pinioned his son's arms with the easy strength of a man who spent his life heaving bales of hay around.

Libby ran to grab Shipley's collar and call Bear back, before the two dogs could join in the melee. Almost as angry as the two young men, she raised her voice. 'Can't you concentrate on what's important? Does it always have to be a competition with you boys? Sarah and Belinda are missing, and you two fighting won't get them back. We know you're upset. Sit down and think sensibly.'

Mike changed his grip on Tim, giving his son a shove that sent him reeling backwards, to crash into a chair. It teetered on two legs before clattering to the floor. 'What would your mother say?' Mike snarled.

Tim regained his balance and brushed his jacket, his face mutinous. 'He started it.'

He sounded like a child.

As Libby stifled a sudden, inappropriate urge to giggle, Max released Robert and sighed. 'What are you, teenagers?'

Robert, avoiding his mother's eyes, subsided into a chair and leaned his elbows on the table, resting his head in his hands.

His father shouted, 'Tim, sit down, shut up for once in your life, and listen.' Tim slouched towards the table and obeyed, shooting an angry glance at the top of Robert's head.

Mike, apparently stirred back to life by the testosterone in the room, laid both hands on the table. 'Now, if you two can stop behaving like ten year olds for a while, Libby here was about to make suggestions. And before you argue,' he forestalled Tim, who was rising from his seat, 'Mrs Forest and Mr Ramshore are the experts. You listen to what they have to say or leave my house. Got it?'

Libby took the sullen silence for agreement. 'I was suggesting we go through any papers that Belinda might have in the house, to see if there are any clues as to where she might have gone. A diary, or something.'

Tim heaved himself to his feet. 'I'll have a look through her desk.'

Max caught Libby's eye, raised one eyebrow a millimetre, and suggested, 'It might be better for Libby to look through Belinda's things. You know, they're both women. I'm sure Belinda would rather have it that way.'

Libby had to admire Max's guile. She wanted to get to Belinda's papers before Tim had a chance, for he was still a suspect, and Max had hit on exactly the best way to make that happen. Men were so nervous about 'women's things'. What did they think they were going to find? It was a clever move.

Tim shrugged. 'If you think you can find things quicker. I guess working as a private eye teaches you how to pry into other people's lives.'

Libby groaned as her son, hands balled into fists, scraped his chair back. She held up a hand. 'Don't start again.'

Max said, 'Tim and Robert, you make lists of Sarah's friends. Tim, you're likely to know her oldest friends while Robert identifies people she sees regularly. With any luck we'll end up with all of them.' He turned to Mike. 'Maybe you could do the same for Belinda? As soon as we've got the names, we can see if they know anything useful.'

14

PATHWAY

Libby sat at Belinda's desk, situated in the corner of the tiny room used as a farm office. Three large filing cabinets stood in a row along one wall, each neatly labelled. 'EU subsidies,' she read aloud. 'Milk 2000 to 2005,' and, 'milk 2005 to 2010'. Deciding to ignore business documents and look for personal information first, Libby pulled open the top drawer of the desk. It was full of neatly arranged boxes of paper clips, Post-it® notes, staplers, scissors, and rulers. The second drawer was more interesting, containing a haphazard pile of documents. Libby lifted them out, elbowed aside the keyboard on the desktop, and began to work methodically through the pile.

Most of the papers were letters received in the past few weeks. It seemed this drawer was used as an inbox, which meant the third drawer was probably an outbox. To test the theory, Libby pulled open the third drawer. It was half empty. Belinda clearly used a computer in preference to pen and paper. Returning to the second drawer, Libby flipped through the first few layers of documents.

Leaflets and government instructions made up most of the

correspondence. She found a couple of 'reply to wedding invitation' cards, both offering apologies from friends unable to attend Sarah's wedding. Remembering Sarah's excitement about her wedding day, Libby offered up a brief prayer that the young woman had come to no harm. Robert's heart would be broken if anything happened to his new wife.

She finished reading the letters in the pile, finding nothing of interest, dumped them back in the drawer, flipped it shut, and turned to the computer.

After the usual wait while the machine slowly woke up, a dialogue box appeared requesting a password. Libby was about to return to the kitchen to ask Mike, when her eye was caught by a sticky note attached to the desk lamp. It seemed Belinda, like most people, had difficulty remembering passwords.

Libby used to keep her own next to the computer, until Max and Mandy joined forces and insisted she set up a spreadsheet with all the passwords she needed, saving it under yet another password. She'd complained, 'What if I forget that one?'

Max had laughed. 'I'll put it in my list. And you put mine in yours. So long as at least one of us manages to remember our password, we'll be all right.'

With an effort, Libby swallowed the lump in her throat. He'd probably be sharing passwords with Kate Stephenson, soon. Startled by her own thoughts, Libby dropped the note. It was jealousy, pure and simple, that was making her angry with Max.

She shook her head. 'Not now,' she muttered, and entered the combination of numbers and letters. It worked. She could now access Belinda's programs. Email. That was the first place to look.

She crossed her fingers, hoping Belinda would not have bothered with more passwords, and sure enough, the inbox opened at the first click. Libby scanned the list of senders. Most of the traffic dealt with arrangements for Sarah's wedding and lunches with friends. There was an exchange with Sarah, discussing the colour of the bridesmaids' dresses, and a note to Belinda's aunt, asking whether she needed help to get to the wedding. 'And, thank you for lending us your jewellery. Sarah would love to wear the pearls,' it ended. They had been the 'something old' worn by the bride.

One name in the senders' list caught Libby's attention. The sender was X. 'Xavier?' she wondered aloud.

With one click, she opened the email. 'Remember not to deviate from the Pathway.'

Libby checked the date. The email had arrived three days ago, the day Belinda disappeared. She printed out the email and set it on one side, her pulse racing, and scanned the rest of the email, but found nothing more from X. She searched with the word Path and Pathway, excited to discover two items. To her disgust, they contained nothing more threatening than a lawn mower adver-tisement and a reference to paving stones. Belinda, it seemed, was a keen gardener.

Max's eyes opened wide when she showed him the email. 'If that's not a threat, then I'm a Dutchman.'

Libby waved the sheet of paper at Mike. 'Is this from Xavier Papadopoulos?'

The farmer's cheek twitched. 'I don't know. I never use the computer – can't abide staring at a screen. I leave all that to Liam. He prints out emails that come for me and I tell him how to respond. I don't know anything about Belinda's account. No idea who she's been talking to.'

He turned away and reached for the kettle. His hand shook so that he could hardly lift it. Max said, 'Don't you think it's time you came clean with us? I think you know more than you're letting on about your wife's disappearance. What's going on?'

The farmer looked from Libby to Max, groaned, and sank into the nearest chair. 'I can't. I can't tell you anything.'

Max said, 'In that case, it's time we called in the police.'

Tim and his father spoke together. 'No!'

Tim licked his lips. 'Come on, Dad. I guess it's time to explain.'

* * *

Mike leaned his elbows on the table, head between his hands, face hidden. 'Belinda hasn't been... Well, she hasn't been herself for a long time. It all started when her mother died. Two years ago, that was. They'd always been close and Belinda took it very hard. She wouldn't talk to me about it, but the church helped. She started going to church of a Sunday.'

The sound he uttered lay midway between a laugh and a moan. 'We'd never really been churchgoers. We were baptised, of course. Everyone was in those days, and we went to Sunday School. Mostly to give our parents a bit of peace at the weekend, I reckon.'

He made a ghastly attempt at a smile. 'We hadn't set foot in the church for years, but the rector came round about her mother's funeral, and he was very kind to Belinda. He came back a few times, to talk about her mother, and Belinda went to church once or twice. She liked it there. Said they were friendly. She wanted me to go too, but I can't abide all that singing and kneeling. Anyway, after a while, it got to be a habit and she was going every Sunday.'

Libby, impatient, longed to hurry him, but she knew Mike needed to take his time. She forced herself to speak quietly. 'Where does Xavier Papadopoulos come in?'

'I'm getting to that. Even though she kept going to church,

Belinda was unhappy. I suppose you could say she was depressed. She could hardly get out of bed in the morning, and that wasn't like her. Even in the spring, when we were lambing, she wouldn't go into the fields. Until then, it was her favourite job. She used to stay out overnight helping the ewes.'

Tim joined in with an awkward laugh. 'Mum was the best for a difficult lambing. She has tiny hands, you see.'

The nerve in Mike's cheek twitched. 'Going to church helped a bit. She got friendly with some of the folks there, meeting them for coffee and so on. Then, one day, she met Olivia Papadopoulos. You met her, remember, that day you visited?'

'Of course. She and her husband didn't seem pleased to find me here.'

Mike fidgeted, rubbing his leg. 'He'd come to... I mean, he was on business.' He shot a glance at Libby, eyes narrowed, and looked away again. 'Not one to chat, Xavier Papadopoulos. He can be a bit sharp, but I owe him a lot. Belinda's recovery was his doing.'

'Really?' Libby found that difficult to believe. Mike's restlessness suggested he was holding something back. Libby glanced at Max for confirmation, and he returned the smallest nod.

'Olivia invited Belinda to their house one evening. They run these groups, you see, of bereaved people, where they all get together and, well, talk, I suppose. It seems to help. It wouldn't do for me but it worked a treat for Belinda.' Libby guessed that a stoic farmer like Mike would run a mile from any talking therapy.

'Is this group the Pathway in the email?'

He wrinkled his nose. 'That's what they called it. The Pathway to Health.'

Max joined the conversation. 'Have you been to any of these meetings, Mike?'

The farmer lurched to his feet, grabbed empty coffee cups

from the table and piled them in the sink. 'Belinda preferred to go alone, and I didn't mind. I was just pleased to have the old Belinda back again.' He dropped a cup. It shattered, the sharp crack reverberating around the kitchen. He made no attempt to pick up the pieces.

He swung round, worry etched on the lines across his forehead and round his mouth. 'Just recently, she's been busy with the wedding and I thought she was back to her old self. She wasn't going to the Pathway meetings so often, being busy on the farm, you see. She even helped with the lambs again.' A brief smile lit his face. 'She had three orphans in the kitchen at one time, giving them the bottle all through the day and night.'

Mike ran his hand over the back of his head, rubbing the hair until sparse strands stood on end. 'Olivia came over to talk to her one day. I was out in the fields, so I don't know what she said to my wife, but Belinda was crying when I got back. In floods of tears, as bad as when her mother died. She wouldn't tell me what was wrong, just that she didn't want to go back to those meetings. I suppose they fell out. That's what happens in these groups. Bickering, you know.'

Libby nodded. She'd seen plenty of squabbles at the Exham History Society, and on her visits to the Knitters' Guild. The atmosphere could be electric. If only she'd been a fly on the wall when Olivia Papadopoulos fell out with Belinda.

Tired of trying to guess what Mike was holding back, Libby strode across the room and confronted him. 'Be honest, Mike. Why were the Papadopoulos couple here, that day I met them. Was it really business?'

Mike looked straight at Libby, at last. 'They came about Belinda. They said she'd agreed to go to a Pathway meeting the day after the wedding, but hadn't turned up. I told them she'd been tired, but that wasn't the truth. She hadn't wanted to go. I could tell something had upset her, and she didn't want anything more to do with them. She told me she was going to the shops instead. She didn't expect them to come round to the farm.'

He flattened his hair with one hand. 'After you'd gone, I told Xavier and Olivia to stop coming around. If Belinda didn't want to go to their group any more, she didn't have to. They gave me a load of bull about letting down the other group members and I said I'd pass the messages on to Belinda. But she never came home.'

Max said, 'So, she disappeared and Xavier Papadopoulos and his wife had no idea where she went?' He was rubbing a finger along his upper lip, a gesture he used when deep in thought. 'Or was that the impression they wanted to give?'

Max didn't trust the strange couple any more than Libby did. The thought was comforting. She said, 'I think we should pay a visit to the Papadopoulos couple. It sounds as though they were putting pressure on Belinda to keep within the group. Like some sort of cult. It sounds a bit sinister.'

'I didn't know about any threatening email until today,' Mike admitted. 'Do you think that's why she disappeared?'

Max shrugged into his coat. 'It's time we found out. Mike, you stay here in case Belinda or Sarah turn up. Robert and Tim, if you've finished those lists, get on your phones and see what you can find out about this group. What did you say it's called, Mike?'

Mike frowned, biting his lip. 'The Pathway to Health.'

'Meanwhile, Libby and I will visit Mr and Mrs Papadopoulos.'

15

MEETING

'I could kick myself,' Libby said, as the car sped away from the farm. 'I've already been to their house and talked to the Papadopoulos pair, but I didn't get anything sensible from them.' She told Max about her previous visit. Her voice rose. 'In fact, that's why I was at the quiz.'

She cleared her throat. Now wasn't the time to quarrel about Max's fawning over Kate Stephenson. 'I thought Belinda would be there, but she didn't show up, although Olivia Papadopoulos behaved as though she expected her. Was she just pretending? I'm beginning to think that couple know a great deal about the disappearance of Belinda and Sarah. Xavier always seems to be in the picture, even at the wedding. I'm sure he was the reason Belinda backed away from me. Then, they both popped up at Mike's farm and spooked him, and now there's evidence they were bullying Belinda. They're right at the top of my current list of suspects.'

'Before we do too much guesswork, let's see if there's a good reason for Belinda and Sarah to run away. Maybe mother and daughter have gone off somewhere on their own. Belinda could be having some sort of breakdown, and Sarah's looking after her.'

Libby snorted. 'That's not likely. Sarah would have called Robert. She was on her honeymoon, for heaven's sake. You don't leave your new husband just after the wedding, to look after your mother. According to Robert, it was just a lover's spat.'

Max's eyes stayed on the road. It was difficult to read his face. 'Are you sure Robert's— well, I'll speak frankly. Is Robert telling the whole truth?'

Libby felt a chill at the base of her spine. How dare Max accuse her son? Her voice was cold. 'What are you trying to say? You can't think Robert—'

'I'm just looking at the facts, as if he were any other young husband having a row with his new wife.'

Libby shifted in her seat to put more space between Max and herself. She heard the ice in her own voice. 'If you're suggesting Robert had anything to do with Sarah's disappearance, you're mistaken. And why would he want to do anything to her mother?'

Max was soothing. 'I'm sure Robert has nothing to hide.'

Libby could have hit him. 'Don't try to placate me, as though I'm a stranger. I'm perfectly aware he'll be under police suspicion if Sarah isn't found soon, but I would think you'd trust him. He's my son.'

She stared towards the hedge, where the branches loomed close enough to scratch the car. Max's hand touched her knee but she pushed it away. How dare he suspect Robert? A tiny throb of anxiety started up at the back of her head. Trevor was the boy's father, and look at how he'd behaved. Like father, like son?

She closed her eyes. Pictures of Robert as a little boy filled her head. There was the day Ali, his little sister, broke his train set. He'd taken an hour to write a letter to Santa, tongue poking from the corner of his mouth, and he was too excited to sleep on

Christmas Eve. Ali trod on his precious train and the funnel broke, but even then, Robert stayed calm.

Libby couldn't remember a single time before today that Robert had lost control of his temper. Relieved, she let out a puff of pent-up breath. 'Robert is one of the gentlest, kindest people I know and I'm proud to be his mother. Tim pushed him too far, today, when he was already wound up over Sarah. I know Robert wouldn't hurt a fly.'

Max navigated a pothole that covered most of the lane. 'I believe you. Anyway, there's no reason to suppose anything's happened to either Sarah or her mother. Until we know why they've disappeared, let's not quarrel about the suspects.' He turned a corner and the house came into view. 'Here we are. Maybe we'll find some answers now.'

Just as before, when Libby had arrived with the cake, the front door was open before they had a chance to ring the bell. Libby muttered, 'It's almost as though Olivia Papadopoulos spends all day sitting by the window, waiting for visitors.'

'Why, Mrs Forest, how lovely to see you again.' Olivia waved them into the house, a broad smile failing to reach her eyes. 'Do bring those lovely dogs inside. They could perhaps wait in the kitchen? And this must be Mr Ramshore. Of course, we've heard all about you from Mandy.' Libby shooed Bear and Shipley into a spacious farmhouse-style kitchen. Olivia put a bowl of water on the floor and closed the door firmly.

Libby, surprised, said, 'Mandy?'

The woman's eyes glittered. 'She came to a meeting with our friend, Kate.' Libby felt a familiar chill at the base of her spine at the thought of Mandy being pulled into the orbit of the sinister Papadopoulos couple.

Olivia took her arm. 'Come through. It's such a beautiful day, let's drink coffee in the conservatory. It's one of my favourite places.'

Libby's thoughts raced. Why had Kate brought Mandy here? Her stomach churned. Olivia did not appear to notice her silence, for Max kept up a calm flow of conversation. 'I expect you know Belinda hasn't been home for a while. Mike, her husband, is getting anxious.' He didn't mention Sarah's disappearance. 'We wanted to talk to you because Belinda often comes to your groups.'

Olivia waved Libby to a wicker chair facing the garden. As she sat, the sun shone full in her eyes and she shifted, uncomfortable, as though under a spotlight. Olivia poured coffee and offered cream and sugar. 'I'm afraid Belinda's enthusiasm for our little group has waned recently.' She gave a theatrical sigh. 'It happens, I'm afraid. Some people take what they need from our gatherings and then leave. Others, of course, stay to help newcomers who need support.'

Max smiled and sipped coffee. 'We'd like to know more about the group.'

Olivia's eyes narrowed, her face suddenly sharp, reminding Libby of a fox. 'Tell me, Mr Ramshore, are you here as Belinda's friend or in some official capacity? I know you work with the police.' She held up a hand, a ring on every finger, the painted nails long, like claws. 'We have nothing to hide, but I think honesty's always best, don't you?'

Libby turned her head from side to side, trying to avoid the sun. 'My son's married to Belinda's daughter, Sarah, who also disappeared yesterday. As you can imagine, he's beside himself with worry. I'm here as a mother. Max and I are not being paid to investigate Belinda and Sarah's disappearance.' They were being paid to investigate Liam's death, but Libby chose not to mention that. As yet, there seemed to be no link between the two, but she refused to believe a suspicious death and two mysterious disappearances were unconnected.

Olivia shook her head. 'Ah. I was never blessed with children. It's my tragedy. Such trials brought me through tribulation to follow the Pathway to Health. My husband has many remarkable qualities as you know, Mrs Forest. One of those is his gift as a healer.'

The door opened. Olivia rose to her feet. 'And here he is. Xavier, you remember Libby Forest.'

'My dear.' Xavier Papadopoulos acknowledged Libby with a cold stare and a brief nod, but spoke to his wife. 'Have you forgotten? Our meeting begins in two minutes.' Olivia moved towards the door, patches of pink on her cheeks. Her husband continued, 'I see we have the pleasure of a second visit from Mrs Forest.' He watched his wife leave before turning his attention to Libby and Max, lifting one hand as though blessing the visitors. The sun lit his grey hair like a halo. Long, loose robes flowed from head to toe, and as he raised his arm, a sleeve slid back to reveal a tattoo. Libby's gaze locked on the design.

He saw the direction of her eyes. 'You're interested in my tattoo?' He uncovered the length of the tattooed snake that wound around his right elbow, travelling up his arm until it disappeared at the shoulder. 'The product of my time in India.'

Libby, horrified and fascinated, jumped as Max's voice rang out. 'So, you follow an Indian guru?'

The man pulled down his sleeve. 'I fear I have no time to chat, pleasant though that would be. I must ask you to excuse Olivia and myself, unless you'd care to join our meeting.'

16

SÉANCE

'Are you crazy?' Max hissed, his mouth close to Libby's ear, as they followed Xavier through the house and up the wide staircase.

'You don't have to come. Not your thing, I suppose.'

'I'm not leaving you alone with this pair. They're stark staring mad, if you ask me.'

'In that case, let's see what happens.'

They passed the door of the music room where Libby had listened to the Rachmaninov, and continued on to the end of the corridor. Muffled voices sounded from behind the heavy oak door as Olivia Papadopoulos pushed it wide, ushering Libby and Max into the room. Heavy curtains blocked all natural light, so that only a single lamp lit the room. A handful of people sat in the gloom, their armchairs arranged in the shape of a horseshoe. They faced a low table, covered in a pristine white cloth, a water jug and glass, a wooden bowl, and two candles.

Xavier Papadopoulos took a position behind the table, his hands lifted in greeting. 'Welcome, my friends and fellow members, as we walk the Pathway to Health. Today, we have two visitors. Some of you may recognise Mrs Forest and Mr Ramshore.'

Did the small collection of smiling faces belong to an audience or a congregation? Libby's heart sank as she saw Kate Stephenson lean forward and wave. 'Hello, Mrs Forest – or may I call you Libby?' With a sweeping gesture of one arm, Kate addressed the room. 'Libby and I have spent time together. Let's welcome her to our small band of friends.' She led a burst of applause. The twitch of Max's eyebrows betrayed surprise at seeing Kate, but not, Libby decided, displeasure.

All the onlookers were new to Libby. Three older women sat close together, a little apart from a young girl with unwashed hair who gazed glumly at bitten nails. The two remaining members of the group were men, one wearing flowing robes similar to those worn by Xavier Papadopoulos, while the other was dressed in a formal shirt, tie, and business suit.

Xavier Papadopoulos held out his arm, fingers elegantly curved, and beckoned his wife. 'Some of you, I believe, have need of our endeavours today. We must try to break through the bounds of this mortal realm and reach out to another dimension.'

Libby and Max shared a wry smile. It seemed Olivia was some kind of medium, purporting to put the dead in touch with the living. Libby shot a longing look at the door. Could she slip away without being noticed? This felt like a bad mistake.

It was too late. Xavier Papadopoulos lit the candles, wafted across the room, and dimmed the lamp while Olivia sat at the table. Max leaned very close to whisper, 'I wonder what's under that table?'

The dose of common sense calmed Libby's nerves. What harm could come from a couple of aging hippies playing at séances?

Olivia stirred something in the wooden bowl, and a sweet

scent permeated through the room. She muttered something Libby couldn't catch in a slow, rhythmic monotone. Her husband, his voice deep and soothing, exhorted the listeners to concentrate on their breathing. A clock ticked, insistent and regular in the quiet room, and Libby's eyes grew heavy. She took a deep breath, squeezed both fists tight, and dug her nails into her palms, blinking hard, willing herself to stay awake.

She stole a glance at Max's face. A small smile crinkled his eyes. At once, the tension in Libby's muscles seeped away. There was no need to panic while Max, sensible and down to earth, was there.

Some of the other attendees leaned forwards, hands on their knees, faces alert, as if expecting something exciting to happen, but others seemed drowsy, as though in a daze. The man in a business suit had his chin tucked into his chest, and Libby could almost believe he was dozing. Maybe he'd had a liquid lunch.

The urge to giggle took her by surprise. It must be a nervous reaction. Desperate not to attract attention, she sucked in both cheeks and held her breath. She felt rather than saw Max look her way, but dare not meet his eye for fear of bursting into hysterical laughter.

Xavier Papadopoulos clapped his hands, shocking Libby back to reality. Under cover of the noise, she coughed and regained control. The two women who'd been leaning forward, apparently entranced, rose and stood one on either side of Olivia. One wore a red kaftan, the other an everyday black jumper and trousers.

In the flickering candlelight, Olivia's face glowed. She closed her eyes and intoned in a deep voice, 'I feel someone near.' She reached out to the two women, taking their hands. 'One of your departed loved ones wishes to contact you.' She paused. The women's eyes never left her face as she raised their hands high above her head. 'His name,' she intoned, 'begins with F.' She paused, but no one spoke. 'Or S.'

The woman in black shook her head, but the red kaftan cried out, 'My father's name was Stephen.'

Olivia Papadopoulos dropped the other woman's hand. 'My dear, your father says you're not to worry. He's happy and reunited with his long-time love, who crossed over before him.'

The woman was nodding. 'My stepmother died a year ago.'

'That's right.'

'Can you a-ask him about my real mother. She died when I was a child, before Father remarried.'

Olivia gave a deep sigh. 'Wait, he's talking. He says your mother is there and all is well.'

'But which one is he with?' The woman was trembling, agitated. 'Which one is his true love? He can't be with both.'

Max whispered, 'Good question.'

Xavier Papadopoulos stepped forward. 'My dear, things are different in the Other Dimension.' His voice awarded the two words audible capital letters. 'On earth, we are bound by convention. Yet even here, people live happily with more than one partner. Your father is in a state of perpetual joy, his soul entwined with everyone he's ever loved.'

The woman's smile illuminated her face. Libby wanted to jump up and shout at the man. How could these people be so gullible?

Perhaps she'd made a sudden movement. Papadopoulos was suddenly watching, his face expressionless. He held Libby's gaze for a long moment. Defiant, she returned the stare as he dropped a hand on his wife's shoulder. 'Do you have messages for others in the room?'

Olivia was silent for a long time, breathing heavily. At last, 'Ah,' she moaned in a quiet, sing-song voice. 'I hear another. A husband who needs to connect. He wants to make amends.' She rose from her seat and paced round the room. Every head turned to follow her progress. 'He needs to contact his wife. He's been searching, longing to let her know how he feels. Is there anyone here whose name begins with B or E?'

The audience looked at each other, but no one spoke. Olivia returned to her seat. She swayed, gently. 'He tells me his wife uses a shortened name. Wait. It grows clearer. The full name is...' she paused. The room lay silent, her watchers holding their breath, waiting. 'The name is Elizabeth.'

The words hit Libby like a punch in the stomach. She stifled a gasp. The businessman further along the horseshoe jerked awake at the sound, turning to stare. Libby's chest felt squeezed tight, as though encased in steel.

Olivia intoned, 'He tells me he was a bad husband. He did wrong. He wants to tell Elizabeth he's sorry and is watching over her.'

Libby could hardly breathe for the pain in her chest. She swallowed, tasting bile. The room closed in around her and she could stand it no longer. One hand pressed to her mouth, she scrambled past Max and ran from the room, clattering down the stairs and out through the front door into the blessed fresh air.

* * *

Libby wheezed, dragging air into her lungs, her head fuzzy, while the ground seemed to sway under her feet. Someone was at her elbow. She recognised Mandy's voice. 'Mrs F. Whatever's the matter?' Sturdy in a pair of heavy boots, hands on hips, face creased in a worried frown, Mandy demanded, 'What are you doing here?'

It took all Libby's self-control to resist throwing both arms around her young friend. She tried a smile. 'N-nothing. It's nothing to worry about.' The wobbly voice sounded ridiculous, as though it belonged to someone else. Libby cleared her throat, aware she'd made an exhibition of herself. 'I had a shock, that's all.'

She'd let that woman's nonsense upset her, but it was all a sham. Olivia Papadopoulos had been playing a mean trick. Well, if she'd wanted to frighten Libby away from investigating the Pathway to Health, she was going to be disappointed. Nevertheless, the shock of a message supposedly from her dead husband, sickened Libby. How did the woman know so much about her? It couldn't just be luck.

She thought back over the séance. Olivia's spiel was well practised. Her husband's hand on her shoulder had been a signal. They'd probably used the trick with dozens of other vulnerable people. Most likely, everyone in the room was hoping for a message from a lost relative or friend. Why else would they put up with the Papadopoulos pair's mumbo-jumbo?

Libby had fallen for a cheap fairground trick. Furious, she waved an angry finger at Mandy. 'You're not going near those con artists and their phony séance.'

Mandy giggled. 'Good to see you're back to normal. Had me worried for a moment, there.'

'Sorry.' As Libby spoke, Max appeared, accompanied by Bear and Shipley. Max's face was creased with concern. He drew Libby close but she caught sight of Kate close behind, stiffened and pulled away. 'I'm fine. It was hot in there and I can't stand the smell of incense. That's all.'

Kate looked at Libby with soulful eyes. 'It's the emotion in the room. It can be overwhelming at first, but so many people find it helpful on their journey.'

Libby ignored her.

Max sounded anxious. 'Well, if you're OK.' He peered into Libby's face, but she was too angry to read whatever message he was trying to communicate. He gave the ghost of a shrug and turned away. 'Mandy, fancy meeting you here.'

'I said I'd pick Kate up after the Pathway meeting. We're having another session today and it's an excuse to drive out here in my swanky new car.'

Max and Kate admired Mandy's new wheels, while Libby fought to control her feelings. Max was on the warmest of terms with Kate. He didn't seem to notice anything strange about the woman, but it was obvious she was close to the Papadopoulos couple and their Pathway cult. Was he blind?

An unpleasant thought struck Libby. She'd wondered how Olivia Papadopoulos had known so much about her late husband. Perhaps Max had talked about him with Kate.

Surely Max would never betray Libby like that. Or would he? She bit her lip. Perhaps she didn't know him as well as she'd imagined. When they'd first met, he'd warned her he was difficult to know. Maybe she'd taken his feelings for granted...

Mandy and Kate were about to get into the car. Libby would think about Max later. For now, she wanted to extricate Mandy from the alternative therapist's tentacles and that wasn't going to be easy. 'Mandy,' she began. 'Don't forget we planned to work on those new flavours today.'

Mandy waved a hand. 'Don't give it a thought, Mrs F. I'll be there in plenty of time. And I'll tell you about Kate's wonder treatment for my phobia while we work.'

Kate, one foot already in the passenger side of Mandy's car, turned to wave. Her bag slid from her shoulder and fell to the floor at Libby's feet, the contents spilling onto the grass verge. With a muttered exclamation, Kate bent to scoop the pile of belongings back into the bag. She grabbed a blue coin-purse, a couple of pens, a tube of extra-strong mints, and several crumpled pieces of paper, probably receipts for petrol or meals. But it was another object, twinkling in the July sun, that caught Libby's attention. A key, just like the one near Liam's body.

A second later, the key had disappeared back into Kate's bag, leaving Libby wondering if she was mistaken. It could have been an everyday front door key, but if not, why would Kate have a key just like Liam's? And if they were linked in some way, did that mean there was more to Liam's death than either Libby or Max had realised?'

Max waved the two women off and ushered Libby and the dogs into the Land Rover. 'I can see you've got something to say.'

Libby shook her head in silence. Her eyes filled with ridiculous tears and she dashed the back of her hand across her face, wishing she kept a clean tissue in her handbag like sensible people did. Her head was full of questions, but for the first time since they'd met, she wondered if she could trust Max. Her feelings were a mess. She wouldn't mention Kate. Better to stick to the Papadopoulos couple.

She took a long breath. 'Those two are the biggest pair of frauds I've seen for a long time.' It was a relief to let her anger have an outlet. 'Do you think they're charging those people for coming to their Pathway?'

'I saw a collection plate on my way out. I presume it's there for contributions, but I didn't stop to give them anything, and neither did Kate. I'm sorry it took a while for me to follow you outside. I wanted to catch the end of that little interlude.'

Intrigued despite her anger, Libby asked, 'What happened after I left?'

'You mean, after that very dramatic storming out?'

Libby was not yet ready to be persuaded to smile. 'They frightened me. I know it was stupid, but that monotonous, ticking clock was like water dripping on my head. I couldn't stay for another moment.'

'You haven't got over the whole Trevor thing yet, have you?'

Libby tried a little laugh. 'I thought I had. I'd almost forgiven Trevor for the way he treated me like a doormat, but when that woman told everyone in the room what a fool I'd been, I was ashamed.'

Max took her hand and, without lifting his eyes from the road, touched it to his lips. Despite the turmoil in her head, she didn't bother to pull away. Max sounded angrier than she'd ever heard him. 'Trevor, far from floating happily in whatever other dimension the Papadopoulos couple describe, deserves to suffer for what he did.'

Libby took a moment. 'No, I wouldn't wish that on anyone, not even Trevor. I don't know what happens after death, but maybe there's a reckoning. Who knows? Anyway, my husband's gone and I'm not going to let him back into my life.'

'Good for you.' Max let go of her hand to change gear. They drove for a while in something that passed for companionable silence.

'By the way,' Max sounded business-like. 'I took a call from Joe as I was leaving the séance. He wants to talk to us and it sounds important. Let's drop the dogs back at my place, first.'

* * *

Constable Evans met Max and Libby at the police station. She knew him well. A big, florid man, overweight and sadly lacking in social graces, he'd probably remain a constable his entire career. He shook Max's hand and grunted at Libby. She sighed. Max always seemed to be accepted as one of the boys, while most of the police seemed determined to resent her.

The interview room, where they were to meet Joe, was a plain cube. It held a coffee table, with a small two seater settee arranged next to it, opposite a couple of armchairs. Two hard wooden chairs leaned against the walls and a camera was fixed high on the wall. Joe nodded towards the lens. 'We won't need to record our interview. You're not a suspect, this time.' Libby opened her mouth, saw the twinkle in Joe's eye and let her jaw snap shut. He was teasing.

A police constable arrived with three coffee cups, all with the battered look of office mugs more used to a quick rinse under the tap than a thorough cycle in the dishwasher. Libby struggled with a small carton of long-life milk. As ever, a few drops scattered across her shirt. She'd never learned the knack of opening those things. She took a careful sip from the mug, tried not to wince, and placed it back on the table.

'Sorry about the coffee.' Joe grinned. 'Not up to your standards, I'm afraid, but I wanted to show you this as soon as possible.' From a cardboard box, he drew out a couple of plastic zip-lock bags and placed them on the table. 'This is evidence, so I can't take it out of the bag, but I wondered what you made of it.'

Max said, 'That's the key you found near Liam's body, I suppose?'

Joe nodded. 'It is, but what I really wanted to show you was this.' He pointed to the other bag. 'We found a box in Liam's bedsit that the key fitted. These were inside.'

Libby and Max leaned forward to look at the slips of paper inside the bag. There were half a dozen lines of printed letters and numbers on the paper. Libby squinted. 'Those aren't real words.'

'Afraid not. I wondered if they meant anything to you.'

Libby shrugged.

Joe said, 'Do you remember that business of the body at the lighthouse?'

She smiled. 'Of course I do. It was the first time we'd met and you thought I was an interfering old woman.'

Joe side-stepped that. 'You solved that crime by working out a code.'

Libby guessed what was coming. 'That was a bit of a fluke, to be honest. It's not as though I'm a crossword puzzler.'

Max was frowning at the letters. 'These look like passwords, to me.'

Joe said, 'That's what we thought. Funny thing is, Liam doesn't seem to have a computer. Just his phone. We tried to find something the passwords fitted, but so far, we've hit a wall. Maybe they're not passwords at all, but some kind of code. Any chance of you helping crack it?'

Max pointed at the cardboard box. 'Is there anything else to point us in the right direction?'

Joe pulled out one more bag. 'Just these candles. As you can see, they're already half burned.'

Libby leaned forward until her nose was almost on the plastic bag. 'I can smell something, but it's faint, through the plastic. Max, can you smell it? Is it incense?'

Joe nodded. 'That's what we thought. Now, why would a young chap like Liam burn incense candles? We wondered if he used them with girlfriends. You know, to set the tone for a romantic evening, but if that's the case, why hide them away?'

Max told him about the Papadopoulos couple, the séance they'd attended, and the smell of incense in the room.

Joe beamed. 'Great stuff. Could be a link between this Pathway affair and Liam. Can I get you another cup of coffee to celebrate?'

'Not likely,' Libby answered without thinking. 'Are there any fingerprints or anything – er – forensic on the box or its contents?'

'Well, apart from Liam's fingerprints and bits of fibres that match bedding and so on from his bedsit, there's half a thumbprint on one of the candles that we haven't been able to match. With a bit of luck we'll find it belongs to one of your Papadopoulos friends.'

17

LUNCH

Glad to be back at the bakery next day, far away from séances, missing women, and dead farmhands, Libby slid a small loaf into a strong paper bag for Gladys from the flower shop. 'Anything else I can get for you? Your usual cream meringues?'

The woman shook her head. 'Can't stop. Too much to do.' She hurried to the door, almost colliding with Max, and scampered down the street, heading to the right, away from her own shop.

Max grinned and spoke to Libby, 'Can I whisk you away for lunch, later?'

They'd hardly spoken since returning from the police station. Libby, still on edge and longing for a quiet evening, had pleaded a headache and the need to talk to Robert, who was currently staying at Hope Cottage. Mandy had insisted on moving to Bristol while Robert stayed. 'Now I can use the car, I'll stay with Mum for a bit. I can get to Exham in less than an hour. Robert needs to be here with you.'

Libby had hoped a good night's sleep would improve her mood, but Robert and she had talked far into the night. He'd heard nothing from Sarah. He'd been calling and texting her all day, but either she'd switched off her mobile phone or it had run out of battery. 'I can't decide which is worse – is she running away from me, or has something terrible happened?'

He'd lifted Fuzzy and buried his face in the cat's fur. 'You were right about the police. They say there's no reason to worry, yet.'

Joe had said the same thing to Libby. A missing adult driving away in their own car, even a newly-wed, wouldn't trigger a major police search for several days.

Robert had continued, 'I've spoken to everyone I can think of. All her friends and work colleagues. Nobody knows what's going on.'

Libby, sick at heart, had struggled to think of something to comfort him. 'Look, Belinda's gone as well. They must be together. That's good, isn't it? I'm sure they won't come to any harm.'

She hoped she was right. She hated to see Robert in such a state of despair. He'd gone from a besotted new husband to a nail-biting wreck. If only she could mother him with ice cream, as she had in the old days when he fell off his bike. 'If she's not back in a couple of days, I'm sure the police will start searching in earnest.'

After persuading Robert to get some sleep, and falling into her own bed in the small hours, Libby had woken tired and despondent. Robert had still been asleep when she'd left the house.

Now, Libby frowned at Max to cover her elation at seeing him in the bakery. Lunch with Max sounded good. It seemed so long since they'd enjoyed anything like a date alone together. It had been business only recently.

She checked no one was around to hear. 'What did you want to talk about? I had a thought about Liam's notes—' She broke off as two schoolboys crashed through the door, fighting to be first to the counter, jostling each other and howling with laughter.

Max leaned against the glass showcase, admiring Libby's chocolates. 'What if I just want the pleasure of your company?'

Libby served the boys with blueberry muffins, their sniggers fading under Max's icy stare. 'We'll have to eat fast,' she said. 'I promised to do the afternoon shift and Frank's in a spin about this new patisserie. He's worried about business, and judging by Gladys's shifty behaviour over her order, I've a feeling he may be right. Could we go somewhere close?'

'Midday, then. At the Lighthouse?'

Once at the pub, they settled at a table in the corner and studied the menu. 'Sometimes, pub food is just what I need,' Max said. 'Not that it's ever as good as yours, of course.'

Libby took a breath, ready to bring up the subject of Kate Stephenson, but changed her mind. She didn't want to quarrel in public. 'Why did you really want to meet? Do you have news?'

Max didn't answer. Instead, he glanced round the room, nodding to a couple of acquaintances at another table. Libby realised he'd deliberately picked a table at a fair distance from anyone else. His expression was grim.

Libby replaced the menu on the table. 'Come on, out with it.' He'd never seemed reluctant to talk before. This must be bad.

'I've found out a little more about your son's new in-laws. I took a look at the farm's accounts.'

'I take it you don't mean the public ones filed at Companies House?'

He gave his lopsided smile. 'Don't ask too many questions about how I found them, but I discovered the official accounts bear little resemblance to another set, hidden behind a complicated series of screens and passwords.'

'Quite the hacker, aren't you?'

'I learned a thing or two from my geeky colleagues in the past. Do you want to know what I discovered, or will you give me up to the authorities?'

'We'll see. Tell me.'

A waitress approached. Libby and Max each ordered a ploughman's lunch, and Max waited until she'd retreated to the kitchen before continuing. 'That farm's doing a great deal better than you'd imagine, given the recent problems with the price of milk and so on.'

'Maybe they've been diversifying. They make cheese and yoghurt.'

He nodded. 'I found all that. They're managing better than most, but not well enough to cover large payments coming in and going out. Nothing illegal, but very lucrative. There are sums of money received from dozens of people, all over the world, described as 'services'.'

'Really? What sort of services. Not...' An image of Belinda dressed as an old-school madam and running a massage parlour sprang into Libby's head.

Max laughed. 'Not those services. I dug a little further and discovered they use a website that sends out automated email sequences.'

'There's nothing wrong with those. I use one to contact customers, check their orders have arrived and tell them about new lines and so on. I write the emails, and the service sends them out at intervals.'

She sat back as the waitress delivered plates piled high with ham, crusty bread, salad and chutney. 'To be honest, I don't really do any of that. Mandy's in charge of it all, updating the business. She understands how it works. She says every business has an on-line presence nowadays, and she's right. Sales have rocketed. Why shouldn't Belinda and Mike do the same?'

Max was nodding. 'Exactly. The problem is, the emails don't go out under the farm's name.'

Libby stopped, a forkful of locally cured ham on the way to her mouth. 'What name are they using? No. Wait. Don't tell me. Not The Pathway to Health?' Max nodded. Libby replaced the fork on her plate, leaving her food half eaten. 'The Papadopoulos cult.'

'Exactly. It seems Mike and Belinda's farm is running a separate, very lucrative business with Olivia and Xavier as partners.'

Libby looked at her watch and swore. 'There's no time to talk more. I've got to get back.'

Max said, 'Come round for supper. Joe and Claire are coming. Joe wants to know what I've found, even though it doesn't appear to relate directly to Liam's death.' He grabbed her hand. 'Maybe we'll find time to talk, soon.'

18

SUPPER

To Libby's surprise, Mandy opened Max's door that evening, beaming, a dog on either side. 'We think you need cheering up.' Libby's throat contracted. She felt wretched. Beside herself with worry about Robert and deeply upset by the séance, she'd pushed her worries about Max and Kate deep down inside, but she couldn't quite forget.

Robert was still at her cottage, unable to bear the thought of living alone in rented accommodation while he should have been touring the West Country on his honeymoon. She'd been tempted to bring him along, but he wanted to spend the evening phoning Sarah's friends again. He'd waved Libby off with Fuzzy cradled in his arms, insisting he would be fine, but he looked ten years older and thoroughly miserable.

Max's friend Reg, bigger and more positive than ever, was leaving for the States in a few weeks. Libby cast a quick glance at Mandy, wondering how she'd deal with the loss.

Claire had brought food, refusing to let Libby near the cooker. 'You cook all the time. I shall never forget your spicy chicken. I've had dozens of meals at your table, so if you don't mind eating simple food...'

Joe snorted, on his way to the fridge for ice. 'She means, if you don't mind your chicken burned to a crisp.'

He ducked as Claire threw a tea towel. 'Of course, he's right,' she admitted. 'I can't cook for toffee.'

Mandy made a noise between a cough and a snort. 'I'm sorry,' she spluttered. 'Toffee? What does that even mean?'

Max patted her on the head with mock condescension. 'You young things...'

Joe spent half an hour in the kitchen, mixing cocktails. Reg accepted a Martini and boomed, 'Is this something they teach at your British Police College, Joe? Vodka martini, shaken, not stirred, a la James Bond?'

Max stuck with beer. 'I need a clear head. There are so many bits and pieces of information to draw together.'

'Personally, I think better after a Margarita,' Libby insisted. 'Or at least, I think I think better. Which probably isn't the same thing at all.'

Mandy leaned over and grabbed her glass. 'How many have you had, Mrs F? You do know that's almost, like, pure spirits, don't you?'

Libby waved a hand in the air. 'Don't mind me. Max is going to tell us what he found out about Handiwater Farm.'

Max flipped up the lid of his laptop. 'I'll show you.' They gathered at his shoulder and he turned the screen so they could all see.

First, he brought up a picture of the farm. 'This is the official website. As you see, it has tabs leading to pages of information about the farm itself, produce for sale, a few moody shots of the cattle coming in for milking at dawn, that sort of thing.'

Joe leaned over and clicked through a couple of tabs. 'Nothing odd there, so far as I can see.'

'That's right. However, if we go to this page of links...' Max scrolled down a long page. 'Here it is. A link to the Pathway. If we follow it, this is what we find.'

The screen changed, opening up a different site. Libby peered at the screen. 'It's a typical New Age sort of page. The kind you'd expect from alternative healers, full of rainbows and unicorns.' She fell silent, thinking of Kate Stephenson.

'That's right. All above board, with offers of astrology readings, interactive fortune telling, and lucky numbers. Silly stuff, but it seems harmless. However, I approached it from a different angle, using what they call the Dark Web.'

Claire's eyes were on stalks. 'Isn't that the place where people buy drugs and weapons? Things not supposed to be for sale?'

Max shrugged. 'There's some stuff on there you really don't want to see. It's a set of web pages hidden from the normal user, where you have to use a special browser to get in. Hackers use it all the time. I dug around and came across some interesting information about the Pathway's activities. For one thing, they have deep, hidden links to the Silk Road, an on-line source of illegal substances. You can't use banks or even PayPal there. They deal in bitcoins, the on-line currency.'

Mandy shivered, theatrically. 'How very sinister.'

Reg's bear hug almost pulled her off her feet. 'Don't worry about it.'

Joe was leaning forward to get a better view. 'Some of my colleagues have to be experts on these areas of the web. It's a constant battle to keep up with all the frauds, phishers, and scammers around.'

His father nodded. 'I'm not surprised. Now, the Pathway appears to have access to sites with information that should be private. For example, databases of names and personal information that are supposed to be secure and encrypted.'

Claire sounded thoughtful. 'I've heard of hackers getting hold of credit card information and pretending to be other people.'

'That's right.' Joe was nodding. 'Identity theft. It happens often, these days. Is that what the Pathway's up to?'

Max stretched, rubbing the back of his neck. 'Not quite. They've been collecting other kinds of information. Personal stuff to use against people.'

As he spoke, Libby's brain clicked into gear. She winced. 'Is that how Olivia knew about my husband, and how she could target me at the séance? She's seen information about me. She knows all about Trevor...' She groaned. The Papadopoulos couple knew her innermost secrets. She remembered Xavier's supercilious smile when she met him at the wedding and the way he'd lingered on her name. The thought brought acid bile into her mouth.

She swallowed. 'How else are they using the information they steal, apart from fake séances?'

'Someone's been running a series of scams.'

'Who? Not Mike or Belinda? Surely, they wouldn't get involved—' She bit off the words. Belinda had disappeared. Did she know about the Papadopoulos couple's scams? If so, she could be in danger, and Sarah with her.

As she pondered, Libby started to collect plates. Mandy jumped up. 'You leave it to us, Mrs F.' Claire and Reg followed Mandy into the kitchen.

'About that list I showed you,' Joe began, seizing the moment alone with Libby and Max. 'I can't talk about police business with everyone here, but I wanted to tell you we had another look in Liam's place, but there's definitely no sign of a computer. We still have no idea what the passwords unlock.'

Libby murmured, 'What if...'

The two men fell silent, watching, but she shook her head. The myriad ideas in her head didn't quite make sense. 'No. I had a thought, but it's gone. I'm getting muddled. Cults and scams and people disappearing. Not to mention Liam's death and his secret passwords. I wonder what we're missing in all this.'

Joe said, 'There's one thing. It doesn't take us any further, but I thought you'd want to know about the ring.'

Max made a face. 'What ring?'

'That fight at the wedding, remember? Over the missing ring?'

'The one Liam stole?'

Libby interrupted. 'Or at least Tim said he stole it.'

'Well, it's a fake. Professionally set, but pure glass. Worth almost nothing. So what the old lady was making such a fuss about, I can't imagine.'

Max raised an eyebrow. 'Another piece of the jigsaw that makes little sense.' He scratched his head with one arm of his reading glasses, leaving his hair in spikes, and yawned. 'It's hard to see the wood for the trees, sometimes. Let's let our minds work on it while we're asleep. Libby and I will talk it through tomorrow morning. If we come up with anything, we'll phone you, Joe.'

Mandy returned, just as he finished speaking. 'Don't forget we're working on those new chocolate flavours tomorrow, Mrs F. Raspberry and ginger. Yummy.'

Libby picked up her bag. 'I'll start Mandy off tomorrow morning and come back here later.'

He shrugged. 'Bear and I will be waiting, but why don't you take Shipley with you? Isn't it time you put those training exercises into practice.'

Mandy arrived bright and early the next morning, to work on the chocolate business. Libby held a finger to her lips and whispered, 'Come into the kitchen. Robert's still asleep.'

Mandy giggled. 'Won't he have a shock when he finds me here again?'

'I'm sure you'll cheer him up.'

She left Mandy mixing ingredients, clipped Shipley's lead to his collar and headed for the car. For once, she felt in no hurry to see Max. She couldn't get Kate Stephenson out of her head.

She let in the clutch, thinking of Kate's annoyingly pretty face. Alternative therapy, indeed. Oh well. She might as well admit it. She was jealous. And with good reason. Even Mandy seemed to think the sun shone out of Kate Stephenson's—

Libby's foot hit the brake as a thought flashed into her head.

The Fiat behind squealed to a halt, inches from the Citroen's rear end. Libby pretended not to see the driver's rude gesture and sat for a long while, thinking. What was it Mike had said? He hated computers. Someone, though, must be using one for farm business. It would be almost impossible for a working farm to exist without computers, and she knew they had a website. Someone must work on it.

Belinda's machine had been full of personal emails and shopping sites, with nothing about the farm. So, where was the farm's computer, and who used it? It clearly wasn't Mike, and his son Tim refused to have anything to do with the farm, so there was only one other likely person: Liam Weston.

With a buzz of excitement, Libby remembered. Mike saying he relied on Liam to print out anything he needed to see. She was right, Liam was the farm's computing expert.

She grinned, pleased to be a step ahead of Max. He could go on hacking into the farm's files, but why should Libby let him have all the fun? If Liam kept the farm records, chances were he was the one working with Xavier Papadopoulos. Libby didn't know what they were up to, but it was certainly secret and probably illegal and, even better, had nothing to do with Belinda, Mike or Sarah.

Liam had no computer at his own home, so all his information must be at the farm. What better place to hide things than on files no one else ever used, hidden in plain sight on someone else's property? Those files would tell Libby what was going on out there in the villages of Exmoor. She was certain of it.

She laughed aloud. She would discover the truth, steal a march on Max and visit him later. She sent him a text:

Having a lazy morning. See you later.

That would teach him to make eyes at Kate Stephenson.

* * *

The Citroen squealed to a halt at Handiwater Farm. Libby ran to the house and hammered on the door, but no one came. Shipley, excited by the activity, leaped at the door. Libby pulled him away and moved to the window. Shielding her eyes from the sun's reflection, she squinted until she saw Mike, slumped at the kitchen table, staring into space.

Libby banged on the door and shouted. Mike turned his head, his red-rimmed eyes betraying despair. Slowly, he rose and let Libby and Shipley into the house.

She bit back a comment on his appearance. 'Did you sleep last night?'

He shook his head. 'I can't manage so much as a catnap without Belinda. She's never stayed away so long before.' He drew a shuddering breath. 'Don't know what I'll do if she doesn't come home. And Sarah as well. Both my women.'

The house was silent, except for the ticking of the kitchen clock. 'Where's Tim?'

'I sent him away. Fussing around, he was, blaming Liam for everything. They never got on, those two.'

Libby longed to ask if he'd said anything like that to the police. Did Tim's own father think he had something to do with the farm hand's death? She'd ask him later. Liam was beyond help, but the longer Belinda and Sarah were missing, the more likely it seemed they were in danger. Upsetting Mike further would just delay matters.

She took a long look at the farmer's gaunt face. Before she could get any sense out of him, he needed help. She doubted he'd eaten a square meal since his wife left. 'I don't suppose you've had breakfast?'

Gathering all her patience, Libby cooked eggs and bacon, feeding Shipley a couple of bites of usually forbidden food, and waited until Mike had pushed bacon round his plate and torn minute pieces from a slice of bread before asking to see the computer.

'In the office. Other end of the house.' The farmer showed no interest in why Libby wanted to use it. The man's lethargy began to grate on Libby's nerves. Why wasn't he trying to find his wife and daughter, instead of sitting in a puddle of gloom? She couldn't imagine Max sitting at home, doing nothing, if she'd gone missing. Not even if his affections had shifted – she clicked her tongue, annoyed at herself. Worrying about Max was a distraction she didn't need just now.

'Come with me, Shipley.' She hurried down the corridor to the farm office, in search of the business's computer. There it was, in plain sight on the desk in the middle of the office. Libby hadn't spared it a glance before, when she'd been concentrating on Belinda's desk.

Libby told Shipley to lie down, and to her amazement, he obeyed at once. She pulled out her notebook, turned to the page of passwords, and switched on the machine.

The computer accepted the second password on Liam's list and a screen full of icons opened. Libby grinned. It felt good to be right, sometimes. The glow of success only lasted a moment or two, though. Where should she go next?

She found the farm website that Max had shown them last night, but clicked away. She'd leave Max to go down that route. She was looking for something more personal to Liam Weston.

For half an hour she clicked through random files, finding nothing beyond innocuous Word files of business letters and Excel spreadsheets, full of animal numbers, milk quotas, and details of subsidy payments. These were the tools Mandy had been struggling to persuade her to use for her business.

Nothing jarred or seemed out of place, and there were only a couple of files left unopened. Libby's neck ached and her eyes itched from staring at the screen. She yawned and clicked on one of the remaining files.

It demanded another password. Libby sat straighter and ran a finger down Liam's password list; the one he'd kept under lock and key. After a couple of false starts, just as she feared another mistake would lock her out of it for ever, the file opened.

At first glance, there was little to warrant such secrecy. The file was a simple list of names. Some were familiar: Belinda, Sarah, Olivia and Xavier Papadopoulos, Kate Stephenson. Libby murmured, 'The Pathway?'

Several last names recurred often. That was common in this part of the world, where families had lived, worked the land, and intermarried for generations. Watson, Meres, Appleby, Hambledon: Libby had met dozens of people sharing those names. She visualised them, trying to imagine each as a member of the cult.

Appleby. She knew an Appleby, but she couldn't place them. She tilted her chair back, rubbing her nose, trying to visualise where she had been when she heard the name. Her mouth fell open. Lady Antonia Appleby was Belinda's aged aunt. Libby could remember her now: Lady Antonia, full of old-fashioned airs and graces but forgetful and vague, making a fuss at the wedding about a worthless ring. The old lady must have known it had no value.

Or did she? She'd been genuinely distraught. She was old, and hardly lucid at times. A twinge of guilt hit Libby. She'd dismissed the woman's panic over the loss of a valueless piece of costume jewellery, putting it down to age and some kind of mild dementia. Instead, she'd focused on the animosity between Liam and Tim and never stopped to wonder about the ring's real value. She must find out about that later.

She pasted the list of names into an email and sent it to her own inbox, while she focused on the last remaining file, hoping it would contain even more information.

Sure enough, she needed the last of Liam's passwords to open the spreadsheet. She held her breath as it opened to show three columns of information. The first was a series of dates, beginning a year ago, and ending in May. The second column was a list of places. She recognised some of them: Dulverton, Williton, and Watchet were all Somerset towns.

Puzzled, she turned to the third column, which contained hyperlinks. She clicked on one and gasped as a photograph opened up. There was Kate Stephenson, her arms round someone with his back to the camera, eyes closed, mouth half-open in the prelude to a kiss. For a second, Libby's stomach seemed to turn over.

She relaxed. The man wasn't Max.

She peered more closely, her heart rate returning to normal, but try as she might, she couldn't identify the man in the photo.

She tried another link from the file, and found another image. Taken from the outside, looking in through a window, it showed Kate Stephenson and the same man. This time, both were naked. Libby smiled as she recognised the curtains in Abbott House, Kate's home.

She pulled a mint from an old packet in her bag and sucked, as a series of events clicked into place in her mind like dots joining up to make an outline; Kate, Belinda's links to the Pathway, her disappearance, and the strange affair of the worthless ring.

Libby swallowed the last of the mint and shut down the computer. Now, she knew where she had to go.

Her phone rang. 'Yes?'

Max said, 'Where are you? I thought you were coming round

earlier this morning. Bear's furious, and I'm...' He hesitated. 'I'm missing you.'

A warm glow flooded Libby's veins, but there was no time to talk. She gabbled, 'I've cracked it. I've been looking at the farm computer and I know what this is all about. Give me Lady Antonia's address and meet me there. Hurry up, I'm on my way.'

'Hold on,' Max shouted. 'Wait for me. Don't do anything until I get there.'

Libby dropped the phone in her bag before he could protest, and hurried to the kitchen.

Mike sat where she'd left him, his face vacant. She hesitated. He was in no fit state to answer questions. Anyway, she had no need to ask. She dropped a hand on his shoulder. 'You should have told us, Mike.'

'What?'

'Never mind. Stay here, I'll be back soon.' Libby left at a run with Shipley at her heels, leaving behind Mike's plaintive voice, begging her to explain what on earth was going on.

20

THE HOUSE

Gravel screeched under the car's wheels as Libby accelerated away, speeding down the twisting lanes until she turned onto the main road and hit the back of a queue of traffic travelling at less than ten miles an hour.

Thumping the steering wheel, she leaned sideways, trying to see the blockage. A tractor lumbered ahead, filling the road, leaving no room to pass. Frustrated, taut muscles screaming, Libby changed down until she was crawling in second gear.

Just as she was about to scream with frustration, the tractor found a lay-by and let the queue of traffic pass.

At last, she reached Lady Antonia's home. Libby steered between two pillars topped with stone pineapples, drove past a tiny church along a narrow avenue, hedged on either side by beeches, and arrived at an impressive Georgian manor house. Libby counted eight rows of windows, dark and uninviting despite the early afternoon sun. Libby's skin crawled. Under other circumstances, she'd think the house charming and old-fashioned, but her heart was pumping with fear for Sarah and Belinda.

She ran up the short flight of carved stone steps to hammer on the door. There was no reply, so she ran round the house to the back garden, where a spacious lawn led down to an ornamental lake. Lilies floated serenely on the surface.

There was no one in sight.

Shipley sniffed round the garden, found a scent, and nose close to the floor, ran down the path and back. 'What is it, Shipley? Can you smell something strange?'

The dog stopped, nose in the air, four legs rigid. Libby knelt beside him. 'What is it?' She followed his gaze. 'Are you pointing at something?'

Directly in the line of the dog's sight was a set of outhouses, probably built as stabling for horses, but no equine heads poked over the half doors today. With an anxious glance back at the house, Libby walked towards the nearest stable, her pulse racing. She had one hand on the wood, ready to push it open, when Shipley barked, once. 'Not that one?'

She moved to the next door, Shipley at her heels. 'Is this the way?'

The door opened easily. The outhouse was full of junk. She saw old chairs and an ancient mangle, a relic from the days of washing clothes by hand. A musty smell emanated from a pile of rolled carpet. Wrinkling her nose, Libby muttered to the dog, 'Is that what you can smell? Old rugs?'

The dog ignored her. Tail in the air, nose to the ground, he pushed past heaps of rubbish to the other end of the building, where he stopped at the wall, body rigid.

At first, Libby could see nothing unusual. Just wooden slats. She looked more closely. One area of wood was cleaner than the rest. She ran tentative fingers across the surface. The wood moved under her hand. She pushed, hard, and it swung open so fast she almost overbalanced.

She steadied herself, grasping at the door frame. The ground below her feet pitched sharply down as steps led away into the blackness. Remembering one of the tricks Mandy had shown her, she switched on her phone to light the way, and set off down the stairs. 'Come on, Shipley,' she whispered. 'I'm not going down there alone.'

* * *

Blood thundering in her ears, Libby descended the steps, one hand touching the wall, the other holding the phone. Shipley, close behind, growled quietly.

The steps turned sharp left and Libby followed, her hand trembling, the light flickering over the walls. What was that? She stopped and Shipley scrambled past, almost knocking her over, and galloped across the floor. Libby shone her phone light around the space, but could see nothing except racks of wine bottles lining the walls. The air in the cellar was cool and dry.

'There's nothing here, Shipley. It's just a wine cellar.' Weak with relief, Libby examined the bottles more closely. Some were covered in dust, while others looked more recent, but there was nothing unusual about any of them.

Shipley snuffled in the corner. 'What have you found?'

Aiming her light with care, she could make out cracks where the walls met the wooden floor. 'Rats.' Libby shuddered. 'That's what you were chasing. And I thought you were leading me to something important. You need more training, I can tell.'

A voice boomed from the top of the steps. 'I hope you haven't disturbed my bottles.'

Libby spun round. 'Lady Antonia,' she gulped, filled with sudden guilt. 'Er, no. I was just-er-just... I'll come back up.'

A different voice laughed. 'Will you, indeed? We'll see about that.'

Libby tensed, suddenly motionless at the threat in the man's voice; a voice she recognised.

John Canterbury, the friendly rector, stood at the top of the stairs, one hand lying heavily on the elderly woman's shoulder.

Libby rested her foot on the first step, shining her light upwards. The rector's eyes glittered bright. 'Time to stop snooping about, Mrs Forest, I think. Antonia, get back inside the house. Make coffee or something.'

Obediently, Lady Antonia turned away.

'What do you—' Libby stopped. 'Where are Belinda and Sarah?'

The rector descended the stairs, slowly, his face intimidating in the single beam of light. 'Not here, I'm afraid. Your dog has led you on a wild goose chase. And you won't be seeing your friends; we're all very tired of you poking your nose into our business. It's time to stop.'

Libby licked dry lips, suddenly scared at the menace in the rector's voice. She glanced from side to side, searching for something to use as a weapon, but there was nothing nearby. She swallowed. Perhaps she could trip him up as he came down the stairs.

'Shipley,' she whispered. The spaniel stood at her feet, mouth open, panting. Libby wasn't alone. She tensed, ready to fight.

'I'm sorry, my dear,' the rector went on. 'We can't tolerate any more of your interference—'

A growl echoed round the cellar. Libby shot a glance at Shipley, but he was silent, at her side.

She looked up to see Bear leaping down the stairs, cannoning into the rector, jolting him forward. The rector's hands grabbed at the walls, but there was no rail and his feet slipped on the narrow steps. For a long moment, he teetered, trying to regain his balance, before falling heavily towards Libby.

She clutched at his jacket as he fell past her, but the weight of his body pulled it from her grasp, and with a sickening crack, his head hit the floor.

Bear, still growling, followed him down.

Then, Max was running down the steps. 'Bear, that's enough.' His hand brushed Libby's shoulder. 'Are you OK?'

She nodded. He crouched by the rector's side and felt for a pulse in his neck. 'He's still alive.' Max pulled out his phone and swore. 'No reception.'

'Let's get out of here. He won't be going anywhere for a while, even if he wakes up. He'd have to climb up and get past me.'

He took Libby's hand, and drew her up the stairs and out into the fresh air.

Libby blinked against the daylight as Max called the police. She gasped. There stood Belinda, face dirty, usually tidy hair in greasy spikes, scrubbing away tears with a grubby handkerchief. Libby laughed aloud. Sarah was outside the stable, too, her phone to her ear, laughing and crying at the same time. 'Robert? It's all over. I'm safe.'

'Where's Antonia?'

Belinda's eyes were red. 'She's lying down. She's even more confused than usual, now.'

'But, what are you all doing here? I mean, I thought we'd find you at Aunt Antonia's, but Shipley took me to the cellar and then...' Libby felt a sob rise in her throat now the drama was over. She bit her lip, determined not to cry.

Max took her hand. 'Shipley needs a little more training if he's going to be useful as a sniffer dog. I imagine he was taking you to the rats. But he wasn't far away from Sarah and Belinda. They were locked in the next stable. The rector drugged them both to keep them quiet.'

Libby made a face. 'The rector had me fooled when I met him. He seemed so...'

'Quite. He put on a good show and took us both in. He would have fooled anyone with his benign rector act. By the way, I'm impressed with your improved IT skills, if they led you straight here. You've been keeping those quiet.'

Libby managed a smile. 'It's Mandy's doing. She gives me lessons. It's just as well, because Liam had put all the information I needed on the farm computer. But, go on. Did the rector kidnap Belinda? And Sarah as well? Why would he do such a thing?'

Max looked at Belinda. She twisted her hands together, as if washing them clean. Her eyes were over-bright. 'My aunt has a vast inheritance stashed away, but she hasn't done anything with it. She just leaves it all in the bank, and over the years, she's become more and more vague.'

Belinda shrugged. 'We didn't notice at first – neither my mother, nor I. I feel dreadful. She's been suffering from dementia for a long time, and when the rector started visiting, he seemed to be so helpful. We trusted him completely.'

Tears rose to her eyes. 'My mother would have been horrified if she'd known he was really looking for way to get his hands on her fortune.'

Her face was scarlet. 'I knew the money would come to us, eventually, and I got into some difficulties. Money, I mean. I didn't want to – to tell Mike, so I came to ask my aunt for a loan one day, and she refused. The rector was here. He must have overheard us – she said we'd get our hands on her money when she died and not before.

'I was getting desperate. I had to pay, you see, to get rid of...' She put her head in her hands, whispering, 'To get rid of the curse.'

'What curse?' Max scratched his head. 'What are you talking about?'

Libby shook her head. 'Pay? Who were you paying? The rector?'

Belinda shook her head. 'No, not John. The Pathway. The Pathway, and Kate Stephenson.'

Libby groaned. 'You don't mean you were hooked by those séances? We went to one and it's all a load of old hokum. The Papadopoulos couple prey on vulnerable people who've lost a partner or a parent. They find out things about you, and fool you into thinking they're in touch with the dead.'

Belinda shot a glance at Libby through misty eyes. 'You too?'

Libby chuckled. 'I could have been taken in, perhaps, but they didn't realise the last person I wanted to hear from was my dead husband. All the same, I can see why you believed them, and they gave me a nasty shock.'

Belinda's smile was watery. 'Olivia said my mother had an important message for me. She said I was in danger, but I could be helped. Kate Stephenson was there that day. She told me she could see an aura round my head, and that someone had put a – a curse on me.' She began to sob. 'I'm sorry, it sounds so silly.'

Sarah put her arms round her mother. 'Don't worry. I know how close you were to grandma. I can't believe how cruel these Pathway people are, preying on grieving relatives.' She put a tissue into her mother's hand. 'Anyway, it's all over, now.'

Belinda took a deep breath. 'Kate said she could help lift the curse, and she'd do it for nothing because we were friends. All I had to do was pay for some special candles.'

'I gave her a few pounds – hardly anything – for the candles. Then she made an appointment and I went to her house. She sat at her little table for a while, telling me about my aura, and how someone must have put the curse on me when I was young. When I was about thirteen, she said.'

Libby winced. 'Everyone has arguments with other children at that age. Especially girls. And they can be cruel.'

'There were a few kids at school who used to bully me. They said I was posh. They used to steal from my school bag, scribble on my homework, that kind of thing. It sounds stupid, now, but it really hurt and I was scared of them. Especially one girl, who was big for her age. She used to come right up to me and spit.'

Belinda's face screwed up in pain as she remembered. 'When Kate told me about the curse, I remembered those girls, and I thought they might have really hexed me. Then, Kate showed me an egg. Just an ordinary egg. She said it was from the chicken in the nearby farm, but it would show if I had truly been cursed.'

She wiped her eyes. 'I can't believe I fell for it.'

Max said, 'You wouldn't be the first to fall for a psychic scam. There are plenty on the internet.'

With a grateful smile, Belinda went on, 'She touched that stupid egg to my head and made me breathe on it, and then she smashed it on a plate. It was horrible. Mostly, it was normal egg white and yolk, all mixed up, but there were also a few black things, like apple pips, in with the yolk.'

Max's voice held an undertone of cold fury. 'You didn't go back there, did you?'

Belinda nodded. 'Kate said there was a definite curse on me, and she could lift it, but—'

Libby interrupted. 'Let me guess. It would be expensive?'

'She had to buy special crystals. She said it usually cost thousands of pounds, but she'd let me pay a little each month to the Pathway, because she wanted to help.'

Max said, 'You handed over the money, but the so-called curse was too strong to be dealt with in one session, so they needed more...'

Belinda nodded, sobbing too hard to talk.

Libby remembered the email to Lady Antonia she'd read in Belinda's inbox, talking about borrowing jewellery. 'In the end, you owed thousands of pounds and you ran out of money. You couldn't get out of her clutches, so you borrowed some of your aunt's jewellery, pretending it was for Sarah's wedding, sold the ring and had it replaced by a fake.'

Belinda blew her nose. 'I was so scared. I'd stopped going to the Pathway meetings, but Olivia kept ringing up and sending me emails. They were threats, really, though not in so many words. I'd plucked up enough courage to ask you for help, but when Xavier saw us talking at the wedding, I didn't dare take it any further.'

'And I,' said Libby, 'didn't try to help you. I'm so sorry, Belinda. Did you tell anyone else about your money worries?'

Belinda bit her lip. 'I told the rector. Mr Canterbury.'

* * *

An ambulance siren sounded in the distance. Max said, 'I'll go down and check on our villain.'

'Not on your own. I'm coming too,' Libby said.

Max descended into the cellar, Libby, Belinda, Sarah and the dogs following close behind. As if on cue, the rector groaned and opened his eyes. He tried to struggle to his feet. Max smiled, his eyes steely. 'Don't bother. The police are on their way. I'm rather hoping you've broken a bone or two.'

'That dog of yours tried to kill me.'

Bear growled, but Max held him tight. 'We know what you've been up to with your friends in the Pathway cult. Psychic scams, that's what they call the business you're all in: you, Xavier and Olivia Papadopoulos.'

'And your lover, Kate.' Libby threw out the words, enjoying the absolute silence that followed. She grinned at Max's startled face, before turning back to the rector. 'Don't try to deny it. Liam kept photos of you both. You've been having an affair, and he found out, and that's why you killed Liam Weston.'

Max's mouth dropped open. Libby smiled at him, enjoying the moment. 'Blackmail.'

She turned to the rector. 'Liam was blackmailing you about your affair. He's been pulling everyone's strings. He had a hold on all of you, one way or another. He was behind the Pathway cult, using Xavier's charisma, his clothes, and Olivia's talent for imitating a medium. They've been working for Liam, not the other way around, at all. He even fooled Mike into believing he was growing the business at Handiwater Farm, when all the time he used it for his own purposes, and at the same time, he learned your secrets and blackmailed you all.'

'Liam?' Belinda's face was a picture of horror. 'But he was such a good worker – and we were all sorry for him, because his family suffered so during the foot and mouth epidemic.'

'It seems he pulled the wool over a lot of eyes,' Sarah said.

The rector scanned the circle of faces, desperation in his eyes. 'Those photos would have finished me. Imagine a man in my position, caught having an affair. My wife would never forgive me.'

The self-pitying whine made Libby shiver as he went on, 'I paid that monster, Liam, to keep him quiet, but he was never satisfied. He wanted more and more money, bleeding me dry, until I couldn't stand it any longer. Liam Weston was evil – pure evil.'

A cunning smile curled his lips. 'He knew everyone's secrets.'

He glared directly at Belinda, a hint of hysteria in his voice as he sneered, 'and you let him into your lives. More fool you.'

Tired of his self-justification, Libby stayed practical. 'What did you use to drug him, so he'd crash the tractor?'

'Rohypnol.' The rector chuckled. 'The date rape drug. It's easy to get hold of it these days, if you know how—'

'Your wife,' Libby interrupted, remembering their conversation at the rector's house. 'She's a pharmacist.'

'Always so pleased to share her specialist knowledge.' The venom in his voice suggested little love lost between the rector and his wife. 'She always thought she was a cut above me. Like so many of you do.'

Max steered him back. 'Let's not waste time on your pathetic self-pity. What about the Rohypnol. How did you get Liam to take it?'

'Easiest thing in the world. I'm the rector. Everyone opens their doors to me. Even though he was blackmailing me, it never occurred to Liam Weston I'd try to harm him, the idiot. Not as clever as he thought, was he?'

He winced. 'I think I've broken my arm.'

'Good,' Max said, with feeling. 'Now, how did you kill Liam?'

'I had a cup of coffee with him before he went off on his tractor. I'd tried it several times. It didn't work at first, but he didn't suspect anything. He just thought he'd had too much to drink.' His smile was cruel. 'It worked in the end, as I knew it would.'

Libby exchanged a glance with Max. 'The poison that leaves no trace.'

Max's mouth was set. 'Not from the Amazon rainforest, but more effective.'

For a moment, she was silent, thinking hard. Finally, she admitted, 'We were wrong about Tim, thinking he was jealous of Liam. What if it was the other way around?'

She turned to Belinda. 'I think Liam hated you and your family for surviving the foot and mouth disaster, while his own father was ruined and committed suicide. Liam was left with nothing, while you had everything. You thought you were helping him, giving him access to everything; the farm, the computer, and the house.'

'We had no idea he felt that way,' Belinda shook her head. 'How could we have been so gullible?'

How dreadful to discover someone knows all your innermost secrets. 'I bet he loved reading your emails,' Libby muttered, 'finding people's secrets and using them for profit. What a twisted man. He knew you'd borrowed your aunt's jewellery. It wouldn't take him long to put two and two together and realise the ring was a fake. He really did steal it at the wedding, and made sure Tim saw him pick it up, so there'd be a fight. He wanted to draw attention to the ring so he could blackmail you, Belinda.'

The rector said, 'The world's better off without that boy. Born wicked, he was. I've done the world a favour.'

The smug grin he flashed at Belinda sent a chill up Libby's spine, but she continued, thinking aloud. 'Liam's probably been stealing from you for years, building up funds for his new herd. With that, the proceeds of blackmail, and the Pathway's psychic scams, he must have had a substantial sum hidden away somewhere.'

Max murmured, 'Under false names and IEP addresses – almost impossible to trace. Still, it should be possible now we know what to look for.'

Libby turned back to the rector. 'You realised Liam was making a small fortune, and you failed to kill him on the first few tries, so you dreamed up your scheme to kidnap Belinda and demand a ransom from Mike. You hoped the money would keep Liam off your back until you put your plan to kill him into operation. When the murder plan worked, you couldn't resist going ahead with the kidnapping.'

The rector snorted. 'No point wasting a good plan.'

It was Max's turn to ask Belinda a question. 'How did he trap you here?'

Belinda sank on the steps, hugging Sarah close. 'He used my aunt's phone. She trusted him, of course. Who wouldn't trust the rector? He'd been worming his way into her life for months, visiting, pretending to help. He even talked to Mike and me about finding a suitable home for Aunt Antonia when the dementia got too bad. We were so grateful to him for helping her. How could we have been so dense.'

Libby said, 'Because he's the rector. Everyone assumes he's a good man because of his position.'

Belinda's eyes blazed. 'I was on my way to a shopping trip when I had a text from my aunt's phone, begging me to hurry over. I didn't even bother to let Mike know. I wasn't worried, as Aunt Antonia often panicked and sent for me, and it was usually because she couldn't work the TV, or she'd lost her reading glasses. When I arrived, he was here.' She jerked her head towards the rector. 'He made me coffee. Next thing I knew, I was locked in the stables.'

Sarah, pale but composed, took up the tale. 'He drugged you, Mum. Then he took your phone and used it to message me. The message said you'd been kidnapped, and I had to keep quiet and come over here. It said you wouldn't be harmed as long as I told nobody.'

Tears sprang into Sarah's eyes. 'I panicked. I should have said something to Robert, but I was too scared.' Her shoulders shook. 'I rang him just now. He's on his way, but I don't know how I'll face him. He'll be furious with me. Maybe he'll stop trusting me.'

As he answered, Max's words beat a path to Libby's heart. 'Of course, he'll trust you. That's what being a couple is all about. You make mistakes, admit them, and forgive each other.'

Belinda added, '"For better, for worse." That's what we say in church. But, sometimes, we forget for a while.'

Libby watched Max's kind, familiar face as he comforted Sarah, and her lips trembled. She had to swallow a sob, suddenly scared to think how close she'd come to losing Max. She'd taken him for granted. Instead of telling him the truth, explaining her worries and fears about marriage, she'd pushed him away; been cold and difficult. What a fool she'd been. It would serve her right if he'd turned away for good, to find comfort with the warm, sympathetic Kate Stephenson.

The look Max shot the rector would have frozen a stone. 'I guess Mike wasn't paying up fast enough, so you thought you'd turn the screw.'

He held up one hand. 'I believe I can hear the police.' He beamed cheerfully at the rector. 'You'll be going away for a good, long time.'

22

CHAMPAGNE

'At last, an evening to ourselves.' Max put his feet up on his coffee table, a glass of wine in one hand. Bear lay spread across the floor, while Shipley rolled happily in a patch of evening sunlight.

As she curled up in one of Max's oldest, most comfortable armchairs, Libby's stomach seemed to be tied in knots. She couldn't even touch the glass of New Zealand Pinot Noir. 'Max, we need to talk.'

He stiffened, and Libby struggled to read the expression in his eyes as she confessed, 'I saw a key, just like Liam's, fall out of Kate Stephenson's bag when she dropped it, after that séance.'

She knew she was blushing, ashamed to have deliberately kept a relevant fact from him, allowing jealousy of Kate Stephenson to interfere with their murder investigation. After the rector's arrest, a police search found gold keys and locked boxes, like Liam's, at the Papadopoulos couple's house.

The pair had talked freely, desperate to distance themselves from Liam's murder. Apparently, all the conspirators had copies of Liam's passwords in identical boxes. The day Libby met the couple at Mike's farm, they'd been hoping to access his files on the farm computer.

'I didn't tell you about the key because...' she fiddled with a strand of her hair, plucking up the courage to tell the whole truth. 'Because I wanted to solve the case myself.' Her voice sounded very small. 'I was jealous when you spent all evening talking to Kate at that horrible quiz.'

Max looked surprised. 'Jealous? But I don't give a fig for Kate Stephenson. You told me you were worried about Mandy seeing her, so I kept an eye on her. We knew each other years ago and I used that as an excuse. You seemed to have your hands full.'

He hesitated. 'To be honest, I was glad to talk to her about Debbie. I don't often get the chance to talk about my daughter with someone from the old days.'

Libby's chest contracted. Max rarely referred to the guilt he felt over Debbie's riding accident. 'Do you speak with Joe about his sister?'

He shook his head. 'Not much. Don't really know how to start, after all these years. We're not good at these emotional things, Joe and I.'

He gave a crooked grin and Libby's heart missed a beat. Max always seemed to be the strong one. So clever and capable; so sure of himself. He'd helped Libby through the bad times uncovering her husband's fraud, but tonight he looked sad and vulnerable.

Maybe she'd taken Max's support for granted, not noticing that sometimes he needed her, too. She moved from the chair to sit beside him.

He took a deep breath. 'Libby, I've been wondering. Are we making a mistake, going into business together? I think I might have talked you into it against your will, and it's seemed, lately, as though you're having second thoughts. I wish you'd tell me the truth. Would you be happier sticking with your cakes and chocolates?'

Libby took a moment to think. 'This isn't about business, is it?'

'Not really.'

She leaned closer, breathing in Max's familiar male smell. 'I need to apologise—'

He turned to look into her eyes and she put her finger against his lips. 'No, I have to say this now. I've taken you for granted over the past couple of years. I've let my history with Trevor frighten me, and backed away whenever you mentioned marriage. I've been scared, you see. Going into business is one thing, but being a proper couple is another.'

His face was very close as he murmured, 'Do you want to be that? A proper couple?'

She smiled. 'When I saw you with Kate Stephenson, I was so jealous I could have scratched her eyes out, but it gave me the shock I needed. I can't expect you to wait any longer for me to decide what I want.'

Max's eyes opened wider. He'd stopped breathing, and in the silence, Libby knew their future rested in her hands. Was she ready to commit, even if it meant giving up some independence and moving out of her beloved cottage?

It took less than a split second to decide. She slipped from the chair and knelt on the floor, her heart hammering against her ribs. 'Max Ramshore, will you marry me?'

* * *

Libby could hardly wait for the next supper night with their friends.

'Everything's changing,' Mandy grinned. 'You two getting married, Reg going back to America...'

'You better come visit, young lady,' Reg interrupted. 'Bring that musician boyfriend.'

Libby stared at Mandy and she blushed. 'Didn't I mention? I saw the therapist Claire suggested, and I managed to go to London on the train, to see Steve. We're not exactly back together, but I'm going to see him again soon.'

Sarah said, 'Mum and Dad are organising a live-in carer for Aunt Antonia. My aunt rather likes the idea of a 'companion.' She thinks she'll be like the Victorian aristocracy.'

Robert put in, 'The companion will be carefully vetted, of course; we've all learned our lessons about people who pretend to help. I wouldn't have that job with Aunt Antonia for all the tea in China.'

Sarah said, 'She's agreed to dig into her bank account to pay for it, and sell some of the jewellery if necessary, and she's going to give Mum a power of attorney. Luckily, she didn't seem to understand that Mum had pinched her ring; or maybe she understood but decided to ignore it. It's so hard to tell, with Aunt Antonia. At least we can stop any more predators getting their claws into her.'

'And that,' said Max, as he slid the cork from a bottle of champagne, with only the gentlest of pops, 'is worth another celebration.'

Bear and Shipley, as though alerted by the sound of the champagne, trotted excitedly round the room, visiting one friend after another, for hugs, pats and scratches from each.

Robert and Sarah, sitting so close together that Mandy had cackled wickedly and told them to get a room, toasted each other.

Robert said, 'Sarah's never to leave my sight again without telling me where she's going.'

Sarah and Libby exchanged a glance and Sarah winked. That state of affairs wasn't going to last long. Robert's new wife, none the worse for being drugged and locked up in an old stable full of mice and spiders, was tougher than she looked. The two of them, at Sarah's suggestion, planned to disappear back to their hotel tomorrow, to complete the honeymoon.

'By the way,' Robert continued, 'we're thinking of moving down to Somerset. Sarah's dad's handing over the running of the farm to Tim, and we're going to live nearby to lend a hand. I can work from anywhere with a decent internet connection, and I fancy a taste of country life. It seems to have suited you, Mum.'

Libby could hardly believe her luck. Life still held plenty of challenges; the new café in town was putting Frank's bakery in danger, and she'd have to think hard about ways to fend off the competition. At the same time, her semi-official role with the police could lead in many directions.

Most of all, she missed her daughter Ali, so far away on the other side of the world. Watching Sarah with Belinda had filled her with longing for her own daughter.

Nevertheless, with Max at her side, she felt she could deal with anything that came her way; and to have Robert living nearby with Sarah would be the icing on the cake.

Joe and Claire were quiet, and Libby wondered if they felt side-lined by all the celebrations. She'd been planning to thank Claire for finding a new, trustworthy phobia therapist for Mandy, who seemed to have made a difference already.

Kate Stephenson was under police investigation for the scam she'd used on Belinda, along with the Papadopoulos couple. Libby still shivered when she thought of Xavier and his wife. They might not have killed anyone, but they'd preyed mercilessly on vulnerable people across the world, making a small fortune from their heartless cons.

She cleared her throat, but before she could speak, Joe rose. 'I want to make a toast.' He stared at Libby through clear blue eyes. His smile was lopsided, like Max's. 'Since you came to Exham, Mrs Forest, you've turned the place upside down. We were a quiet little backwater and you've transformed us all. Dad's been like a new man since you met, and I can't think of anyone I'd rather have in the family.'

Max took Libby's hand as Joe raised his glass. 'To my new stepmother.'

MURDER AT THE CASTLE

AN EXHAM-ON-SEA MYSTERY

1

FRUIT CAKE

Max Ramshore descended the last few steps of the ladder, panting with effort. He dumped a massive cardboard box on the floor, rubbed his back, and sighed. 'How many more boxes are up in your loft?'

Libby chuckled. 'I warned you I had plenty of stuff.'

'You weren't kidding. I thought you downsized when you moved to Exham.'

'You should have seen the amount I threw away. These boxes are full of important items—'

She broke off as Max flipped the lid off the box. 'Soft toys? Really?'

'They belong to Robert.'

'Why are they in your loft and not his?'

Libby wriggled. 'I'm not sure he's told Sarah about them yet.'

'Your son's been married for months. Time for him to confess, I would have thought, and take back his own – er – toys.' Max held aloft a battered tiger. One eye was missing. 'This one's seen action, I suspect, and a ride or two in the washing machine?'

Libby retrieved the toy and slid it gently back into the box.

'Robert promised to come over this afternoon to help me clear the cottage.' She gestured vaguely around the tiny landing. 'He thinks I'm too old and infirm to pack up my own belongings and move to your place...' Her voice faded as she leaned over Max, who'd squatted down to sort through the medley of toys, books, and CD cases. She snatched a soft, blue-covered book from his grasp and flipped it open. 'He used this when he was in primary school. Look, a drawing of his sister.'

'Love Ali's pigtails.'

'She must have been about five when he drew this. He was eight.'

Max laughed. 'Not bad artwork for an accountant.'

Libby stood up. 'Even so, I can't keep everything. I'm making a fresh start when we get married and Robert will have to decide what to do with his belongings. Tell you what, I'll get one of those memory boxes for things I want to keep and the rest is up to him.'

'A small one.'

'Well, medium-sized. If things won't fit, I'll let them go.'

Max pushed the box to one side and set off up the ladder once more.

Libby looked again at the drawing and her stomach flipped. She recognised that stab of anxiety. Ali was grown up and sensible, and Libby liked that she was engaged in voluntary work, but South America seemed so far away.

Even Robert and Sarah's wedding had failed to entice Ali home, and according to her latest email, she wouldn't be back any time soon. She was totally engaged in her voluntary work, and if it weren't for the regular emails she sent home, Libby would suspect she'd lost interest in her family. Would she even get home for Libby's wedding?

Maybe it was Libby's own fault. Determined not to pressure Ali, she'd made light of her wedding, pointing out it was only going to be a quick registry office affair. She'd had quite enough of the 'bells and whistles' approach to matrimony, with her first, deceased, husband, Trevor, and look how that had turned out; he'd been demanding and controlling, and deeply involved in money laundering for a gang of criminals.

No, Libby's second wedding was going to be nothing like the first.

She snapped the book shut and put it back in the box. She wouldn't admit, even to herself, how much she missed her daughter. To stave off the familiar wave of sadness, she slipped into her bedroom to look at her wedding dress. The wedding would be quiet, but it was still an excuse for a new outfit. In knee length navy silk with a pattern of bright red poppies, the dress hung behind the door in a cloud of protective plastic. She'd even bought a hat and red shoes and was planning the cake. Something suitable for an autumn wedding, perhaps, incorporating elderberries.

A contented smile spreading over her face, she shouted up to Max, 'Cup of tea?' and ran down the stairs of the cottage. Bear, the enormous sheepdog, raised his head from the box he shared with Fuzzy, her marmalade cat. He was hoping, as ever, for a titbit. 'No chance. You're starting to get fat.' With a heavy sigh, Bear closed his eyes and went back to sleep.

Shipley, Max's recently adopted springer spaniel, was racing in circles round the garden. Libby hoped he'd work off some of his excess excitement. He'd shown himself to be a talented sniffer dog, and Max was delivering him soon to a specialist trainer, to hone his skills and learn to be calm. Recent attempts to improve his behaviour by attending obedience classes with him had been only mildly effective, and Libby didn't hold out a great deal of hope.

She pottered happily in her kitchen, spooning the tea Max

preferred into a teapot. When she made tea for herself, she stuck lazily to teabags. Opening a cake tin, she cut a hunk of fruit cake, then shaved off a third. Max couldn't resist her home-made cake, and she'd noticed his shirts were just a little tighter over his chest, these days.

Libby leaned on the counter and admired the room. When she was finally installed in Max's old manor house, she'd miss Mandy, her lodger, who planned to stay on for a while, renting the property cheaply while she and Libby continued to run the chocolate business from there. She couldn't bear to leave the professional kitchen, which she'd designed herself. After her husband had died, she'd used up all the money she had, incorporating all the latest kitchen gadgets to help her build up her cake and chocolate business.

Eventually, there would be plenty of room in her new home for an even more splendid workspace. She flipped through a glossy catalogue; one from a pile she'd amassed. Maybe two big ovens, she mused as she delivered tea and cake to Max. But there was no hurry. One step at a time. Marrying Max was more important.

2

COFFEE

Late autumn sun bathed the ancient stones of Exmoor's Dunster Castle in a warm glow. Inside, peace and tranquility reigned. That was just how Margery Halfstead liked it. She shifted a pair of heavy spectacles further up her nose, careful to avoid putting smears on the lenses, and grasped the small, soft brush more firmly. With a satisfied smile, she registered the click of her wedding ring against wood, and breathed in a lungful of slightly musty air.

Surrounded by formidable portraits of other people's ancestors, she felt at home. On the days she worked as a National Trust volunteer, she daydreamed about living in this castle on top of the hill, overlooking the hills and valleys of West Somerset. You could even catch a glimpse of the sea – well, the Bristol Channel – when you looked out of the right windows.

Her husband, William, was here with her today. Humming tunelessly, Margery selected another book from the pile. With a gentle, practised flick of the wrist, she released a year's worth of dust from the top of the pages. The dust motes danced in a random ray of sunlight, finally subsiding invisibly onto the floor. Could there be any better way to spend the day? Margery glanced at William. 'I wonder why dusting old books in a stately home is such fun when...'

'When there's so much housework to do at home,' William finished. They often ended each other's sentences. Hardly surprising, after forty years of marriage. 'Wedded bliss,' William called it.

'Birds of a feather,' her father had called them, years ago.

Margery's brush hovered in the air. She'd often wondered what Father had meant by that.

She gave a mental shrug and carried on with the job. William would never set the world alight, but he'd been a solid, dependable husband. He'd understood his wife's longing for the bigger house they couldn't afford, and he'd put money by. There wasn't enough for a new place, but they were planning an extension. A bigger sitting room, with floor to ceiling windows so Margery could look out on the garden, and one more room upstairs to use for sewing. Mind you, some of the neighbours weren't keen. Mrs Whatshername down the road said she was going to object and stop the planning permission.

William would sort it out. He'd think of a way. Margery rewarded William with a fond smile. Reliability; that's what she liked most about her husband. When you'd known someone for years, you could trust them.

The clatter of heels on wood disturbed the peace as a stranger, a younger woman in her early forties by the look of her, burst in from the passage, gabbling in breathless haste, 'So sorry to butt in. Mrs Moffat, the housekeeper, sent me over here. She said you'd show me the ropes. It's my first day here, you see. I'm Annabel.' She beamed and held out a hand.

Margery suppressed a grimace. She'd raise the issue of proper flat shoes later. Even those ghastly trainers the young people wore would be more suitable than this woman's highly polished, pointy toed boots. She tried to be gracious, putting down the brush to shake the woman's hand. 'You're very welcome, Annabel.' Annabel, what sort of name was that?

William blinked behind horn-rimmed spectacles. 'You'll soon pick things up. I'm William, and this is my wife, Margery. She's the boss when it comes to cleaning.'

The skin tightened on Margery's face; he sounded like a hen-pecked husband. 'William usually shows visitors around the castle, but we're closed between October and February. Just a few pre-arranged groups are allowed.' She shot a glance at her husband. Neither approved of out-of-season tours, for they disturbed the winter peace of the castle.

William wasn't listening. His eyes were on stalks, staring at the stranger. Margery spoke louder. 'A special party of students from the local school will be here shortly. William will lead the tour, but meanwhile...'

'I thought I'd lend a hand with the cleaning,' William cleared his throat. 'Plenty to do.'

Margery nodded. 'The more the merrier.'

'Many hands make light work.'

'No man is an island—' Margery broke off. The newcomer was biting her lip with small white teeth, as though stifling a giggle. Incensed, Margery took a long, slow breath. How dare this newcomer laugh at them?

She narrowed her eyes, summing up Annabel. Almost pretty, except for that snubby nose. Brown hair in a tidy bob, quite suitable. Wide blue eyes, the exact colour of that expensive looking sweater – not cashmere, surely, to come cleaning? A pair of rather expensive, well cut jeans. Margery patted her own fringe into place and sniffed. 'Did they give you an apron?'

Annabel nodded. 'Not that I need it, really. These are my oldest clothes. By the way, Mrs Moffat said you might like a cup of coffee. Can I get you one?'

William looked at the watch Margery gave him last birthday. Nothing too showy – a solid, reliable British watch. He laughed, a little too loud. 'That'll hit the spot, coffee. Can't bring it in here, of course, but I'll come with you, make sure you find the sugar. Are you coming, dear?'

Margery shook her head. 'I'll finish up here. You go on.'

He was already on his way, 'The biscuits are hidden in the cupboard on the right...'

His voice faded away. Margery, alone in the sudden silence, clicked her tongue, replaced the newly dusted book, and reached for another.

* * *

William and Annabel returned, chattering like old friends. Margery flicked a book with harder-than-usual force. Horrified, she watched a page flutter to the floor. She'd never damaged castle property before, not in all the years she'd been volunteering. She shot a wary glance at Annabel, but the younger woman was too busy listening to William telling her about the castle to notice. Margery slipped the page back inside the book.

William hadn't noticed, either. He beamed at his companion, raking a hand through thinning grey hair. Margery remembered when he'd had a blond fringe flopping over his forehead. That was a few years ago, now. Still, he'd aged well.

Annabel's eyes sparkled. 'I'm so excited to be here. I loved history at school, but other things got in the way. Life.'

Curiosity piqued Margery's interest. 'Family?' she suggested.

'Just one son. He's thirteen, now, and it's time I got my life back. I'm a widow, you know. My husband died in a car accident when Jamie was five.' Annabel's hands were clenched.

William's head wagged in sympathy and Margery swallowed. 'That must have been difficult.' She paused. 'Your son must be a great comfort to you.'

Annabel gave a watery smile and started dusting books. 'He is. He's a great kid, but a child's not the same as a husband. I miss his father dreadfully.'

Margery coughed awkwardly, never very comfortable dealing with personal matters. How could she know what to say? 'Now, it's time for you to let these students in, William. Goodness knows why Mrs Moffat made a special arrangement, just for them.' She sniffed. 'Something about history exams, I think you said?'

'Quite right, dear, but I can't stand here all day. We're starting off in the modern butler's pantry, so the students can try out the speaking tube.' A favourite feature of the castle, the tube allowed the butler to speak to kitchen staff, downstairs in the servants' quarters. 'Then, I'll take them round the rest of the castle, finishing with a Victorian tea party later. Mrs Forest will be bringing a cake.'

Margery hesitated, every vestige of her earlier contentment destroyed by Annabel's arrival. She wouldn't spend any more time with this superior younger woman if she could help it. She replaced her brush in its bag. 'I'll give my husband a hand, if you're happy to carry on here.' She'd be glad to join the tour, and some of Libby Forest's cake would be just the job to cheer her up.

* * *

Heaving teenage bodies filled the tiny butler's pantry. They shuffled, giggled and – Margery sniffed the air – passed wind. She wrinkled her nose. A tall lad, towering over his companions, disproportionate height miraculously supported by a skeletal frame, bent over to place his mouth against the speaking tube and affected an exaggerated upper class accent. 'Hello. Who's there? I'm talking on behalf of Mr Haddock, the butler. To whom am I speaking?'

A distant, tinny voice filled the room. 'Elsie 'ere. I'm the scullery maid.'

William hissed in the lad's ear, 'Use your script.'

Face pink as he struggled with self-conscious giggles, the youth pulled a crumpled sheet of lined paper from his pocket. 'I'd like to speak to the cook.'

The voice replied, 'Ooh, she's out, I'm afraid. Can I 'elp, at all?'

Margery raised an eyebrow. She knew that voice. Beryl Nightingale, a fellow volunteer, was a timid little woman, not someone Margery would have chosen for an acting role. She supposed William thought he was doing Beryl a favour. Maybe he was right. Beryl sounded unusually confident today.

As the student continued to read from his script, William hissed at Margery. 'I've left some handouts in the car. Can you take over here? Send everyone downstairs to the old Victorian kitchen when they're finished here. I'll do the tour of the castle afterwards. I've given them maps.'

'B-but,' Margery wanted to argue. She hated dealing with visitors, and schoolchildren were the worst of all, but she was too late. William had already gone.

The teenager, enjoying himself, went on speaking through the tube. 'Mr Haddock, the butler, wishes to confirm tonight's dinner menu.'

The menu was almost lost in his companions' gleeful snorts. Margery could hear Beryl listing elaborate dishes, from partridge soup and potted crayfish to scotch woodcock. She began to think the catalogue would never end. Beryl was relishing the starring role. Finally, the litany came to an end, '... and queen of pudd—'

The disembodied voice fell abruptly silent. The young man shouted into the speaking tube. 'Hello. Are you there?'

More silence.

Margery stepped forward. 'It gets blocked sometimes. Try blowing into the tube.'

The boy puffed and the device produced a loud raspberry, but there was no reply. The scullery maid, it seemed, had gone.

'Right, never mind.' Margery swallowed. She wasn't good at handling groups of students. They made her nervous. She tapped one of the boys on the shoulder. 'You come upstairs with me. You can tug the bell-pull while the rest go down to the servants' quarters, find the row of bells on the wall, and wait. Mr Halfstead will join you there.'

'Will they ring downstairs? Like in Downton Abbey?'

'Exactly.'

Margery climbed towards the bedrooms, an excited teenager in tow. Her knees ached.

As one foot reached the landing, a single cry rang through the castle. Another volunteer, a big woman, poked her head out from a nearby doorway. Neat black hair framed her face. Her blouse was printed with bright swirls that made Margery's head spin. 'What's that?'

'Party of schoolchildren.'

Another cry interrupted. The two women's eyes met. Without another word, Margery turned and, forgetting her painful knees, ran down the stairs to the servants' quarters.

She burst through into the old kitchen, the young lad close behind. William was already there, bent over, peering behind the huge metal-topped table that dominated the room.

Margery pushed past the knot of schoolboys. 'What is it?'

Her husband looked every day of his age as he turned an ashen face to his wife. 'It's... she's...'

But Margery, knuckles stuffed into her mouth to stifle a scream, had already seen Beryl Nightingale's motionless body.

3

PINEAPPLE CAKE

'Time to drive over to Dunster Castle.' Her head still full of plans for her new kitchen, Libby shooed two excitable dogs away from her purple Citroen, 'But I'm not taking them with me.'

Max, brushing dust from his ancient baggy brown jumper, wore a mock puzzled expression. 'But they'd love it. All those enticing visitor smells.'

'Exactly. Bear will chase up and down the stairs and gallop through the woods, while Shipley will go into sniffer dog mode and frighten all the volunteers. He'll bark like crazy if he picks up any sort of suspicious scent.'

'It's true he hasn't quite got the hang of only following one smell at a time. Maybe he's too old to learn new tricks. Are we asking too much of him?'

'We'll find out. He just needs time. Springer spaniels are notorious for bounding around, I believe, but they're very intelligent.' Libby considered Bear's mournful brown eyes. 'Not that you aren't just as clever, Bear,' she added, pulling a treat from her pocket. 'You're like a jealous child.'

'Good job we're too old to have our own kids,' Max pointed

out. 'It's enough trouble dealing with the three we have between us, plus the dogs. And Fuzzy, of course. Mustn't forget the cat, even if she does spend all day in your airing cupboard at the moment. I hope she finds mine as desirable.'

'Anyway.' Libby was firm. 'If you'll look after the dogs this morning, I'll get the cake over to Dunster Castle and be back for lunch. Then you can deliver Shipley to the trainer.' The cake was another reason for leaving the dogs at home. Three layers, iced, with a Victorian-style sugar pineapple perched on top – what was this Victorian thing about pineapples? The sweet smell alone would drive the dogs crazy, quite apart from the health and safety issues of letting animals anywhere near her catering.

'Ah, lunch.' Max rubbed his stomach. 'By the way, I found some fishing tackle in your loft. Robert's, I suppose?'

'Not mine, that's for sure. Did you want it?'

'No, but seeing it made me think. There's a local club. We used to have competitions, but it all got a bit nasty. You won't remember, because it was just before you arrived in Exham, but there was some bad feeling. People accused of weighting the scales.'

'Really? Why would anyone care that much about fishing?'

'You'd be surprised. I just thought I might take it up again.'

Libby laughed. 'Good idea. It'll keep you out from under my feet. Isn't that what old married couples say?'

She climbed into the car and waved goodbye through the open window as she rounded the corner into the road, watching in the mirror as Max and the dogs vanished from view. The mirror reflected her ridiculous grin. Contentment. That's what she felt. It had taken her months – years, almost – to realise marrying Max would not necessarily mean loss of independence. She was embarrassed to remember how she'd dithered and hesitated, and done her best to drive Max away. At last, recognising she'd lose him if she didn't make up her mind, she'd proposed to him.

They'd made plans for the ceremony and given notice to the registry office, so they could marry whenever they chose. There was no hurry. Her son Robert's wedding had ended in drama, but Libby was determined to have as quiet an event as possible, and Max hated any kind of fuss. He had breathed a sigh of relief. 'If you're sure that's what you want, it will suit me fine. We'll go to the registry office on our own and do the deed. They'll supply witnesses.'

'For the first time in my life,' Libby had confided to her friend, Angela, 'I don't feel under any pressure to do what other people want me to. I'm free, at last.'

Angela, long a widow, had looked wistful. As Libby drove, she mentally ran through a list of men she knew, wondering if any would be suitable for her friend. Oliver, perhaps, who'd been at school with Max? Or Reg, the African American basketball player who came over to Exham at every opportunity. He'd dallied with Libby's apprentice and lodger, Mandy, but that relationship had fizzled out. Reg was in his thirties, about halfway between Mandy and Angela, but maybe Angela would like a toy boy?

A ray of sunshine broke through the late autumn clouds, adding to Libby's glow of well-being. Her own happiness made her want the same for everyone but she'd try not to interfere in other people's lives. She had enough to think about with the cake and chocolate business, and the private investigation partnership she'd established with Max. Angela would have to find her own way forward.

Libby changed gear. On the other hand, it would be nice to see Angela happy. Perhaps she could try on-line dating?

The purple Citroen screeched to a standstill. Dunster Castle was in uproar. A police car, blue lights flashing, blocked the driveway as white-clad figures moved purposefully around the entrance, securing police tape across the road.

Libby recognised a crime scene when she saw one. She climbed out of the Citroen, leaving the cargo of cake, keen to find out more, only to hear a harsh voice. 'Wait there.' The familiar, unwelcome, figure of Police Constable Ian Smith levered an over-weight body from the front seat of the police car.

His small eyes were screwed into pinpricks of malevolent light and Libby's heart sank. He'd never liked her. For one thing, she'd succeeded in solving several murder investigations, leaving PC Smith and his colleagues with egg on their faces. Some in the police force had slowly grown used to having Libby around, and afforded her a reasonable measure of respect. It had helped that Max's background as a financial consultant, often working for the government, was valuable to the local police service. Recently, as Libby and Max's standing as private investigators gained traction, they'd been invited to undergo a trial period working for the increasingly stretched police force. They were rather grandly described as civilian investigating officers. What's more, they were paid for their work.

PC Smith disagreed profoundly with a policy of allowing 'muggles' anywhere near investigations. 'Sorry, Mrs Forest. Not this time.' He looked as though he could hardly speak civilly to Libby.

'Actually, I have my official badge with me.'

She kept her voice friendly and tried hard not to look smug as she pulled out the laminated card, but Smith's lip curl made it plain she'd failed. 'You're not involved in this one yet.'

Libby's pulse quickened. Not involved yet? So, she was likely to be? Her stomach lurched and she drew a sharp breath at the familiar mix of excitement and foreboding. 'Might not even be a murder,' he continued. 'The old woman probably had a heart attack after walking up that road.' He pointed up the steep slope that led towards the castle's thirteenth century gateway.

'Someone's dead?'

PC Smith folded his arms across a beer gut. His face flushed red. Clearly, he'd given away more information than he intended, so keen to put Libby in her place he'd forgotten to watch his tongue. 'They won't let you in to the scene,' he grumbled.

Libby stepped round him, wondering how he'd ever managed to pass a fitness assessment. 'We'll see.'

She climbed through the gateway and up a flight of steps, arriving breathless at the entrance to the castle. Detective Sergeant Joe Ramshore, Max's son, ducked under the yellow police tape to greet her, pulling off white gloves on the way. 'Well, news really travels fast around here. Nice to see you, step-mother-to-be. Is your partner-in-crime here too?'

'Not today. Max is involved in some of these bitcoin mining frauds. He spends most of his time tracking down computer viruses, trying to find their source. It's going to take weeks, if not months. Some of his old government contacts sent the work his way, and as you can imagine, he's loving it.'

Joe laughed. 'That sounds like him. Never happier than gazing at a screen, fingers on the keyboard. Rather him than me. But what brought you to our latest crime scene? Are you developing second sight or did someone tip you off?'

'Pure coincidence. I'm here on bakery business, delivering cake for a group of visiting schoolchildren, though it looks as though they won't be eating it. What's up?'

'Elderly lady dead in the kitchens.'

'Anyone I know?'

Joe clicked his tongue. 'I'm afraid so. Beryl Nightingale. She belongs – well – belonged to the Exham on Sea History Society. Was she one of your friends?'

Libby had not known it was possible to feel colour drain from your own face. She'd been a member of the society since she arrived in the area, so she knew Beryl. Last time Libby saw her, the older woman had perched like a small brown sparrow on a wooden chair, nibbling on cake crumbs and whispering with her old friends, George Edwards and the Halfsteads. 'Beryl? Not really? What – I mean how did she die?'

'We don't know if it's natural causes yet, or something more sinister. It could be a stroke or heart attack. There's no obvious sign of foul play, but we'll wait to hear from the pathologist.'

He made a wry face. 'Unfortunately, we have a gaggle of schoolkids here, and if I'm not mistaken they'll already have texted the whole of Somerset with lurid gossip, so our friends in the press will arrive at any moment.'

He paused to take a deep breath, before finishing with a dramatic flourish. 'What's more, one of the boys is that new local member of parliament's son.'

Libby's mouth formed a soundless whistle. 'An MP? Now, that's going to cause some complications, if Beryl's death turns out to be anything other than natural causes.'

'Sure will. What's more, the lad was talking to Beryl when she had her seizure, or whatever it was. His dad's not going to like it.' Joe raised his eyes to the heavens. 'Tell you what, if you want to sit in on young Jason Franklin's initial interview, I could use your input. In your new official capacity.'

* * *

Jason Franklin's long, bony body perched on a wooden chair in one of the offices at the back of the castle, well away from the public areas. His arms and legs, sticking out at odd angles, reminded Libby of the spider her son had once kept as a pet, against Libby's better judgement. She'd always hated the beast, shuddering every time she passed the tank in his bedroom. Robert insisted spiders were harmless. Libby did not believe him.

The boy's uniform marked him out as a pupil at the local comprehensive school. The regulation tight grey trousers failed to quite cover bare ankles, and he wore no socks. Did young people not feel the cold? Whether the shortness of the trousers was due to a teenage growth spurt or simply current fashion, Libby had no idea.

Jason's intelligent, sharp featured face was alight. Excitement or nerves? He waved his hands in the air as his voice veered between a deep, adult brown tone and occasional adolescent crackles.

A young detective constable, neat in black trousers and jumper, with long fair hair tied in a ponytail, sat opposite Jason, nodding at his answers. She looked up as Libby entered, her face blank. Recognition dawned and her expression hardened. 'Mrs Forest. Can I help?'

Libby's heart sank at the sight of another resentful police officer. What had she done to annoy this one? They hadn't met, before today. She fixed a friendly smile on her face and held up her pass. 'DS Ramshore wants me to sit in, if that's OK, Detective Constable?'

The young officer raised an eyebrow, and Libby's spirits dropped further. She was not welcome here.

A police radio crackled, and the young detective constable fiddled with it for a few seconds before she spoke. Her otherwise pleasant voice held a hard edge as she spoke. 'Very well. I'm Detective Constable Gemma Humberstone. There's tea and coffee over there.' She nodded to a tray on a nearby table. 'Jason is just explaining what happened. Of course, this is only to get a feel of things. If we need to talk more, we'll organise an appropriate adult to be with us, as Jason is a minor.' Libby nodded. The detective constable clearly intended to proceed according to the book. Well, that made a refreshing change from PC Ian Smith's slap-dash methods.

Libby tilted the coffee pot over a cup. Liquid dribbled out, the colour of treacle. It must have been brewing for some time. Preferring not to give herself palpitations, Libby took another cup and used a teabag instead.

The DC raised her voice. 'Now, this is just a preliminary chat, as I was saying, Jason.' Libby caught the implied rebuke and subsided quietly into her seat, sipping lukewarm tea. DC Humberstone continued. 'You were all together in the butler's pantry?'

The boy nodded. 'We were – I was – talking into the speaking tube. It goes from the butler's pantry to the kitchens. Everyone was there. I mean, all of us from school.'

He paused, and the DC waited, but he said no more. She asked, 'Did you have a teacher with you?'

'No. Mr Halfstead was in charge. He works here. I think he's a course leader, or something.' DC Humberstone nodded and made a note as he talked. 'There were a couple of other people as well. People who work here, I think. I'm not really sure.'

'Don't worry. We'll get names and so on before people leave. Just tell me what you remember. In your own words.'

The teenager scratched at his chin, leaving a pink mark. 'Well, nothing much. I mean, like, I asked her what was on the menu for dinner – pretending to be part of the staff, you see.' He screwed his eyes shut, obviously trying to be precise. 'She talked about food – different courses – one was something called a shape. I was going to ask her what that was, but I didn't get a chance. She gave a sort of hiccup and stopped talking.' He frowned. 'I wasn't really worried, and Mrs Halfstead didn't seem too bothered, anyway. She sent us down to the servants' hall and then she took one of the others up to the bedrooms to ring a bell. They have this full set of bells on the wall, like in the servants' quarters, so the family can summon help when they need it...'

His voice faded away. 'We didn't know what had happened. We all ran down the stairs. Mr Halfstead was already there. He turned and shouted at us to stay where we were, but we'd already seen what looked like a bundle of rags on the floor. Someone screamed, I think.' He shrugged. 'I didn't see the lady's face, just a bit of her skirt and that. It was all a muddle, with people shouting.'

'Did anyone try to revive the lady?'

'I think he did – Mr Halfstead, I mean. He bent over her, like he was giving her mouth to mouth.'

'OK. That's fine, Jason.'

As DC Humberstone rose, Libby put in, 'Do you mind if I ask a question, Jason?' She ignored the DC's cold stare. 'Can you tell me exactly what you said to Ber— I mean, to Miss Nightingale, through the speaking tube?'

He reached inside his back pocket. 'I had a script. Here.' He hesitated, then offered it to Libby.

To avoid further antagonising DC Humberstone, Libby shook her head. The police officer held out a plastic bag and Jason slipped the sheet of paper inside. Libby would have a chance to scrutinise it later. 'Did you write this yourself?'

'With my mates. We had a session at school about coming here today. Mr Halfstead gave us a talk on the history of the castle and that, and then we wrote down what we'd say.'

'Just one more thing,' Libby asked, feeling the atmosphere in the room, already chilly, cool by several degrees under the detective constable's continued disapproval. 'Why were you the one talking through the tube? I mean, how were you chosen?'

Jason beamed, and for the first time, Libby caught a glimpse of his personality as pride overcame his shock. 'I won it in a competition.'

'A competition? Organised by...'

'Mr Halfstead.'

4

SHORTBREAD

For the first time, Libby was allowed into the Incident Room in the police station, a sign of her new status as an official adjunct to the police. Joe Ramshore led the way, pushed open the door and stood back to let her in. Libby looked round the room, her heart sinking at the sight of PC Ian Smith, leaning against a wall. His eyes had narrowed to virtual invisibility and his upper lip curled in a sneer. By his side sat DC Humberstone. She glanced round at Libby, then turned back, her face stony.

Joe made the introductions. 'Some of you already know Libby Forest. She helped with the recent murder case over at the bridge in West Somerset, and DCI Morrison's asked her to work with us on this case. We can use her in the investigation, but you need to remember she's a civilian. DCI Morrison will be here soon, and he's keen we welcome her properly.'

Libby felt her face burn as PC Smith snorted, loud enough for her to hear. 'Always around when there's a suspicious death, isn't that right, Mrs Forest? Anyone would think you know it's coming.' Another officer slurped a mouthful of coffee and sniggered.

Joe raised a hand. Before he could come to her defence, Libby stepped forward. She needed to stand up for herself. 'I help when I can.' She took a breath. 'I've brought cake.' Someone made an appreciative noise as she pulled the tin from her over-sized tote bag. 'This was intended for the school party at the castle. They won't need it now, and I thought you might like some. Oh, and some shortbread.'

The coffee drinking constable took the tin, opened the lid, and sniffed. 'Smells OK. What's this pineapple on the top for?'

Libby followed him to a side table. 'It's part of a Victorian theme. The students intended to visit the old Victorian kitchen and the Victorians were fond of pineapples – something about one-upmanship if you could grow them in your orangery.' The constable cut a huge slice, swallowed it in two bites, and murmured through a mouthful of crumbs, 'Not bad.' Libby had a theory that when people eat food you've cooked, they feel obliged to be civil, at least. So far, so good.

The door opened. 'Right, if you've all finished stuffing your faces, let's get on.' Detective Chief Inspector Morrison had arrived. Libby had met the senior officer several times before. His deeply lined face wore the crestfallen expression of a man who expected very little from the world and was seldom disappointed. Nevertheless, his reputation for clearing up crime on his patch brought grudging respect, even from the likes of PC Smith.

The detective chief inspector opened the discussion. 'We don't have a report yet from the pathologist but he gave a few hints. First thoughts about the cause of death are unclear. No wounds of any sort. The victim appeared to be alone in the kitchen, by the speaking tube. There's no chair, so she must have been standing, which suggests she felt well. Not much more to tell, at this stage, I'm afraid.'

The crime scene manager, a short, cheerful woman wearing baggy black trousers and solid, flat shoes, described police activities at the unusual scene. 'This may not be a crime scene, but given the deceased lady's good health and a few preliminary thoughts from the pathologist, we decided to treat the death as suspicious and collect as much forensic evidence as possible.'

She glanced at Libby. 'We don't want to dismiss this as natural causes and look like fools.' That had happened more than once in the past couple of years.

'Unfortunately, dozens of people visit the Victorian kitchen every day, so finger marks are not likely to lead us anywhere, unless we take prints from everyone who's visited the castle this year.'

Someone groaned. 'We won't be going down that route yet, not without extra resources,' DCI Morrison confirmed. 'Do we have any other leads?'

'We're testing the victim's possessions. She's not allowed to have a handbag with her in the castle, apparently, but she had a few things in her apron pockets. Nothing very interesting. Mints, purse, a diary with very few entries – the usual things. Plus, some personal souvenirs – a small silver photograph album, the kind that takes just two photos, and a hip flask. One picture is of an old lady bearing a very strong resemblance to the victim – perhaps a relative – and the other is of a young man. That photo's in black and white, and judging from the lad's clothes and haircut, a proper short back and sides with a neat parting, it was taken back in the fifties. We may get something useful from them.'

DC Gemma Humberstone and PC Ian Smith reported on their initial conversations with the volunteers and schoolboys. Most had been brief, placing people at various points around the castle. All accounts confirmed that Beryl Nightingale was alone in the kitchen.

Libby shut her eyes for a moment and imagined the scene. Beryl, who'd so often longed to take centre stage in the history society meetings, must have been thrilled with her starring role in the little drama. She could never have dreamed it was about to end so tragically.

DCI Humberstone displayed the sheet of A4 the schoolboy had handed over, still encased in its protective plastic bag. 'This is Jason's script. He was reading it as he spoke to Beryl Nightingale through the butler's tube. He took the main part in their little drama, after a competition organised by William Halfstead. That's the Halfstead who discovered the body. We took his statement at the scene.'

Ian Smith said, 'Sounds like a suspect, to me.' The cake eating officer, a young man with spiky hair and the pink face of someone who hardly needs to shave, nodded, but DCI Morrison held up a warning hand.

'Now, let's not jump to conclusions. At this stage, we ask questions: who, what, when, how, where and why. We need to know everything about the key witnesses. Remember, although we may have suspicions, we don't even know yet if this is a murder. We're still waiting for confirmation from the pathologist.' He turned to Libby. 'Mrs Forest, you knew the victim. One of your history society members, I'm told. What can you tell us about her?'

Libby's neck tingled as she tried to think, conscious of every eye on her. 'The society stopped meeting over the summer. The next discussion's due in a couple of days, as it happens, so I haven't seen Beryl there for a while.' She remembered something, 'She's been coming to the bakery more often than usual, recently.'

'Any reason why, so far as you know?'

'I'm not sure.' Libby thought back to a remark heard in the shop. 'I think she recently retired. I'm hoping to find out more about her at the meeting. Some of the members have known her for years. She's always been so quiet.' She wracked her brain for ways to describe Beryl, but the woman's personality had been so withdrawn Libby hardly knew her. 'She likes carrot cake.' PC Smith's lip curled in a sneer and Libby stopped talking, annoyed at sounding unprofessional. They didn't need to know that sort of gossip.

DCI Morrison followed the direction of her gaze. 'Ian. You have something to add?'

PC Smith folded his arms across his chest and stared at the floor like a sulky child. 'No, sir.'

The DCI nodded, tasked a couple of officers with taking full statements from the volunteers at the castle, and set a date for the next conference. 'But, before you all go, I have an announcement. DS Ramshore will be leaving us. He's passed his exams – not before time, I might add.' He scowled with mock severity at Joe. 'He's moving on to West Mercia as a detective inspector.'

5

SALMON

That afternoon, Shipley's absence on a few days training made Max's house seem eerily quiet. 'I'm looking forward to his return as a reformed character,' Max said. 'In the meantime, let's give Bear some exercise. There's an hour or two before the light goes. He can have our full attention, for once.'

They headed for Brent Knoll, one of the peculiar rounded Somerset hills that rise from the Levels as landmarks, visible for miles around. The unseasonable warm weather of the past few days had faded. Libby shivered. 'The nights are drawing in, fast.'

Max stopped, drew in a huge lungful of air, and stretched his arms towards the sky. 'I love this time of year. I like wearing cosy clothes, there's a hint of melancholy, the trees have finished turning, and there's the promise of Christmas just around the corner.'

Libby's spirits rose. 'We'll be an old married couple by then.'

Max slid his arm round her shoulders, pulled her close, and kissed her. 'Now, do you feel warmer?'

She drew back to study Max's face, tracing with her finger the laughter lines round his eyes and the dent in his chin, all as familiar, now, as her own features. She leaned in again, drinking in his warm, masculine scent and the sharp hint of aftershave, recognising it as one of her presents to him.

'Why are you laughing?' Max asked.

'Because I'm happy. And astonished at my good luck.' She'd arrived in Exham on Sea, released by widowhood from an unhappy marriage, never expecting to find real love at this late stage of life.

Bear, who'd been trotting ahead, stopped dead. He hesitated, then bounded over and reared up on his hind legs, aiming his wet tongue at Libby's face. The romantic spell was broken and Max let her go. 'He's jealous.'

'Come on, Bear.' Laughing, Libby chased ahead, Bear matching his pace to hers. Before long, she had to admit defeat, gasping, 'That dog could keep going for hours.'

'It's the breed. His ancestors travelled miles, watching sheep on the Carpathian hills.'

Bear, tail aloft with pleasure, turned his attention to sniffing at hedgerows. Max asked, 'How did the police conference go?'

Libby kicked at a stone. 'Not brilliant, if I'm honest. Some of the officers think I'm just playing at investigations. They don't want me, especially now Joe is moving on. I'm pleased for him, of course, but things could be tricky.' Suddenly furious, she burst out, 'They think I'm an impostor, no matter how many cases I solve. They believe I should stick to the chocolate business.'

Max nodded and walked on a few paces, deep in thought. 'It's not surprising some of the – well, the less enlightened among the police resent you. They feel threatened, because you've been the one catching murderers. They're not all so inflexible. DCI Morrison wants you there. He thinks a great deal of you.'

It was true, Morrison gave every sign of listening when Libby spoke. She kicked through a pile of fallen leaves. 'I wish Ian

Smith didn't dislike me so much, and Gemma Humberstone's almost as frosty.'

'They'll get used to you. The sensible ones will see you're good at your job, although I fear Ian Smith might never get it. He's a lost cause, but that's his problem. If justice was left to the likes of him, it would never be done.'

'You're right. It's almost as if his attitude has affected the others, so the best way to prove myself is by finding out what happened to Beryl. Morrison believes her death's suspicious, at the very least. I'm sure the pathologist would have recognised a stroke or heart attack straight away. Suicide seems unlikely, given she was in the middle of a conversation.'

Libby paused as a familiar mix of excitement and horror kicked in once more. That feeling never failed to grab hold at the beginning of a new case. With a burst of determination, she announced, 'I won't let Ian Smith and his childish buddies intimidate me. Besides, I owe it to Beryl to get justice, if she was murdered.' She walked faster. 'I'm back on the case, Max, which is just as well. You're too busy to work on this one, but it helps to talk it through.'

'And that's why we're a team.'

Libby's brain clicked into gear. 'Let's think. Why would anyone want to kill a helpless old lady like Beryl?'

'That's the puzzle,' said Max. 'How much do we know about her?'

'Hardly anything. She's like people's old aunts. You know, always there on the side-lines, but no one takes any notice of them. They don't seem to matter, not in the rush of day-to-day life. I hardly knew her, although she was always at the history society meetings. She never said much, just sat in the corner, eating cake, waiting to be asked to give a talk about her ancestors.

I don't know much about her background. Do you? You grew up in Exham.'

He shook his head. 'Not really, though I knew the name. I was more interested in football than middle-aged spinsters, and our paths never crossed, but I can tell you who will know all the detail.'

'Go on, then, who?'

'Your friend, Angela. She's known Beryl all her life.'

'Of course.' Angela Miles, born and bred in Exham, knew the history of everyone in the area. 'You're right. I'll talk to her tomorrow. Then, the rest of the society's getting together in a couple of days. I should get some useful background from them.'

Max stopped at a railway bridge and leaned on the wall, watching for trains. 'While you're in this positive mood, how about setting a date for the wedding?'

'Mm.' Libby thought of the dress, hanging patiently in her cottage, and her belongings all packed in boxes. 'Let's do it soon.'

'How soon?'

Libby tried to analyse her feelings. What was holding her back? She was dying to get married to this man. She loved everything about him, even his fondness for poring over a computer for hours at a time. Moving into his manor house and learning to call it home felt like an adventure, so why was she hesitating? She pictured a wedding, bigger than the one they were planning, surrounded by their children – Robert and Joe, with their wives, Shipley, and Bear, of course, but something was missing. 'Ali,' she murmured. 'I wish Ali could be there.'

A train thundered past, shaking the bridge under their feet, drowning Max's response.

'What did you say?' Libby asked.

'I said, have you asked your daughter to come?'

'I mentioned it, but I know she can't come all the way from

Brazil, just for my wedding.' Ali was happy and her voluntary work was worthwhile, even though, according to her emails, she was permanently broke.

'I'm being silly. Let's not wait. How about two weeks on Saturday?'

'Perfect.' Max landed a kiss on her cheek and set off at a run. 'Meanwhile, race you to Brent Knoll.'

* * *

Libby spent the evening in her cottage, packing. Now they'd set a date for the wedding, there was plenty to do. Libby checked she had ample supplies of coffee so the cottage would smell enticing when they arrived. She'd bake bread, as well. If that didn't sell the house, nothing would.

Fuzzy, her aloof marmalade cat, reacted to Libby's return with a cold stare. She deigned to nibble at a tiny mouthful of the best salmon, stalked from the room, and returned to the airing cupboard to curl up in her favourite spot. She was an aging cat, almost sixteen, and her muzzle displayed a mix of original ginger and grey fur. 'Oh, Fuzzy, don't you go getting old. I couldn't manage without you.' With a sudden overwhelming rush of emotion, Libby plucked the cat from her nest on a pile of recently ironed duvet covers and buried her face in the soft fur.

Like all cats, Fuzzy despised unnecessary emotion. She struggled out of her owner's arms, but allowed Libby to stroke her back as she settled back to sleep, warm and happy. 'Sometimes I wish I was a cat,' Libby muttered. 'Life would be much simpler.'

She worked fast, for once unhindered by the attentions of the dogs. The process was far easier in their absence. Only the other day, Shipley had stolen one of Libby's favourite red sandals, sloped off to a corner, and chewed the leather to shreds.

With half the contents of her house neatly packed in boxes, Libby sank into a chair, exhausted, to watch the news on television. She hardly heard a word; her brain was too full of Beryl. Why would anyone want to harm such a gentle soul? Unmarried, Beryl had led a quiet, solitary life. Libby had arranged to visit Angela the next day. With luck, her friend would share a few details.

Libby sighed, switched off the TV set, and made a cup of hot chocolate, ignoring the automatic pang of guilt. She'd walked a long way with Max, so she had calories to spare. A few mouthfuls of chocolate wouldn't stop her fitting into the wedding dress.

As she sipped, guiltily savouring the drink's sweet richness, her phone rang. The caller ID was blocked, so it was probably the police. Maybe the news would be good.

'Mrs Forest, it's Detective Constable Gemma Humberstone here.' There was an edge of excitement in the DC's voice that set Libby's heart pumping.

'I'm sorry to call so late, but DCI Morrison wanted you to know as soon as possible—'

'Yes?' Breathless, Libby cut her short. 'Know what?'

'The pathologist telephoned again. He won't entirely commit himself yet, but he's pretty sure Beryl Nightingale died from nicotine poisoning.'

6

HOT CHOCOLATE

Libby's hot chocolate cooled, untouched, as she scoured the internet for everything she could find on nicotine poisoning. It was past midnight before she slept, but the next morning she rose early, watching the time tick slowly past. She forced herself to wait until a reasonable hour before she locked the cottage and set off to visit Angela.

Her friend looked charming and elegant as always. Even in the early morning, her hair shone and subtle makeup brightened her face. Libby had tried, but she could never match Angela's easy style.

She welcomed Libby graciously with freshly brewed coffee and a plate of Libby's own shortbread. 'I think you're one of my best customers,' Libby pointed out. 'How do you stay so slim?'

'Genes. I can't help it, I was born lucky. My mother lived to be ninety-five, and I'm planning to last even longer.' Angela flicked an invisible speck of dust from the coffee table. 'Now, what did you want to ask me about? I'm sorry you had to make a special journey, by the way. I know you're meeting the rest of the history society, but I've promised to go over to Wells Cathedral for an extra session tomorrow. They have more visitors than ever, these days.' Angela worked as a guide, showing sightseers round the building. She pulled a face. 'I wonder whether there's a degree of notoriety adding to visitors' interest, ever since – you know – that awful business.'

Libby shot her friend a sharp glance, diverted for a few minutes from the purpose of her visit. Her inbuilt detection systems were on the alert. Angela had not seemed so lively for months, not since she was involved in the murder at the cathedral. 'Come on. What's happened to cheer you up? Something special – or someone?'

Angela beamed. 'I'm not sure, yet. I'll tell you in a while. It might all fizzle out.' She made a show of crossing her fingers. 'But, you didn't come to talk about my social life. I imagine you need to discuss Beryl.'

'You're right. I'll let it go for now, but you're not off the hook. I'll be back! I hope things work out.'

'If I end up half as happy as you and Max, I'll be delighted. By the way, I haven't forgiven you for wanting a tiny wedding with no guests.'

Libby grinned. 'Maybe we can make an exception for you.'

Libby pulled out a battered spiral pad and a pen. Taking notes helped to draw a line between friendship and investigating. 'I need to know everything about Beryl. Her life story, if you can fill in the details. You never know what may be important. I'm working officially with the police on this case. DCI Morrison's teams are collecting the hard evidence, forensics and so on, but they've asked me to gather general information from people who knew Beryl. As her only interest seems to have been the history society, and volunteering at Dunster Castle, I'll be talking to all the members, to hear background details.' She paused, anticipating the effect of the announcement she was about to make. 'Beryl died from nicotine poisoning.'

Angela's eyebrows shot up. 'Nicotine? You mean, from cigarettes? But, she didn't smoke.' She frowned. 'Was it an accident, or – or something even worse?'

'I'm afraid either accident or suicide is unlikely. It would be an odd way to kill herself, and if she didn't smoke...' Libby explained the few facts she'd learned. 'It's not difficult to distil the poison from cigarettes, but there would be plenty of easier ways to do away with yourself. It's been used in the past for murder, though, because cigarettes are easily accessible in large numbers. Beryl must have eaten or drunk something tasting strong enough to disguise the nicotine.'

Angela's eyes were stretched wide, her face horrified. 'Who would do such a thing to Beryl? And why?' she whispered. She fell silent, rolling the hem of her jumper between agitated fingers. She opened her mouth, then closed it again while Libby waited, sure her friend had something important to say.

After a moment, Angela leaned forward. 'I don't like to tattle about Beryl, especially now she's dead. You know, never speak ill...' Her voice trailed away.

Libby nodded encouragement. 'It's so important to find out all I can about her. If she had secrets, they may be the reason she was killed. In any case, whatever you know will help.'

Angela wrinkled her nose. 'I'm sure you're right, and you'll probably find out from someone else. You see, Beryl had a secret. She – well – she had an occasional drink or two. Alone. During the day. In fact, I suppose you could say she was almost an alcoholic.'

Libby bit her lip to hide disbelief. Mousy Beryl? Surely not? Then, she remembered that the police had found a silver hip flask in Beryl's bag. She let her breath out in a long sigh. Perhaps Angela was right. 'What did she drink?'

'Well, I believe she's been seen with a supermarket trolley full of bottles of whisky.'

Libby ran a finger round the rim of her cup, thinking it through. 'A good slug of whisky would mask the taste of nicotine.'

The two friends stared at one another. Angela winced. 'There's quite a story to Beryl, I'm afraid. Oh dear. I hate to gossip even more...'

Libby let the pause lengthen, allowing her friend to gather her thoughts. Eventually, Angela leaned forward, replaced her bone china plate on the polished occasional table by her elbow, and gave a small shake of the head. 'I can see you need to know the full story, to understand what made Beryl tick. It's a sad tale, and it goes back a long way.'

Libby scribbled fast as Angela talked. 'Beryl was born during the Second World War, in a family that had once been wealthy, but declined over the years. Her father died a few days before the war ended, leaving her mother to raise Beryl, the baby, and her older brother. She was a widow on a tiny pension and no real marketable skills. They went on living in a big house, but it was a draughty old place, it cost a fortune to heat, and they survived on a shoestring.'

Libby, growing up within living memory of the war, had heard many such stories. 'After the war, when education and health improved, did things look up for them?'

'Beryl's mother prided herself on caring her best for Beryl and Cyril. She made a small living with her sewing machine, altering clothes, and the children did well in school. Beryl was a clever girl, especially good at maths. She could have gone to university, but the family was still struggling and Mrs Nightingale persuaded her to get a job, here in Exham, as a secretary. Cyril, of course, being the son, went to university. Exeter, I think, where he gained a respectable degree in law and started to make his way up the ladder as a barrister. Beryl and her mother both doted on Cyril.'

'Beryl stayed quietly at home in Exham, looking after Mrs Nightingale?'

Angela nodded. 'Exactly. But, Beryl had hopes. Cyril's friend, Geoffrey, was also a lawyer, and he and Beryl fell in love. They became engaged and she was all set to marry, set up home in Exeter, and live happily ever after.'

Libby groaned. 'I can sense this isn't going to end happily.'

'You're right. Cyril bought himself a little car. One evening, after a successful case, he and Geoffrey celebrated by driving across the Somerset Levels, visiting public houses. They sped round a corner, straight into a cow that had wandered out from a nearby field. The car pitched into a rhyne, upside down, and both the young men died.'

Libby drew in her breath. 'Those ditches can be treacherous. I've ended up with my front wheels in the water before now.'

'It's easily done, and it was even easier back then, with no lighting in the countryside. The sky was overcast so there was no starlight. No one even found the car until the next morning. Beryl was distraught and Mrs Nightingale was never the same again. They'd both worshipped Cyril, and Beryl truly loved Geoffrey. All her dreams of the future died with him.'

Libby stopped writing, the tragedy of Beryl's loss made more poignant by her own happiness with Max. She made a silent promise never to take her luck for granted. 'That explains the photographs Beryl carried around. The young man must be her old flame. No wonder she kept his picture close. She was left with no qualifications, no fiancé, a dead end job, and a grieving mother.'

'She looked after her mother for years, as Mrs Nightingale

grew more infirm. They became inseparable, with all those shared memories. Beryl never found anyone else to love. She seemed content enough, until her mother died. Mrs Nightingale was well into her eighties, but it came as a dreadful shock to Beryl. She was left all alone in the world. I think that's when the drinking began.'

She fell silent. Libby prompted, 'Come on, you can't stop now.'

'No, I suppose not. The talk in town was that alcohol had always been a problem in the family. I heard Beryl's father was – well – practically an alcoholic as well. Although nothing was certain, the general belief was that Cyril drove the car while he was drunk, and the accident was his fault. People did drink and drive, in those days, before the law changed. There were no breathalysers.' She gave a rueful laugh. 'Folk used to talk about having one more drink before driving. "One for the road," they called it.'

Libby was puzzled. 'I never heard the slightest hint. Not even from Gladys in the flower shop, and she's the biggest gossip in Exham.'

Angela poured more coffee. 'That's the way, around here. We love to gossip, but we're protective of each other when—' She stopped and blushed.

'I know what you mean. When strangers or newcomers are around. Like me.'

Angela's lopsided grin was apologetic. 'There's always been a sort of conspiracy to hide Beryl's problem. Everyone was sorry for her.'

Libby thought back to the society meetings. Beryl had so often offered to give talks about local history, but the talks had never taken place. Other group members always suggested a reason to move on to another topic. Once, Beryl had pulled sheets of lined A4 paper from her bag, but before she could speak, George Edwards had begged for another slice of Libby's cake, to take home to his invalid wife. Margery Halfstead had joined in, praising Libby's baking, and somehow Beryl's talk had been forgotten.

'Are you telling me that when Beryl sat quietly in the corner, waiting to give her lectures, she was sozzled?'

'I'm afraid so. That's why we always found a way to prevent her from starting the talk. I once caught a glimpse of the notes – not even notes, really – merely the stack of paper she kept in her bag.'

Libby nodded. 'Her lecture notes. She used to pull them out and wave them.'

'They made no sense at all; just a few scribbled sentences and a dozen blank pages. Beryl could no more give a talk in public than fly.'

'I had no idea.' Stunned, Libby fell silent. How little she'd understood of Exham's ways. What else did the town gossip hide? 'It's a lot to take in.'

Angela rose and collected cups. 'I think we need more coffee. I suppose we were all – what is it called these days? – enablers. We let Beryl get on with her drinking while we watched out for her, and covered up if she was in danger of embarrassing herself.'

'To save her from strangers like me.' Libby let her breath out in a rush. 'There I was, thinking I'd finally made it into Exham society, but there's so much going on under the surface I don't know about.' She smiled at her friend. 'I won't take it personally. I'm sure any small town's the same.'

While Angela brewed more coffee, Libby thought through the implications of the news. If everyone in the local community knew about Beryl, it would have been easy for her killer to visit on a pretext, and seize a moment when Beryl left the room to slip a dose of poison into a bottle of her favourite tipple.

She followed Angela into the impeccably clean and tidy kitchen. 'Do you know anything about Beryl giving up work? She'd been around town more, recently, popping into the bakery almost every day. Did she just retire, or perhaps she had to leave?'

Angela shrugged. 'Because of the drinking? I didn't hear anything, but some of the others might know. I know she stopped working at the racing stables a few months ago, but she was old enough to retire long ago. She'd worked well beyond retirement age. She'd been with the stables all her life, and I imagine they let her stay on as long as she wanted to. I'm not sure how useful she would have been, in recent years. Another example of mistaken sympathy, perhaps, letting her carry on.'

Angela led the way out of the kitchen. 'We were wrong to ignore her drinking. If we'd been tougher, maybe she could have dealt with the problem, and would still be with us. So much for helping your neighbour. I'm afraid many of us bear a little of the blame for Beryl's sad life.'

Libby remained silent for a long time, thinking, until, seized with a longing to talk it all over with Max, she finished her drink, gathered up her bag, and stood, ready to leave. Angela took her arm on the way out. 'There's something I need to tell you.'

'Not more lurid revelations?'

Angela smiled. 'No, but you won't like it. You remember that smarmy Terence Marchant?'

Libby groaned. 'A while ago he was threatening to start up a rival patisserie in Exham, but he seems to have lost interest, I'm pleased to say.' The look on Angela's face stopped Libby in her tracks. 'Or has he?'

'I heard he's back, and the patisserie will definitely open in a few weeks. He's planning to overwhelm Exham with French pastries, and he's employing a genuine French pastry chef. He thinks you'll be closed down within six months.'

Margery Halfstead sat on the chintz covered settee, knitting needles clicking like chattering teeth. From time to time, she glanced over at William, but he seemed engrossed in the televised golf tournament that slowly played itself out in the drizzle of a northern golf course. Margery pressed her lips more tightly together and knitted faster, tugging hard at the wool after every row, obsessively counting stitches.

William had hardly spoken since Beryl Nightingale's death. He'd talked to the police, but refused to discuss anything about the brief interview at the castle, beyond remarking that constables seemed to get younger every year. Margery tried to feel sympathetic. He'd found the body first so he was bound to be upset, but his actions bothered her.

He'd behaved oddly, that day. He'd left the schoolboys alone and she'd had to step in. Then, he hadn't prevented them from seeing the body. There'd been chaos, for a while, with teenagers shouting and screaming. She wouldn't be surprised if there were complaints from parents. Maybe William would lose his position as a guide. That would upset him, she knew. 'Are you all right?' she tried. William just grunted.

Margery went back to her knitting. They'd never been ones for talking about feelings, neither of them. It seemed a bit un-British, really. Even when she'd lost the baby, all those years ago, they hadn't said much. What was there to say? Talking wouldn't change the fact of the miscarriage. In Margery's opinion, people these days were a bit too inclined to throw their private sorrows in everyone else's face.

She stopped knitting. She hadn't thought about that time for months. At first, she'd not been able to forget the baby who never was. He'd been in her thoughts all the time. They'd planned to call him Oscar. Margery was sure he was a boy, though the doctors had never said.

Thrusting a knitting needle into the ball of fawn coloured wool, she decided to finish the sweater later. She didn't feel much like knitting anything today. Her thoughts slid back to those dreadful days, after she came back from the hospital. She supposed William had given away the little jackets she'd knitted for Oscar. He never said, and she never asked where they went.

She zipped up her knitting bag. This was ridiculous. Beryl Nightingale's death was making her maudlin, and sitting in silence wasn't helping. Better to do something. 'Do you want another cup of tea?'

William grunted. 'Not just now.'

Margery heaved herself to her feet and set off towards the kitchen. She'd have one anyway, and a chocolate biscuit to boot.

She looked back. William had pulled his mobile phone from his pocket. He was scrolling through the screen.

Bet he's ringing that Annabel.

The conviction sprang into Margery's head, as if from nowhere, and immediately, she was sure it was true. A noise started up in her ears, like a storm of wind, and for a moment she felt quite dizzy. She steadied herself with one hand on the kitchen table and let her thoughts run free.

She'd been suspicious from the first moment that Annabel woman had come into the room at the castle, all high heels and lipstick. William already knew her, Margery was quite sure, she could tell from the way he grinned at her. He'd fallen over himself to look after her. A hollow, sick sensation took a grip on Margery's insides. The death of Beryl Nightingale hardly seemed to matter compared with William's treachery.

Forgetting to make the tea, Margery staggered back into the sitting room on wobbly legs and opened the knitting bag again. She tried to work but her eyes wouldn't focus.

She drew a long, steadying breath. 'I hope Annabel isn't too upset. Fancy having someone die on your first day. Bet she won't be back at the castle in a hurry.' Talking about the woman was like picking a scab. She knew it was going to hurt, however William answered, but it was impossible to stop.

He glanced up from his phone. 'Sorry? What did you say?'

Playing the innocent.

The sick feeling was turning to anger, boiling inside. She almost shouted, 'I said, what about Annabel.'

'What about her?'

Pretending not to understand, that was his game, was it? 'Tarty little thing.' Margery almost gasped at her own spite.

'I wouldn't say that.'

Under normal circumstances, Margery admired William's ability to keep calm, but today, she wanted a fight. 'I said,' she raised her voice even more, 'I reckon she's no better than she should be.'

William studied her, as if seeing her for the first time, a

puzzled frown on his face. 'I wouldn't know. What makes you say that?'

The doorbell rang. William said, as he always did, 'I wonder who that could be.'

Margery usually replied, 'There's one way to find out,' but instead, forestalling her husband, she jumped up to answer the door herself.

She had her mouth open, ready to say, 'We never do business at the door,' as William always did, but before she could make a sound she stopped, mouth hanging open at the sight of a pair of police officers, a few respectful feet away from the threshold.

The older one, an overweight man of around forty, said, 'Is your husband at home, Mrs Halfstead? My colleague and I would like to talk to him again, if you please.'

The young blonde woman at his side smiled. 'It won't take too long.'

Margery blinked. Of course, the police had said they'd be coming back, but she hadn't expected to see them again so soon. She stepped aside to let them in, just as William appeared from the sitting room. 'You'd better come in.'

* * *

An hour later, the police left. Margery watched as they drove away. She couldn't swallow; her mouth felt like sandpaper. Her hands were shaking. She crossed the room to the settee, but she couldn't sit. She returned to the window, looking down the empty road. The police car was out of sight, now.

She paced from the hall to the kitchen and then back to the sitting room, her head spinning.

What had just happened?

She revisited the scene, trying to make sense of it.

The interview had begun in a friendly way, like a conversation, with the police offering sympathy. 'We know it's a shock to be involved in a sudden death. We just want to clarify exactly what happened.'

William told them about the morning in the castle, and the arrival of Annabel and the schoolboys. Then, Margery mentioned how William had gone ahead with the boys to the butler's pantry. The two officers exchanged a glance. 'You were with the boys, then, Mr Halfstead, while they talked to Miss Nightingale?'

William glanced at Margery and stammered a little. 'Not exactly. I had to collect some notes from my car, and I left the boys to talk. My wife was with them, so they were quite safe, and there was a script. Young Jason had prepared what he wanted to say.'

Margery licked dry lips. At the time, she'd been annoyed that William left her to cope. Beryl's death had overshadowed the incident and she hadn't given it another thought, but now she wondered why he'd been so keen to leave. That wasn't like him at all. He was always conscientious, and she'd never known him leave documents in the car. In fact, she was sure he'd had a file with him all the time he was in the castle.

What if he'd lied to her, so he could get away on his own? Why would he do that?

Try as she might to think, she could only imagine two reasons for William to abandon his charges. Had he left the boys to go down to the kitchen? Maybe to check something? But, if so, he would have told her, instead of making up an excuse.

Margery chewed a rough nail, struggling to think straight. If William had gone to the kitchen, he was there when Beryl died.

Margery shuddered, on the verge of tears. That would mean he might have – no, she couldn't finish the thought. It scared her.

Surely, he had no reason to harm Beryl Nightingale? She closed her eyes. There must be another reason for his absence.

Yet, to her mind, there could be only one other possibility: that he was with the new volunteer, Annabel. The more she considered his behaviour that morning, the more certain she became.

Now the police had gone, she had to know the truth. She faced William, hands on hips. 'Why did you leave the boys alone? You didn't need to fetch any handouts, did you? Where did you go?'

For the first time in all the years they'd spent together, William looked shifty. Margery could think of no other word for it. He looked away, shuffled his feet and cleared his throat. His glance flickered towards the door, as though he was contemplating escape. Margery put her bulk firmly between her husband and the exit. 'Tell me,' she demanded. 'Right now.'

He coughed. He spluttered. Margery waited until finally, he spoke. 'I went to speak to someone.'

'Someone? Who?'

'It was...'

He'd never been able to lie. Margery poked a finger at his chest. 'You went to see that Annabel, didn't you?'

His face registered surprise – no, horror – and Margery felt sure her suspicions were correct. He licked his lips, then rubbed his chin, as though playing for time before answering. 'I just wanted to check on her. You know, dear, on her first day and all. I thought she'd like to come and meet the boys, maybe talk down the speaking tube as well, or operate the pulley for the serving lift. Get a flavour of the house.'

Margery closed her eyes. 'You went after that – that hussy. I knew it. How long has it been going on?'

'Going on? I-I don't understand.'

'This affair with that woman.' As she spoke, Margery almost believed she could hear their marriage crashing to the ground. All those years together counted for nothing. The shared, never mentioned sorrow at the loss of their baby, the quiet evenings watching TV over a plate of shepherd's pie. It was all a sham.

William was having an affair.

The words seemed to stand out in Margery's brain, like a neon sign. Her husband took a step forward, but she threw out her arms to ward him off. 'Don't you dare come near me, William Halfstead, unless you can deny you went to find that woman – Annabel whatshername.'

The colour drained from his face. 'You've got it wrong. I mean —' He gasped for breath, clutching his hands to his chest. 'I-I...' He lurched forward, mouth open in a soundless scream as he tore at the sweater she'd knitted last Christmas. Eyes fixed on his wife's face, he tottered a few steps, stopped, gave a howl of agony, and dropped to the floor.

Margery screamed.

8

SPAGHETTI CARBONARA

'William Halfstead's in hospital.' Libby put her phone back in her pocket. 'That was Ian Smith. The horrid man's gloating because I can't talk to one of the main suspects. Or at least, not until he recovers from a heart attack, poor chap.' She was in Max's house – so soon to become her own home – eating dinner. They'd hoped to host his son to celebrate his promotion, but Joe and Claire, his wife, had been forced to cancel. The new job had already begun, and Joe was working on a series of armed robberies. 'We'll do dinner for Joe when he has a spare evening,' Libby had said, 'but let's toast his success anyway.'

'Good idea. Any excuse for one of your special feasts. And tonight, we can enjoy a candle lit dinner for two. I'll put on some romantic music. What's on the menu, by the way?'

'An avocado and smoked chicken starter, followed by spaghetti carbonara, and then...'

'Please, say it's bread and butter pudding.'

'Of course it is – but once we're married, I'll have to train you to eat some different desserts. Oh, and Somerset Brie afterwards, if you can manage it.'

'You know your dinners are the only reason I'm marrying you.'

'Actually, you're marrying me because I asked you to.'

'And who am I to disagree?'

Max put the last morsel of spaghetti carbonara in his mouth and moaned with delight. 'No, sorry, it's definitely because of the food. Bring on the pudding.'

'We'd better not eat like this every day. I don't want you keeling over with a stroke, or a heart attack like William Halfstead.'

Max carried the plates out to the kitchen, returning with a dish full of fragrant, spiced pudding, bursting with sultanas, and topped with crisp brown bread slices. 'At least I'd die a happy man.'

'That's not funny. It does happen, you know.'

Max waved the champagne bottle at Libby. 'Let's hope we've both got a few more years in us. Cheers.'

Libby took a deep breath. It was time she told the truth. 'Actually, I've got a confession to make.'

Max replaced the bottle on the table. 'That sounds serious. Should I be worried? What terrible thing have you done in that murky past of yours?'

'I didn't like to say, before, but I don't want to keep secrets, now we're getting married.' She sighed, theatrically. 'The truth is, I really don't like champagne.'

'No! Really? 'Well, who'd have thought it? I guess our marriage will be full of shocks like that.'

He opened a bottle of Australian Pinot Noir for Libby's approval and they returned to William Halfstead's heart attack. 'Do you think he had the attack because he's guilty of killing Beryl and he's feeling remorseful, or because he's innocent and thinks people will blame him anyway?' she asked.

'Or maybe it's neither and he's just unlucky.'

Libby thought about that. 'His wife must be beside herself.'

Max finished the bread and butter pudding. 'Well, as you're officially involved in the investigation, you can question people as much as you like and find out. Just remember what Joe always says. Don't jump to conclusions, just...'

'Follow the evidence. I will. Also, Beryl's not as squeaky clean as we thought.' She told Max about her conversation with Angela.

He frowned. 'Angela's a mine of information. I always knew the Nightingales had their troubles, with the brother's death, but I didn't know them well. I must have left Exham before Beryl's drinking took hold. No one mentioned it when I eventually came back after – well, you know.' Max had only returned to Exham after his daughter died in a riding accident and his marriage broke up. If Joe hadn't followed, complete with job and wife, determined to sort his father out, no one knew what would have happened to Max.

He stood up. 'Shall we finish the wine in my study? It's cosier in there. Come on, Bear.' He looked around, but there was no sign of Bear.

Libby pointed. 'He's usually behind that chair.'

'Was he there earlier? I thought it was quiet this evening, but I put that down to Shipley being away with the trainer. Bear was in the garden this afternoon. We'd better call him in, as it's starting to get dark.'

They stood at the back door, looking out over the garden and fields beyond. Max shouted Bear's name, but nothing happened. No giant dog hurtled up the path. 'That's odd. He never strays.' Max was frowning. 'He must have escaped through the fence.'

'I'm sure he'll be home soon.' Libby tried to sound confident, but she could see Max was unconvinced. Bear was the most faithful and loyal of canine companions, rarely leaving his humans. 'Let's come back out in a quarter of an hour or so, see if he comes home.'

Neither could settle and the last of the wine remained untouched. Together, they filled the dishwasher and tidied the kitchen, each of them frequently, surreptitiously checking their watches.

'Come on,' Libby said at last, and led the way outside. 'Let's give it one more try.'

Finally, hoarse with calling Bear's name, they were forced to admit defeat. Libby squeezed Max's hand. 'I'm sure he'll be back by morning. He must be off on a spree. Maybe he's scented a female and he's hearing the call of the wild.'

'Maybe, though it won't do him any good. The vet's seen to that. I suppose there's nothing we can do tonight,' Max agreed. 'I'll leave the back door open, just in case.'

9

TOAST

Next morning, Bear was still missing. Libby and Max phoned or sent a text to every friend or neighbour they could think of, but no one had seen him. By the middle of the morning, anxious and sad, they had to admit he'd disappeared. 'But, where could he have gone?' Libby wondered aloud. 'I know he can walk for miles, but surely someone would have seen him.' Mechanically, hardly aware of what she was doing, she made coffee and toast.

'I have a really bad feeling about this,' Max confessed. 'But before we panic, let's go back over his whereabouts in the last couple of days.'

'He was with me two days ago,' Libby remembered. 'Then I left him with you while I went over to the castle to drop off the cake.'

'While you were with Angela yesterday, I took him out on the beach. We walked for about eight miles. It's not as though Bear didn't get his exercise. After the walk, I'm sure he fell asleep behind the chair, as usual, and I drove out to buy champagne while you cooked dinner.'

Libby tried to visualise the time she'd spent alone in Max's house, with Bear. 'The doors were open so he could go in and out. I don't remember seeing him at all, really. I was too busy in the kitchen.'

Max screwed up his eyes in concentration. 'I haven't seen or heard him since. He must have wandered off while you cooked.'

'We're not sure that's when he disappeared. He might have followed you when you went out to get the champagne. You usually take him with you.'

'I only popped out for twenty minutes. I thought you'd be watching him.'

Should she have been? Libby felt a little sick. She loved Bear, but it wasn't her fault he'd gone missing. She didn't live here, yet. She defended herself. 'I can't watch him every minute and this is your house.'

'He spends more time with you these days.'

Suddenly annoyed, Libby pushed herself up from the table, spilling half a cup of coffee. Ignoring the mess, she turned her back on Max and made for the door. 'Maybe I look after him better.'

Max said, 'If you took him out more often for proper walks...'

She swung round, an argument on her lips. As she opened her mouth, she suddenly registered the pallor on his face, and the network of worry lines round his eyes. Her harsh words melted away, temper fading as fast as it had appeared. 'Why are we quarrelling?' She returned to the table, pulled a tissue from her pocket, and mopped up the coffee spill.

Max laid his hand on hers. 'Sorry. There's no need for us to argue. It's not your fault.'

She squeezed his fingers. 'Nor yours. We both kept as much of an eye on Bear as we do normally. I expect we're exaggerating things.'

'Pre-wedding nerves?' Max threw his arms round her, giving one of the hugs she loved.

'I can't understand it.' She nestled into his arms. 'He's never escaped from the garden before. I hope nothing's happened to him, that's all.' Max walked to the window. He peered through the glass, arms folded, miles away, deep in thought.

'Wait a minute.' He left the room at a run. Libby waited patiently. He'd had one of his ideas, and he'd tell her what it was, soon enough. He returned, clutching a glossy magazine full of Somerset news, pictures of impossibly elegant, stately home gardens, and advertisements for houses that no one she knew could afford. 'I'm sure I saw an article...'

Flipping through the pages, he stopped near the end and turned the magazine until Libby could read it.

MISSING PETS

Seven Somerset residents have reported the loss of family pets in the past month. Mrs Johnson of Williton told our reporter her shi-tzu went missing from her garden two days ago. 'He's been with us for years. Of course, he's a pedigree animal, registered with the Kennel Club, so he's worth a lot of money in the market. But we keep him as a family pet, and my two children are devastated.

Martin Anderson, a farmer in West Somerset, reported his Border collie stolen, two weeks ago. The animal, a working sheepdog, lived in a specially built kennel near the house. 'They must have drugged him,' Mr Anderson insisted. 'He'd never go willingly with anyone. He's a highly trained, tremendously valuable dog who's won prizes in television's One Man and his Dog.'

Max's eyes met Libby's. 'It looks as though someone's stealing valuable animals.'

A painful lump took up residence in Libby's throat. If Bear

had been stolen, he might be gone for good. He'd become almost as important to her as Max and her children. He'd been with her on all her adventures. In fact, it was the dog who first introduced her to Max. Idiotically, she said, 'What will Fuzzy do without him?' After an initial spat, the marmalade cat had become firm friends with the giant dog.

Max heaved a sigh. 'Well, we're supposed to be private investigators. It looks as though we'll have to do some investigation on our own behalf, this time. The bitcoin fraud will have to wait. I'll start with Google, if you'll speak to your friend, Tanya the vet. Maybe she knows about this.' Tanya had once nursed Fuzzy's broken leg, and was one of Bear's devoted friends.

'Has Bear been chipped?' Libby asked. 'I never thought to ask.'

'Yes, I had it done when old Mrs Thomson died and I adopted him.'

Libby slipped on a waxed jacket. 'I'll print out some poster-sized pictures of Bear and visit Tanya now to find out what she knows, but then I have to spend the rest of the morning in the bakery. I promised Frank I'd work this shift with Mandy while he does some special deliveries on the other side of town. Oh!'

'What is it?'

'I'll have to tell Mandy. She'll be devastated.'

* * *

The vet was full of sympathy as Libby showed her the magazine article. She knew Bear well. 'I've heard about this; several animals have disappeared, and the thieves seem likely to be professionals, if they're able to whisk huge animals like Bear out of sight.' She nodded. 'The victims are mostly valuable dogs, so the police have been involved. Have you talked to Joe?'

Libby clicked her tongue in annoyance. 'Do you know, I never thought of that. Are the police taking it seriously?'

Tanya shrugged. 'They came to see me, but I couldn't help. They sent Constable Ian Smith, though, and I can't imagine he'll put himself out too much over missing animals.' Her expression made it plain PC Smith was no more popular with her than with Libby. 'He loves to catch children riding their bikes on the pavement on the way to school, but he's too lazy to go out of his way to offer a helping hand.'

The vet sighed, 'I miss the old days of policemen on bikes. We have a pair of community police officers who call in from time to time, and they're more sympathetic than PC Smith, but it's not the same.' She laughed. 'I'm showing my age. Anyway, I reckon the police have more important things to worry about. Like this business up at the castle.' She looked at Libby, a question on her face. She was always in the market for gossip.

Libby hesitated. She had to be careful not to give away unauthorised information. Sometimes it was harder working with the police than independently. Still, there seemed no harm in telling Tanya the bare bones of the story, leaving out any information that could identify the schoolchildren involved. Tanya had helped her out before, with information leading to the exposure of the Glastonbury Tor killer, who'd recently begun a sentence of fifteen years in HM Prison Exeter.

After some thought, she even told Tanya about William's heart attack. He was a well-known figure in the area, one of the members of the recently reformed Exham on Sea History Society, and a popular guide at the castle. The vet might be able to throw some light on the man and his wife.

Tanya made a sympathetic face. 'I've been on a tour of the servants' quarters with him at Dunster Castle,' she said. 'He's a charming man, although his wife can be difficult. They used to bring their Highland terrier here, but sadly, he passed away a few months ago. I don't think William and Margery have got over it. That dog was like a child to them.'

That gave Libby an idea. She wanted to talk to Margery about the death at Dunster Castle, but she needed an excuse to visit. Now she had one; if she was a dog lover, she'd be sympathetic about Bear. She'd probably be willing to put up a poster in her window.

The idea wasn't brilliant, but the best Libby could dredge up for the moment. In any case, she wouldn't be visiting until tomorrow. It was past time for her to start work in the bakery, and she refused to let Frank down.

Tanya made a suggestion. 'Why don't we organise a proper search for Bear?'

'We're planning to put up posters on lampposts and so on. That was how I found Mrs Marchant's missing cat.' Libby felt a familiar twinge of anxiety, for Mrs Marchant's son was the same Terence Marchant who seemed determined to put Brown's Bakery out of business.

She didn't have time to think about Terence Marchant today. She was too worried about Bear. 'Here's one of the posters. Would you put it up in your waiting room?' The sight of Bear's face, so big and gentle, with enormous, soulful brown eyes, almost broke her heart.

Tanya took the poster. 'Of course, and I'll ring round other dog owners on the books. You know they'll all be willing to turn out and search. It makes walking the dog more interesting than usual, and the weather's respectable today. In any case, plenty of my clients know Bear, and everyone loves him. I'm not too busy today, apart from the surgery.'

She waved in the general direction of the waiting area, which was filling fast with an assortment of over-excited, yappy young dogs, grumpy cats in baskets, clearly wishing they could escape and see off the puppies, and a couple of sickly looking hamsters.

By the time Libby made her way to the door, through the throng of sympathetic pet owners, she was horribly late for work, but at least five people had promised to get out into the fields and woodland around Exham and join the search. If Bear was anywhere near Exham on Sea, Libby was confident he'd soon be found.

Mandy was busy tweaking the display of Mrs Forest's Chocolates in the bakery window. Despite her wild black hair, which was styled today in a series of spikes, the slash of purple lipstick across her mouth, and her status as Exham's resident Goth, she was a popular member of the Brown's Bakery team. Even Frank, the proprietor, had grown used to her weird appearance.

She greeted Libby's arrival with a sympathetic hug and a barrage of questions. 'I couldn't believe it when I got your text. Did Bear just wander off? Have you made posters? Will you be able to get him back, d'you think?'

'I'll find him, or die trying.' Libby explained the situation to Frank. 'I'm so sorry to be late,' she finished.

'Don't you worry. Mandy and I have been managing just fine.' He hesitated. 'Since you arrived in town, Libby, with your cakes and chocolates, the turnover in this place has trebled. If there's anything I can do to help, just let me know.'

Libby had to blow her nose, suddenly overcome with emotion. Frank never wasted words, and he avoided emotion like the plague.

As Libby attached posters to every spare space, inside and outside the shop, Frank pulled loaves from the kitchen oven, visibly relieved to get back to business. 'That's the lot for today.' He peeled off his gloves. 'If you're ready to take over, I'll leave you two alone this morning while I make my rounds. I'll tell everyone I meet about Bear, and don't you worry about that animal. He can look after himself.'

Mandy nodded vigorously. 'Of course, he can. He probably got himself stuck in an outhouse overnight. He'll give someone a fright when they open the door.'

Frank untied his apron. 'Those new chocolates are selling brilliantly.'

'Well, I can't take the credit,' Libby confessed, determined to be business-like. 'They were Mandy's idea. I'd never have thought of treacle tart flavoured filling.'

Mandy, blushing through her makeup, stacked loaves of bread on the shelves to hide her face, just as the bell rang to herald the daily flood of lunchtime customers.

'Here we go,' said Frank. 'I'm off.' He hated chatting to customers. He'd find any excuse to leave the bakery during the rush for sandwiches.

Libby welcomed the sudden influx of business. Maybe it would take her mind off Bear.

Every customer had plenty to say. Even if they weren't dog people, there was a lot to discuss: Bear's disappearance, the death at the castle, and William Halfstead's heart attack were all hot topics.

'It's a funny thing,' Libby murmured, passing Mandy on the trail of pizza slices for a group of hungry teenagers. 'Have you noticed how we double our customer numbers when there's something for them to gossip about?'

Before long, Gladys from the flower shop arrived and pointed at Bear's poster. Libby's heart missed a beat, as it did every time she looked at the dog's face beaming down from the wall. 'That's why I would never have a pet. It's too easy to get fond of them.'

Mandy muttered to Libby, 'I can't imagine that woman being fond of anyone or anything.' Libby suspected the reason she came into the bakery was to pick up on the day's news, so that she could pass it on, with embellishments, to her own customers.

Libby whispered, 'In her defence, she's good at her job. She sold me a beautiful autumn bouquet of dahlias – or, were they chrysanthemums, I never know the difference – last week.'

Mandy scoffed. 'Aren't chrysanthemums the flowers people put on graves?'

Libby paused, disconcerted, a half-wrapped cob loaf in her hands. 'Are they? I didn't know that.'

'They are in Belgium, anyway. We had a school trip there, to see the battlefield at Ypres, and they told us. It's bad luck to give them as a gift.'

'Really? Oh dear, I gave them to the new doctor's wife a while ago, when she invited me to tea. Don't laugh. I've had an idea, though.' She raised her voice. 'Could you make me up a rather special bouquet of flowers for Margery Halfstead? I want to visit her later today. But no chrysanthemums, thanks.'

'How about Michaelmas daisies and Chinese lanterns?'

'Perfect. I'll pick them up this afternoon.'

Gladys had a theory about William's heart attack. 'It's the cholesterol,' she said, taking possession of two pastries in a paper bag.

Libby avoided Mandy's eye, for fear of bursting into laughter. Gladys clearly didn't see the irony in her high cholesterol purchase. 'But I hear the heart attack happened just after a visit from the police.'

The woman's eyes flittered between her listeners. 'Those

police officers may have a case to answer, if I'm not mistaken. Harassment, you know.'

James, the newsagent, hurrying to collect his lunchtime sandwiches, paused a moment to add his thoughts before rushing from the shop. 'Annabel Pearson was up at the castle when Beryl Nightingale died. She told my wife Mr Halfstead looked fine at the time.'

Libby listened to the gossip without contributing. The bakery often produced useful titbits. When she talked to customers outside the shop, they remembered her job as a private investigator and grew tight-lipped, but inside the shop, they seemed to regard her as part of the furniture.

Gladys showed no sign of leaving. 'I can't imagine why anyone would want to kill Beryl Nightingale. She never did any harm in her life, though she didn't do much of anything, come to think of it.'

Mandy rolled her eyes at Libby. It seemed Gladys was perfectly happy to speak ill of the dead.

At least she didn't appear to know about Beryl's secret drink problem.

A couple of cashiers from the bank juggled sandwiches, cakes, and bottles of pop to take back to their colleagues. Marianne, the youngest, a girl of around Mandy's age wearing an impossibly tight skirt, her hair scraped into a ponytail on top of her head, said, 'Beryl was a sort of relative of my mother. She used to do the books for the racing stables until she retired.'

'Retired? Is that what she called it?' Her colleague, Adrian Waller, an older man wearing horn-rimmed spectacles and a baggy blue suit, snorted.

Gladys turned at the hint of gossip. 'Go on. You can't stop there. It sounds as though there's a story to be had.'

Adrian Waller was already in full flow. 'There was a discrepancy. In the books. That's what I heard.'

Gladys gasped, her eyes glittering with excitement. 'No. Really? Who would have thought it?'

Marianne looked close to tears. 'I don't know where that story came from, but Aunt Beryl was as honest as the day is long, so there.' She elbowed the door of the shop and left, slamming the door in her colleague's face. He grimaced and followed meekly behind.

'He'll be wishing he kept his mouth shut,' another customer observed.

The bakery fell silent, and Gladys took her leave. 'I'm sure none of us meant any harm.' She hesitated at the door. 'I'll make up that bouquet for you right away, Libby. I'll make it special. No one can say I don't do my bit in the community.'

At last, the shop was empty. 'Well.' Mandy let her breath out in a sigh. 'That was interesting. Will you be investigating Beryl Nightingale's death, Mrs F, or are you too busy looking for Bear?'

Libby, scribbling in her notebook, hardly heard. Mandy shook her head. 'If only you'd learn to make notes on your phone, you'd save yourself, like, hours of work.'

11

LAYER CAKE

While Libby had spent the second half of the morning at the bakery, Max had abandoned his computer in favour of the search for Bear, co-ordinating with the vet's band of volunteers. He returned cold, wet, and dirty, but with no good news. 'If Bear's anywhere between here and Taunton, we'd have found him.'

He looked as despondent as Libby felt. She fed him coffee while he listed the places the helpers had searched and told her about a call he'd had from Joe, 'He filled me in on the reported animal thefts in the area. The cases are still open, but he says the police don't have enough manpower to prioritise them. We'll have to find Bear ourselves.'

He took another mouthful of coffee. 'That's better. How about a slice of toast? Or, even better, coffee cake?'

As Libby cut a hefty slice, calculating that hours in the countryside had earned Max a decent reward, he talked with renewed enthusiasm. 'I've tracked down a string of similar disappearances across the south-west, mostly valuable animals. No ransom demands, so far. That's good, I think, because it means the animals must be of use to the thieves.' That was something to hold onto.

'Several are trained sheepdogs, like Bear,' he pointed out. 'Would they have some sort of market value as working animals? No one's tried to take Shipley, even though he's a much better sniffer dog. He's only got another day or two with the trainer, by the way. He'll miss his canine mate.'

'Don't write Bear off like that,' Libby pleaded. 'We'll get him back. We just need to work a bit harder.'

'I'm doing all I can.'

'I know.' Libby tried to smile. She was taking her feelings out on Max again, although she knew it wasn't his fault. 'Sorry.' She kissed his cheek.

Max enveloped her in his arms. 'We're both upset, but we're professional investigators. We'll find him. You follow up on Beryl's case, and I'll keep tracking down other missing animals. There must be common links, and if there are, I shall find them. They don't call me Meticulous Max for nothing.'

Reluctantly, Libby laughed. 'I've never heard anyone call you that.'

'No. I made it up. Now, you're looking more cheerful. Go and find out more about William Halfstead.'

Libby was eager to visit Margery Halfstead, to find out the truth about William's heart attack. She stopped on the way to pick up her flowers. They were beautiful. Gladys surprised Libby. 'I'm giving you a 50 per cent discount.'

'That's far too generous.'

Gladys blew her nose. 'I think I was a little harsh this morning. I'm sorry about William, and Beryl too, of course. Give Margery my regards.'

She travelled through a maze of small streets on the modern housing estate where Margery and William Halfstead lived, trying not to think of Bear. He should have been in the back of her cramped Citroen, slobbering on her seat. Instead, he was missing.

Margery Halfstead answered the door wearing an apron and carrying a duster. For a moment, Libby wondered if her husband had come home from hospital, and things were back to normal in the Halfstead household. Then, she remembered her own mother's habit of undertaking vigorous housework at times of stress. Libby used baking in the same way. She'd spent the previous evening constructing an elaborate layer cake that neither she nor Max would ever eat.

Margery peered out suspiciously. 'Are you from the police?'

'I'm Libby Forest. I work with the police, but I'm not a proper officer. I mean, I don't arrest people, or anything.'

The fierce lines on Margery's face relaxed. 'In that case, you can come in. I won't have the police in my house, not after what happened to my husband.'

'I heard. We're all very sorry, in the history society, and other people too. Here, these are from me and – er – the lady in the flower shop.'

'Gladys? Oh, yes, we've known her for years. Come in.'

Libby followed her into the house, and Margery took the flowers out to the kitchen while Libby sat on a fifties style G Plan sofa, watching coloured blobs of lava rising and falling in a nearby lamp. When Margery returned, holding a tall jug in which she'd arranged the flowers, she nodded towards the lamp. 'That was a wedding present. It's still working, after all these years.'

Libby made approving noises. 'You've been married a long time, Mrs Halfstead.'

'Call me Margery. Yes, and never a cross word.'

'Really?' Libby blinked. She and Max argued endlessly. The truth was, she rather enjoyed their sparring bouts, and they always led to a happy reconciliation. What must it be like never to disagree?

Tears glistened in Margery's eyes. 'Not until the other day, that is. I – I was angry with him.' She took a shuddering breath. 'It's all my fault he's so ill. It wasn't the police that made him ill. It was me.' She burst out crying, sobbing with such heartbreak that Libby had no idea how to help. Instead, she sat in impotent silence, waiting for the storm of grief to pass.

Margery blew her nose. 'I'm sorry. Look at me, I must be a mess.'

'No, not at all. Of course, you're upset and worried. You've a right to a few tears.' Libby longed to know the cause of the quarrel, but hardly knew how to ask.

Luckily, Margery wanted to talk. 'I was stupid, and – and jealous. I said some dreadful things. I accused him. I accused William of having an affair. As if he would.'

Libby stole a glance at the black and white wedding photograph on top of the old-fashioned television. Even on his wedding day, William Halfstead did not look like the kind of man to have affairs. He was neither handsome nor dashing. A touch overweight, with a gigantic nose and long ears, thinning hair, and crooked teeth, he gazed with devotion down at his short, plain bride. Still, it was not looks that mattered. Perhaps William had a dashing personality.

'An affair?' she prompted.

'Yes, with that hussy – Annabel thing.'

Annabel Pearson was half William's age. Surely, his wife was imagining things. Was that what happened when you'd been married for years? It wasn't going to spoil things with Max – Libby caught herself up. Hadn't she been ridiculously jealous of Kate Stephenson, the 'alternative therapist' he'd spent time with recently? And hadn't his interest been just a matter of furthering their investigation? Surely Margery Halfstead was allowed to be as foolish as Libby.

Margery was talking about the day of Beryl's death. 'There were several volunteers there, that morning, getting on with the annual clean. I didn't recognise all of them, because Mrs Moffat had taken on new people. Annabel was there for the first time and William went off after her when he was supposed to be looking after the schoolboys.' Her hand flew to her mouth, as though she wanted to take back her words.

She glared at Libby, fierce as a tiger protecting her cubs. 'Now, don't you go telling people that. It was only a second or two he was away from them, and they were safe with me. I don't want him to lose his job.'

Libby said nothing. If William had been responsible for Beryl's death, whether deliberately or not, losing an unpaid volunteer position at the castle would be the least of his worries.

'Anyway.' Margery sniffed. 'I'd gone upstairs to set off one of the bells the family used to call their servants. The boys would hear it jangling, down in the servants' quarters. There was another woman upstairs, one of the other volunteers. I don't know her name. My head's a bit woolly. Anyway, I was on the verge of telling her about the bell when we heard a scream. Ooh, such a dreadful noise. It gave me the shivers. I ran down the stairs and into the Victorian kitchen, and there was Beryl on the floor.'

She dusted a porcelain figure, one of a pair. A shepherd and shepherdess, so far as Libby could see. She asked, 'That volunteer you saw at the castle. Can you remember more about her?'

Margery paused. 'I've seen her before, once or twice, but she's not friendly. Shy, I suppose. I like to live and let live. Funny clothes, the ones she wears. Bright, you know, and summer frocks even at this time of year. Too much makeup, I've noticed, but her hair's nice. Black and glossy.'

'You don't know her name?'

'We were never introduced. Funny, though, she reminded me of someone...'

Libby waited, but Margery shook her head. 'No, I can't think.'

Libby stood. 'I hope your husband gets well soon.'

Margery had regained some composure. 'At least the doctors say he's only had a mild heart attack – more a bit of angina, they said – and he can come home tomorrow.'

'And you can make up your quarrel.'

Margery peered round the room. 'I need to make the place spick and span for him.'

Libby took the hint, handed Margery a business card, and left. She hadn't even had to use Bear's posters as an excuse.

* * *

Margery closed the door behind her guest, sought out a pot of Brasso, and began work on the door handles, buffing them to a brilliant shine. She'd always said, a clean home is a happy home.

As she worked, pictures of that day at the castle ran through her brain, like watching a film. They'd been working together so happily, William following her lead in the cleaning, waiting until it was time to look after the students. She smiled, remembering the frown on his face as he'd tried to copy her practised flick of the wrist when dusting ancient books.

Then that woman had arrived. Margery's hand froze in mid-polish. She could still hear the heels clacking on the floor, and smell the woman's flowery perfume. Annabel. Annabel who? What was the woman's last name? Had she even told them? And why would a woman like her, young, pretty – even Margery had to admit she looked good – turn up to volunteer in a stately home. Had she come specifically to see William, or was there some other attraction?

Margery sat down. She needed to be comfortable to think. Who else had been in the castle that day? There were the other members of the history society, of course, and a volunteer or two unknown to Margery. Beryl, William and herself, Annabel, and Angela had popped in for half an hour. Libby had not been there until later, with the cake. There were the paid staff, including Mrs Moffat. Then the students had arrived for their visit.

There was nothing unusual about any of it, except that the castle should have been closed for cleaning. For some reason, it had been reopened for Jason Franklin and the other students. Was that because he was an MP's son? Margery hadn't given the matter much thought. She vaguely remembered William talking on the phone, arranging the schoolboys' visit.

A nasty suspicion entered her head. Could it have been Annabel on the other end of the call? And if so, why had she and William wanted the schoolboys in the castle that day?

Margery looked down at her hands. They were trembling. A terrible fear had closed its grip. Was Beryl's death part of a plan, something diabolical Margery did not yet understand? Had the unfortunate woman stumbled upon a secret, and died as a result? And, if that was so, could it possibly be – no, she wouldn't even think it. William would never...

Margery could sit there no longer. She had to find out. She couldn't ask her husband outright, even when he recovered. She was sure of nothing, and nobody, any more. She would have trusted William with her life, but what if he'd been pulling the wool over her eyes for years over an affair with Annabel? What if it had led to a plot involving schoolboys and MPs' sons, uncovered by silly, innocent Beryl who'd had to die as a result?

It was all too much for Margery to deal with on her own. Her head was spinning. She rested it in her hands, the thoughts whirring round, too dreadful to contemplate. She needed help in working things out.

Shakily, she took out the piece of card from her apron pocket.

She dialled the number and heard it ring on the other end. There was a click. 'Hello,' said a voice. Before Margery could answer, her own doorbell rang. 'One minute,' she said into the phone, laid it carefully on its side, making sure not to scratch the polished table, and hurried to the front door.

The visitor wore a big coat and a headscarf. Margery peered at her. 'Can I help—'

She hardly saw the metallic flash of the knife before it plunged into her body, just below the pocket of her apron.

She staggered back, clutching her side, where blood already seeped through her clothes. Her mouth stretched wide as she made a sound between a scream and a gasp, before she tumbled through the door into the sitting room.

As the world turned dark, the last thing she heard was a tinny voice from the phone calling, 'Hello? Who's there? Is everything all right?'

12

ASPIRIN

The phone line was still open. Libby listened with growing horror as she heard the grating, gasping cry, followed by a crash, and sudden silence. 'Hello,' she called again. 'What's going on?' But there was only the empty sound of a telephone line.

'Max,' she shouted. 'Come here.' He came running, and she pointed to the receiver. There's someone on the other end, and – well – I think they've collapsed, or died, or—'

Max took the phone from her hands, listened a moment, then pulled out his mobile. 'We'd better keep the line open while we get help. Who's on the other end?'

'I don't know. They didn't say a word. I just answered the phone and there were all these noises. Ooh, Max, it was horrible. Like someone dying. We have to get help.'

He was already talking on his mobile. 'Right, let me know.'

He clicked off the phone. 'The police will trace the call. Good job you kept the line open. I wonder why they were ringing on the landline. Hardly anyone uses that, these days.'

Libby cried out. 'Oh, Max. I gave the number to Margery Half-stead when I left. I think she's been taken ill.'

'Let's get over there.'

In moments, they were in the Land Rover, speeding through the lanes, but at Margery and William's neat little house on the estate, they found the police had arrived first, along with an ambulance. The paramedics bundled someone into the ambulance, but Libby couldn't tell if the patient was alive or dead.

'Max, if she's dead, it will be my fault. She was contacting me to tell me something vital, I'm sure. I should never have visited her.' The words flew from her lips in a jumbled stream, hardly making sense even to Libby.

'Let's not panic until we have to,' Max advised, gripping her hand. His fingers were large and warm, and Libby clung on as though her own life depended on keeping him close.

PC Ian Smith came over. 'Thought I recognised the car. You again, Mrs Forest?'

Libby was too distraught to care that it was PC Smith. 'Is she OK?'

'She's still alive, at least.'

'Oh, thank heaven.' Relief rushed over Libby's body.

'She's not at all well, though. She's been stabbed.'

Libby gasped. 'She was on the phone. She rang me.'

Smith's habitual expression of faint disbelief changed to excitement. 'You mean, you heard what happened?'

Within seconds, he'd bundled Libby into the back of the police car to give her statement. As she finished the story, he snapped his notebook shut. 'You can go, now. We'll get back to you.' He gave a short bark of a laugh. 'You know the procedure, by now.'

* * *

'Maybe you should take the rest of the afternoon off.' Max was feeding Libby tea and biscuits.

'I'm quite all right,' she insisted, and grimaced. She sounded tetchy. A dose of aspirin had failed to cure the pounding in her head. 'I shall go home and feed Fuzzy. I've been neglecting her, recently, and she'll be missing Bear, too. I'll feel better if I'm doing something.'

'If that's what you want, I'll come with you.'

Tempted, for she felt calmer in Max's presence, Libby made herself turn down the offer. 'We need to push on. There's so much to do. I promised the police I'd talk to the other members of the history society. They'll be horrified; William and Margery are both founder members. I'm sure they'll know a lot more about Beryl, especially her – er – private life.'

'You mean, the secret drinking?'

'Exactly.'

'Good idea. Meanwhile, I'll go and visit Shipley with his new trainer, and track down some of the other people who've lost dogs. They may know what's going on.'

'Shipley. Do you know, I'd forgotten? He should be a fully paid-up sniffer dog by now.'

'He'll never reach the heights of expertise of some of the police dogs. His training came too late. An old dog, you know, and new tricks.'

'Nonsense. Shipley's very talented, and still young. He just needs a little direction. He'll be a star, working with the police. Oh.' She sat up straight, struck by the obvious. 'Maybe we could use him. Not just to find Bear, but in the business.'

'It's a thought. Meanwhile, I'm sure he can help lead us to Bear, if only we knew where to look. If anyone will know Bear's scent, it's Shipley.'

13

CHOCOLATE CAKE

Libby was keen to get to the history society meeting the next day, at George Edward's house. It would help take her mind off Bear. Besides, the attack on Margery, while Libby was listening, had shaken her to the core, and the members of the society must know more about Beryl than anyone else in Exham. The society had been a huge part of her life.

The prospect of meeting George's wife, Deirdre, piqued Libby's curiosity. The woman was surrounded by an air of mystery, for she rarely attended meetings. Ill health prevented her from getting out much, but Libby had only the vaguest idea of her illness. One of those 'female things' George's generation was reluctant to talk about. George often left meetings early, to look after Deirdre. He'd developed a habit of claiming the final portion of cake, supposedly for his wife.

Libby, the main contributor of that cake, had brought a crunchy, chocolate affair today. It was designed to cheer any members distressed by Beryl's death, William's illness, and the attack on Margery. Libby found chocolate was a great cure for mild depression.

The small group huddled in the Edwards' home seemed diminished, not only in number, but also in spirits. There were two new members: Joanna, the young wife of the newly arrived local doctor, who was also the recipient of Libby's flowers, and Annabel Pearson. As Libby arrived, Joanna was moving from one member to another, flirting with the men and telling the women about the latest escapades of her two children. She took a substantial slice of cake and gushed, 'Mrs Forest, how lovely to see you again. I've heard so much about your baking. In fact, my husband insists I call in to the bakery at least once a week. He's determined to sample your whole product range, one cake at a time.'

Mrs Moffat, the castle housekeeper, not required at the castle., was also there. Even the winter cleaning had been suspended for a few days following Beryl's death, while police enquiries continued, and the housekeeper was enjoying her freedom. 'Joanna's been showing me photographs of her delightful children,' she enthused. 'Mine are grown up, now, and would you believe I miss their noise and mess? My house is far too tidy, these days.'

She turned to Annabel, who sat quietly on an uncomfortable looking chair. 'You have children, too, I believe?'

'Just one. James.' Annabel bit her lip, as though unwilling to chat.

Mrs Moffat tried again. 'I wanted to thank you for helping out at the castle. It's so nice to have younger people involved. Most of us are a little "over the hill".'

Annabel nodded in silence, and Mrs Moffat, clearly tired of making the effort to be friendly with so little reward, resumed her livelier conversation with Joanna, gossiping excitedly under their breath about Beryl's death and William Halfstead's heart attack.

Libby circled the room, serving cake. It was a useful way to observe people without becoming embroiled in conversation.

From time to time, Joanna glanced her way. Checking what kind of impression she's making? A bit too eager to please for Libby's liking.

Annabel looked depressed. Libby, aware that William's heart attack had followed a quarrel with his wife, and knowing Annabel was the cause of the argument, used a general conversational hum as camouflage to murmur, 'I'm so sorry about what happened at the castle, on your first day.'

Annabel gave a tired smile, as though making a special attempt. 'Thank you. It was a shock.'

'And then, poor William's heart attack.' Libby made a pretence of struggling to balance the cake plate on a miniscule table, measuring the younger woman's reaction through half closed eyes.

Annabel gulped. 'He was very kind to me on my first day. A lovely man, I thought.'

What did her wide-eyed expression mean? Simple distress, sadness that a good man was gravely ill, or evidence of a closer, clandestine relationship?

Libby moved on, listening to the small talk in the room. Joanna seemed determined to admire everything and everyone. 'I love this room,' she gushed. A print on the wall caught her eye. 'Is that Dunkery Beacon?'

'By a local artist. We have almost as many painters in Somerset as in St Ives.'

'And those trophies?' Joanna had moved on to a group of three silver cups in a sideboard.

'Oh, those.' George moved in front of the cabinet, blocking Libby's view. 'Just a few fishing trophies. I belong to the Exham on Sea club. When we're not sea fishing, we go over to Wimbleball Lake.'

George's wife, Deirdre, raised her voice for the first time.

'George is one of the club's champions. Always winning prizes. Some of the local landowners are members of the club, you know. And I believe our MP takes part, from time to time. He was there, that time someone accused you of cheating. So unfair! As if you would do such a thing.'

George fidgeted, shifting from one foot to the other. 'No one wants to know about the fishing today, dear.' He took his wife's hand, solicitous. 'Are you quite comfortable there? Not in a draught?'

'Dear George,' his wife murmured. 'Always so considerate.'

Deirdre Edwards intrigued Libby. Lying back in the largest armchair in the room, she wore an all-enveloping dress in a vibrant floral material, including, it seemed, every colour shade in an artist's armoury. Her head leaned back against the chair, as though she lacked sufficient strength to keep it upright.

George sat close, handing her teacup to her whenever she needed a sip, constantly checking whether she was too hot, or a little chilly so near the window, whether she would be more comfortable on the sofa, or if she was tired and needed to rest.

To each of his inquiries, Deirdre replied with a gentle smile and a murmured, 'I feel quite well, at present. I can manage a few more minutes, I think.' Her eyes belied her languid pose. An unusual shade of blue green that appeared to change colour according to the light, they flickered tirelessly from one speaker to another, watching. She was an attractive woman. Her black hair, perhaps an unusually bright black for a woman of her age, was beautifully styled and curled gently round her face.

George patted his wife's hand and stood, addressing the group members with unusual authority. 'Thank you all for coming today. It seemed right to meet, in honour of our dear friend, Beryl, who passed away so sadly. Some society members were present at the castle that morning,' he nodded to Mrs Moffat, the housekeeper, 'and were privileged to be the last to speak to Beryl. My wife, Deirdre, has been a long-time friend to Beryl, and she suggested a memorial.'

Deirdre raised a hand in acknowledgement. 'Beryl was such a support when I returned home from hospital. She used to arrive every week with a big container of beef stew.'

Libby wished she'd taken the time to discover what had been wrong with George's wife. She'd assumed her poor health had been just an excuse, used to avoid social events she preferred not to attend.

She offered another slice of cake. Deirdre shook her head. Her hair stayed oddly still, in the same neat style, and Libby realised it must be a wig. How could she not have noticed before? She'd thought Deirdre dyed her hair, the colour a little dark for her pale complexion, but then, who didn't? The poor woman must have been having treatment, probably for cancer. And you call yourself an investigator?

Joanna said, 'I think it's wonderful that you've all gathered here today. I only met Miss Nightingale once, but I found her completely charming.'

Libby fought back an inappropriate smile. Charming was one of the last words she would have chosen to describe mousy little Beryl, even before Angela's revelations.

George continued. 'We must also acknowledge the dreadful tragedies that have fallen on our friends, Margery and William Halfstead. I can hardly believe what happened.' His weather-beaten face fell into such a desolate expression that Libby feared he was about to cry. Instead, he turned to her. 'I'm pleased we have Libby Forest with us, not just for the cake, of course.' He gave a short laugh, but no one joined in, and he cleared his throat before continuing. 'In her role as a private detective, she may know more about the events of the past few days.'

Caught unawares, Libby was forced to point out she could not divulge any information from the police. 'Really,' she confessed, 'I'm here to find out more about Beryl and Margery, as I suppose there's a high probability whoever killed Beryl was responsible for the attack on Margery.'

Her words unleashed a torrent of anger, sympathy, and horror, as the group members debated, with great vigour and animation, in the absence of any factual information, what could have led to the attacks.

'Beryl never hurt a fly,' George stated. 'At least, not when she was herself.'

George's wife, Deirdre, roused herself enough to remark, 'Actually, I found her a little strange.' A hush fell on the room as though a silent agreement had been broken. For a moment, the stillness lasted, until, liberated from politeness now the words were out and the conspiracy broken, the group began to tell the truth.

'She could be difficult, sometimes, especially if she was, well, under the weather,' George said.

'She wasn't always the best time keeper,' Mrs Moffat added. 'She was often late arriving for her shifts at the castle, and once or twice, she seemed just a little...' She swallowed. 'A little unwell. But her heart was in the right place.'

George gave a short laugh. 'Unwell, indeed! It was the demon drink that got Beryl. She could be spiteful when she had a tipple. It loosens the tongue a bit too much for my liking.'

His wife put a hand on his arm. 'Poor Beryl,' she said.

George patted his wife's hand and shook his head sanctimoniously. 'Yes indeed. Sad, very sad. Good thing she had friends to look out for her.'

His words acted as a brake on the group's chatter. They fell to a discussion of a suitable memorial. A collection, they agreed, would be appropriate, spent on an appropriate reminder of Beryl. 'Perhaps a bench in the seafront gardens?' Joanna ventured.

George announced he would make a visit to the hospital with Mrs Moffat, to take chocolates to Margery and William as soon as they were well enough, and the meeting seemed about to break up in a spirit of agreement when Joanna, her clear voice rising above the chatter, said, 'Of course, when we arrived in Exham, we were told about that unfortunate business with Miss Nightingale and the accounts.'

A hush fell, and all heads turned. Libby ventured, 'Accounts?'

Joanna glanced from one to the other, eyes very blue. 'Oh dear, have I spoken out of turn? I thought it was common knowledge that poor Miss Nightingale was asked to leave the racing stables she worked for. A matter of finance, you know. So sorry. Perhaps I'm mistaken.' The half smile on her lips belied her words.

Libby narrowed her eyes. That one knows exactly what she's doing. Did that make her a suspect, or just spiteful?

'I'm sure it was a misunderstanding,' George said. 'She told me she wanted to retire, to spend more time researching her family tree.'

'Of course.'

'A misunderstanding,' he repeated.

'Nothing to be concerned about,' someone else murmured.

The housekeeper turned to Libby, as though searching for a different topic. 'Now, the other matter is your missing dog. We've all heard about him, and we'd like to help. Is there anything we can do, my dear?' The relief in the room at the change of subject was almost tangible. Full of enthusiasm, they debated the best way to find Bear, the suggestions ranging from advertisements in the local paper to the offer of a huge reward.

'If you could all check your sheds and outhouses, that would help, although we're almost sure he's been stolen.' Libby's voice wavered on the last words. She tried not to worry about Bear, but to concentrate on the group members. She'd detected undercurrents in the room she didn't quite understand.

She made a show of looking at her watch, promising to let them know as soon as there was progress in the search for Bear, and left, saying she needed to visit a few other people who may have seen him recently.

As they waved her away, she sensed a lightening of tension, as though at least one person in the room was glad to see her leave. She had the strangest feeling something important had happened, but no matter how many times she ran the conversation through her head, she couldn't think what she'd missed.

14

A BOX OF CHOCOLATES

Mandy's car in the drive was a welcome sight, when Libby returned to the cottage. The car belonged, officially, to the business, but it was Mandy's pride and joy. 'Mrs F, your fiancé said you'd be coming here.'

'My fian—? Oh, you mean Max.' Mandy always managed to make Libby laugh. This evening, there was something odd about her. It took Libby a moment or two to work out what was missing. 'Your hair!'

Mandy ignored the comment. 'I've got instructions to cheer you up. He's going to be away overnight. Apparently, he's chasing some leads to do with the stolen dogs and he doesn't want you feeling sad. He has Shipley with him, so you don't need to go over to the big house, and I'm here as his – what's the word? – his proxy, bearing gifts.' She led Libby into the kitchen, where a bottle of Libby's favourite red wine was prominently displayed next to a giant vase of flowers and a box of chocolates. 'Those are another company's chocolates. It didn't seem right to bring you a box of your own.' Mandy giggled.

She insisted Libby sit down. 'The dinner's in the oven. Have a glass of this and spill all the beans.'

'You know I can't...'

'Mrs F. This is me. How many mysteries have we worked on together? You know I won't blab.'

'Well, apart from Max, you're the only one I tell real secrets to. I know you won't let me down. But first, why the change of style? No black lipstick? No white face powder? Ponytail hair? What's going on?'

'Well spotted. I've had a makeover. Not sure I care for it, really.' Mandy tugged at her demure shift dress. 'I've been to Steve's end-of-year concert in London. Only just got back. Thought I wouldn't embarrass him in front of his posh musician friends.' She let out a peal of laughter. 'Needn't have bothered. They're a right scruffy bunch up at the College of Music.'

'Mad musicians, you mean?'

'You have no idea. Tomorrow, I'm getting back to normal. Steve said he hardly recognised me without my – er – my stuff.' Mandy and Steve had been together, barring quarrels, since Steve finished his studies at Wells Cathedral School. Things were clearly getting serious. 'He said he likes me grungy.' She settled in an armchair. 'Now, fill me in and I'll lend you the benefit of my medium-sized brain.'

Libby frowned. 'What did you mean, Max is chasing leads? What's he up to? Why didn't he ring?'

'You know what he's like. He was in a rush when I bumped into him. Said he'd ring you later, and not to worry.'

Max was notoriously bad at keeping Libby informed. He hated broadcasting his whereabouts, even to her. Still, maybe he was on to something. Perhaps he'd be back soon, bringing Bear.

'I hope he's taking care.'

'Course he is.'

A familiar knot of worry tied itself in Libby's stomach, but there was nothing she could do, except relate the events of the last couple of days to Mandy and wait to hear from Max. She took a swig of wine and dropped two comforting chocolates in her mouth at once.

* * *

Max did not telephone that evening. Libby waited until midnight, persuading a reluctant Fuzzy to join her on the sofa by hand-feeding cat treats. She did not want to be alone, tonight.

At last, knowing he was unlikely to call her so late, she sent a text:

Off to bed. Hope all's well. Shipley OK? Phone me tomorrow.

She steadfastly refused to use text speak.

She expected to toss and turn all night, worrying in turn about Bear and Max, but in fact, she slept soundly, and woke with a renewed determination to get to grips with her problems. There was no answering text from Max. Maybe his battery had run out? Unlikely. Max was an organised man. Meticulous, as he put it. She grinned at the memory. If only he'd told her where he was going.

She scrambled out of bed, showered and dressed, and ate a lonely breakfast. Not long to go until the wedding, she remembered. Her heart sank. Without Bear? Come on, Max. Tell me what's happening.

The phone rang. Startled, she fumbled it from her pocket and dropped it on the floor.

It was Joe. 'Sorry, did I wake you?' he asked.

She forced a smile into her voice. 'No. I thought – oh, nothing.' No need to worry Joe.

'Well, I've been looking into these stolen dog gangs.'

'Really? Isn't it a bit low-level for you, now you're a grand detective inspector?'

'Very funny. I just had a quick look at the files. I found another missing Carpathian Shepherd dog report.'

'You're kidding.' Libby's thoughts whirled. 'You mean, someone's deliberately targeting the breed?'

'Looks like it. They're rare in the UK, so it would be stretching coincidence a bit far if another was stolen randomly.'

'Is it local?'

'Sadly not. Hereford.'

'Isn't that in your new area?' Libby had a thought. 'Did you tell Max? He's gone off to talk to other owners, but he didn't tell me where he went.'

Joe tutted. 'Typical Dad. Bet you'll have a few choice words in his ear when he gets back. And yes, Hereford is in West Mercia. I'll be there shortly, and if I can help, I will. Unfortunately, it's highly unlikely we'll be able to offer any resources – but since when did you and Max need help?'

Libby thought aloud. 'He might have found out about it on-line. He's been googling dog theft. Do you have an address?'

'I do, but don't tell them I sent you.'

'Wouldn't dream of it.'

By the time the call ended, a smile had spread over Libby's face. No need to panic. If only Max were better at telling her what he was up to. She blamed his time on government work. Even though his skills were financial, she knew he'd sometimes put himself in harm's way. 'Need to know,' he called it. Libby would work on that habit when he returned.

Finishing her coffee, she spooned cat food into Fuzzy's bowl and thought about her business. She hadn't given Angela's news about Terence Marchant much thought. If he was back in town, and planning the opening of a rival establishment, she should act. She couldn't afford to lose business. Cakes and chocolates were her main source of income, and Mandy's apprenticeship depended on the business continuing. And what about Frank? He'd poured his life into the bakery.

Libby had met Marchant on several occasions and disliked him more every time. He was rich, had no taste, and always looked Libby up and down as though imagining her with no clothes on. She shivered at the thought.

Should she visit him and appeal to his better nature? She dismissed that idea. He'd use the 'this is business, not personal' defence. No, she must fight fire with fire. Frank's bakery was hugely popular in Exham, and people loved Libby's chocolates. Satisfied customers would be the best weapons to fight a threat to the business.

She rang Angela. 'We're going to have a party. A huge affair. We'll get the press involved, with giveaways and raffles, and cake decorating competitions. It'll be the biggest event Exham's ever seen, promoting all our wares. We'll scare Terence Marchant off, before he's even begun.'

'Then, we need to hurry. His place is opening in two weeks.'

* * *

It took Angela no time at all to start planning the party. Libby arrived at the house to find her friend, fingers poised over a laptop, with a pile of printouts of various lists. 'I knew you'd be the right person to organise things,' Libby admitted. 'I'm having trouble with my own wedding.'

'Not having second thoughts again, are you?' Angela glared over half-moon specs.

Libby held up a hand. 'Definitely not. We were going for a day in a couple of weeks time, but I don't see how we can have a wonderful day without Bear. Maybe we should wait a while longer. There's no hurry. I'll see what Max thinks.'

'Why don't you concentrate on getting Bear back? I'll rope Mandy in to help with the party. I thought a wine and chocolate theme would go down well. In fact, I've got an idea that might work...'

Libby laughed. 'I knew I could trust you. I'll leave it in your hands.'

'Just set the budget and I'll do the rest. And, tell Max you want to postpone the wedding for a while. He'll understand. He waited long enough for you decide you wanted to marry him.'

A weight lifted from Libby's shoulders. 'You're right. He already said there's no hurry. Why am I getting so wound up? I'll talk to him next time. Oh—' She remembered he'd disappeared. 'I think I need to track him down.'

Angela pointed to the door. 'Go.'

15

TEA

Margery Halfstead's head ached and her chest hurt. The doctors told her she was lucky, the knife hadn't hit any important organs, but had slid off her ribcage. She'd endured seven stitches to the wound and an overnight stay in hospital. 'I want to see my husband,' she told the nurse, as she was woken at some ridiculously early hour to have her blood pressure taken.

'I'm sure you can, a little later, if the doctor's happy with your vital signs.'

'Vital signs, my eye.' Margery swung her legs out of bed. 'The doctor said it was just a scratch. I'm getting up.'

'Now, wait until you've had breakfast, why don't you?'

'Nonsense.'

Margery pulled back a curtain to find an elderly lady lying in the next bed, mouth hanging open, barely conscious. Margery replaced the curtain. The nurse raised her eyebrows, shrugged and left her alone, while Margery searched the tiny wardrobe at her bedside, looking for clothes. The dress she'd been wearing was missing. She clicked her tongue. The police had taken it for evidence. She contorted her body, stretching her arms back the short distance she could reach, given the pain of stitches in her side. She winced, struggling to untie the knotted string at the back of her flimsy NHS-issue nightgown, admitted defeat, and shuffled across the ward.

A sign in the corridor pointed the way to two other wards, but the names meant nothing to Margery. She took a chance and pushed open the nearest door. A nurse looked up. 'I'm sorry, you're in the wrong ward. The women's beds are next door.'

'I want to see my husband.'

'I'm sorry?'

'My husband. He's in here, I think.' She looked along the row of beds. 'Mr Halfstead.'

The nurse's expression changed. 'Oh, William's your husband? He's over there, by the window. Such a lovely gentleman.'

Margery frowned. She hated this modern habit young people had, of calling everyone by their first name. 'I'll see Mr Halfstead now, thank you.'

'Well, it's not visiting time, but I suppose, if you're here too.' She looked more closely at Margery's face. 'Are you feeling faint?'

'Most certainly not. I just wish to see my husband.' She was not sure where this determination had come from. All she knew was she had to make things right with William.

She stalked down the ward. William lay asleep. He looked old and tired. His face was grey. Margery, a rush of affection bringing a tear to her eyes, kissed his cheek. 'I'm so sorry,' she whispered.

His eyes flickered. He opened his mouth and said something his wife couldn't catch. She leaned closer. 'I'm here, William. It's me.'

A smile flitted over his face. 'Milly,' he croaked.

The words might as well have been a punch in the stomach. Margery staggered back. 'Milly? Who's Milly?'

William's eyes had closed once more. Margery clapped her hands over her mouth, afraid she might be sick. Mouth trembling, she turned away from the bed and shuffled back across the ward. She could hardly see the nurse for the tears filling her eyes. She'd been right. William had other women. Not just Annabel. Someone called Milly, as well.

Out in the corridor, she leaned against the wall, struggling to catch her breath. She must get home. She couldn't spend another minute in this hateful place. She longed to be in her own cosy home, surrounded by her precious possessions, while she thought this through.

She shook her head, struggling to clear it. Who could she call, to get some clothes sent in? The intruder, stabbing her at her own front door, seemed like no more than a bad dream, except for the pain of those stitches. No matter what became of her, she wanted to be in her own home. She hurried back to her bedside, grabbed the phone and business card from her bag, and punched in the number. Libby Forest would help.

* * *

Despite her determination, it wasn't easy for Margery to convince the staff she was ready to leave hospital. As the nurse explained, with forced cheerfulness, a doctor would be in to see her, but he was very busy this morning.

'I can discharge myself, can't I?'

The nurse squirmed. 'You can, but you'll have to sign a disclaimer.'

Margery fixed the nurse with a steely gaze. 'Then bring me whatever I should sign, as soon as possible.'

She waited, sitting by her bed, staring into space. Her world had crashed around her ears and she wanted to go home. How long would she be imprisoned in this place? It seemed the nursing staff were in no hurry to let her go, and she was losing the energy to fight. Just as she was about to roll back into bed and cry her eyes out, the nurse returned, with Libby in tow.

The nurse pointed to Margery. 'Please take her,' she muttered. 'You've saved my sanity.'

Even so, it was an hour before Margery was finally allowed to leave, clutching a paper bag containing painkillers and wearing a skirt and jumper she would never have chosen for herself. Libby confessed they were the first clothes she'd laid her hands on. At least she'd had no trouble finding the key under a loose paving stone, just as Margery had directed.

Margery sat in silence on the way home, relieved to find her companion did not insist on talking. No doubt she mistook Margery's mood of seething fury for a reaction to the trauma. Margery had met the first tentative enquiries about William with a short, 'He's on the mend,' in the tone of voice that forbids further enquiry.

Libby helped her through the front door, although she felt perfectly capable of walking alone, and made a cup of tea, asking questions as they drank. Margery tried to remember what had happened. 'I wanted to talk to you, that day, before – before I answered the door – because I needed to clear my head. I was starting to think all kinds of stupid things.'

'Tell me what happened. Who was at the door?'

Margery screwed her face up with effort. 'I've been trying to remember. You see, I only got a quick glimpse and she was wearing a big coat and a headscarf —'

'She?' Libby interrupted. 'You mean, it was a woman?'

'Why, yes. But she was big. Not tall, exactly, but well built. Strong.'

'How old was she?'

'Hard to tell. She was wearing big glasses and a headscarf, with just a little dark hair poking out round the sides. That's how I could tell it was a woman.'

Margery's lip trembled and Libby poured more tea. 'You don't need to talk about it any more , just yet.'

'I've been thinking, and I'm sure she didn't really want to kill me, you know. It was just the one blow, and it wasn't aimed at my heart. She could have stabbed me again. I think she was expecting to see William, and I took her by surprise.' Margery's determined smile wavered. 'I think I'm going to have a little sleep soon, if you don't mind. Thank you for bringing me home, but I'd like to be alone.'

'Of course, if that's what you'd prefer. I'll let myself out and come back later, to see how you're getting on.'

Margery finished the tea, feeling a little better. Maybe Libby Forest wasn't such a fool, but Margery had wanted to get rid of her. She didn't want to think about the woman who'd stabbed her. It was only a scratch, after all. No real damage done. She cared more about William's behaviour. If he was having an affair, she had to know.

She climbed the stairs, slowly, feeling the stitches in her side pulling painfully on the bruised skin. William's clothes hung neatly in his wardrobe, or were folded in drawers. Margery insisted on a tidy home.

A twinge of guilt prompted a moment's hesitation as she felt in his pockets, but she hardened her heart. William deserved it. Besides, she had to know the truth, no matter how much it hurt.

There was nothing out of the ordinary in any of the pockets; just the odd bus ticket and imperial mint. William wouldn't be so foolish as to keep evidence of his treachery where Margery would be likely to look.

She sat on the bed, and thought. Where did he go, that she did not follow? Where might he hide things?

A slow smile spread over Margery's face. Of course. The shed, that was it. William insisted every man had to own a shed. His wife was not allowed to clean – or even tidy – the small wooden building in the garden. The shed was William's den.

'Right,' Margery said aloud. 'That's where it will be.' She had no idea what she expected to find, but the urge to know the truth kept her going.

She searched through pots of nails sorted by size, and cans of half-finished paint. They yielded nothing out of the ordinary. Margery pushed them aside, and pulled out the glass jars arranged behind them in a row on a metal shelf. Odds and ends, that's all she found. Coins, buttons, a broken ruler, and several pencil stubs. Until, almost ready to give up the hunt, she picked up the last jar. It seemed to be full of cotton wool.

Margery frowned. What in the world would William be doing with cotton wool?

She tipped the jar's contents onto the only table in the shed, her fingers scrabbling. In the middle of the bundle, a key gleamed.

Her fingers trembled as she picked it up and looked around for something to unlock.

Next to the table, she saw a tarpaulin covered chest, placed instead of a chair. Margery pulled aside the cover. The box was ornate – a perfect match for the key. It was elaborately carved from some foreign wood – sandalwood, Margery guessed, sniffing the faint, pleasant wood fragrance.

She slipped the key in the lock. It turned smoothly. She took a deep breath and opened the lid.

* * *

When Libby returned, tired and dispirited after two hours distributing lost-dog posters in a nearby town, she found Margery on the sofa, gripping a small wooden box, sobbing as though her heart would break.

'What is it? Are you in pain? Shall I call the doctor?'

Margery shook her head. She held out the box. Libby took it, hesitant, expecting Margery to snap out one of her sharp comments. Instead, Margery covered her face with her hands.

Libby lowered herself to sit at Margery's side and opened the box. Inside were a tiny pair of bootees, a baby's white nightgown, and a folded muslin square. 'For the baby,' Margery whispered.

'Baby?' Libby touched the bootees, delicately. 'Whose baby?'

Margery cleared her throat. 'Ours. We were going to have a baby, but something went wrong. I never knew William had bought these things. He didn't tell me. He must have hidden them, all those years ago.' Her voice quavered. 'He hid them so as not to upset me.'

One by one, she lifted the clothes and handed them to Libby. 'Look.' She showed Libby a small, much folded piece of paper. 'He wanted a little girl. I wanted a boy. I had a list of boys' names, but this is his.' There were just two names on the paper: Margery and Milly. 'Milly was the name he wanted for our baby.'

Libby supplied copious amounts of tea and sympathy. Margery blew her nose, folded the baby clothes neatly in their tissue paper and began to talk, relief clearly making her garrulous. 'I've been so silly. How could I have mistrusted him?' She gave a watery smile. 'I always thought William was too good for me, that's the truth. He's such an attractive man. I've never quite believed my luck that he wanted to marry me. When I get him home, I'm going to spoil him rotten. I'll even let him go fishing again.'

She locked the box, smoothing the surface with gentle hands.

'He stopped fishing after that last competition. He was sure he'd won. He caught an enormous rainbow trout, over six pounds, he reckoned, but the scales let him down. He said they were weighted. I told him not to bother with a club where there were cheats.'

The colour had returned to her cheeks. 'I know he misses his mornings by the water. I'll buy him some more fishing kit, that's what I'll do. He'll like that.'

Libby slipped away, leaving Margery searching out old fishing leaflets from a magazine rack.

16

CHERRY BAKEWELLS

Libby had never understood Margery's conviction that Annabel and William were having an affair. Annabel was so much younger than him, and had showed no signs of pining for him. Libby wasn't at all surprised to discover it was all in Margery's imagination.

However, his uncharacteristic disappearance, when he was supposedly in charge of the schoolboys, remained unsolved. Where had he gone? Could he have been with Beryl? Nicotine, Libby had read, can act fast. It was perfectly possible to imagine William offering Beryl a drink of whisky containing enough poison to kill her within minutes.

Was William really the killer? He'd had the opportunity, but what was his motive? Libby hadn't yet tried to uncover whether he had the knowledge to distil nicotine, but he had worked all his life in teaching. He was nobody's fool.

The only fact that pointed suspicion firmly away from him was the attack on his wife. No one could dispute his alibi, as he was in hospital, but Libby's fertile brain conjured up various ways he could still be responsible. An accomplice, perhaps? Someone working with William for some unknown purpose? Or perhaps, even if the older man had no interest in Annabel, he could be having an affair with someone else. What about the mysterious volunteer Margery saw? Had the police tracked her down?

Libby longed to talk it over with Max. If only he'd get in touch. She hesitated, tempted to find out where he'd gone and follow him.

As she hesitated, her phone pinged.

Max. It was almost as though he'd heard her thoughts. The text was brief, but at least he was in contact:

On the trail. Terrible reception here. Will contact if any news. Shipley helping.

Libby almost cried with relief. Max was fine, just busy and out of range. She hadn't thought of that. A niggling voice whispered that he couldn't have been out of range all the time, and she'd have something to say about his silence when he came home. Still, if only he could find Bear, things would be perfect. She grinned, anticipating a short argument, followed by an enjoyable reconciliation.

Suddenly full of hope, her spirits leapt. She would concentrate on enquiries into Beryl's murder and the attack on Margery. She wanted to prove William innocent, for Margery's sake, but she reminded herself of Joe's advice to follow the evidence, even if it led in a direction she disliked.

She planned to follow up the reason for the school party's presence in the castle on the morning of Beryl's murder. Was it a coincidence? William had been responsible for arranging the visit.

She telephoned Jason Franklin's school. The receptionist was reluctant to make an immediate appointment, but Libby was ready with hints at possible consequences for the school if the students' supervision at the castle had been inadequate. The receptionist suddenly found a window in the headteacher's diary. She could see Libby straight away.

Libby ended the call and set off for the school. Max would be proud of her assertiveness.

The school was a comprehensive of over a thousand students, spread over a large campus backing onto open fields. It seemed a pleasant place to go to school, although Libby's quick googling of its most recent Ofsted report showed it 'required improvement' in several areas. The sixth form, apparently, needed more 'stretching'.

Libby left her car in the staff car park, pressed a buzzer, and asked to be admitted. She got a kick out of showing her police credentials to the receptionist, who reluctantly disappeared to check whether the head teacher was available.

Mrs Bass, the head teacher, arrived without unnecessary delay. She was an upright, smart looking lady, probably within a year or two of retirement age. 'How can I help?' she asked, her manner business-like rather than warm, as she ushered Libby into her office. 'Is this to do with that unfortunate death at the castle? My boys were very shocked, as you can imagine. I've organised counselling, should any of them require it, but so far, they seem to be coping remarkably well. We have a strong and supportive environment in this school.'

'I'm sure that will have helped,' Libby said, aiming for diplomacy. She was disconcerted by memories of her own headmistress's study. How did people manage to build such a forbidding aura, even in rooms barely different from a doctor's surgery or solicitor's office?

She coughed and concentrated on the business at hand. 'I work with the police as a civilian officer,' she explained, 'and I'm gathering background information about the day of the castle visit. The boys who were present have given statements, and I was there when Jason Franklin was interviewed. Today, I'm just trying to understand how they came to be in the castle that day. It was a little unusual, because the castle was officially closed.'

The head teacher nodded. 'It was a special occasion. As you will know, Jason's father is our local MP. He gives an extraordinary degree of support to the school.' I bet he does, Libby thought. Best way to make sure his son gets preferential treatment.

As though reading her mind, the head teacher continued. 'That does not mean Jason gains any kind of advantage over the other students.' Mrs Bass shot a look at Libby that defied her to argue. 'Thomas – Mr Franklin – also supports the Trust that manages the castle. They were willing to allow an exceptional visit, on this one occasion.'

'Of course.' Libby let it go for now. Mrs Bass's coolness made it clear she was not interested in sharing gossip, but a spot of colour in her cheeks alerted Libby's instincts. How well did the head-teacher know the MP? She chose her words with care. 'Apparently, Jason was chosen to take part in the short drama. You know, writing a script and speaking to Miss Nightingale to discuss the fictional menu.'

'That was down to Mr Halfstead. He organised a short essay competition among the boys – something about the plight of domestic servants in Victorian times, I believe – and Jason produced the best entry. The visit had been planned for a different day, but when Jason discovered he would be absent that day, his father requested a special outing. Jason was due to visit Oxford University. Several of our students apply each year to the pinnacles of academia, and I'm rather proud to say that two boys were successful last year – one to read physics at Cambridge, the other, classics at Oxford. Jason is hoping to take a history degree.'

Mrs Bass sounded so pleased with herself that Libby could not resist asking, 'The school's improved since the most recent Ofsted report, then?'

The head teacher's manner cooled. 'I was not in charge when that inspection took place. I was employed subsequently, and my remit has been to improve the weaker areas of the school. I'm pleased to say that yes, the school has indeed improved. We expect Jason and one or two others of our current sixth form to make us even more proud, this year.'

'So, Jason is a star pupil?'

'One of them.'

The receptionist entered, bearing refreshments on a tray. Two cherry Bakewell tarts looked suspiciously like Libby's own work.

The head teacher, perhaps noticing Libby's smile, allowed her manner to soften a little. 'Your fame as a cook has travelled before you, Mrs Forest. Perhaps we will be able to persuade you to give a talk to some of our students, one day.'

Clever woman. How could Libby possibly refuse such a request, if she wanted more co-operation within the school? No wonder Mrs Bass had improved the school's performance. She was someone to reckon with. 'I'll look at my diary,' Libby promised. "I'm sure I can help.'

The head teacher, with an air of satisfaction, stirred her tea and took a neat bite from a cake. Libby seized the moment of rapport to find out more about Thomas Franklin. 'I expect it's useful to have the MP's son doing so well in your school…'

'He's certainly a credit to his father.' She positively beamed. 'Thomas Franklin really is a most interesting man. He's only been the local MP for two years, but he's lived in the area much longer. He's a most amusing speaker. He drew quite a crowd when he opened our annual fête.' Libby had seen the man on television talk shows, where he certainly knew how to charm the audience. Judging by the headteacher's increased animation, Libby suspected Mrs Bass's interest went beyond the professional.

That, however, did not imply anything suspicious about the man's request for a change of date for the castle visit. That seemed to have nothing to do with the headteacher. Once again, the key seemed to be William Halfstead. Libby turned the conversation back in that direction. 'Mr Halfstead used to teach here, I believe.'

'Before my time, but yes. He retired shortly after I was appointed.'

'Was that early retirement?'

Mrs Bass let her gaze slide sideways. 'A year or so, I believe.'

Libby silently noted the head teacher's discomfort. 'Forgive me for asking, but was there any particular reason why he was encouraged to retire?'

'No scandal, if that's what you're suggesting. If there had been, Mr Halfstead would most certainly not be allowed to guide our students around the castle. No, it was simply a change in ethos and methods. I had to bring the school up to date, in some ways. For example, more account taken of studying contemporary texts in history lessons, and rather less in the way of dressing up.' The head teacher stopped talking, a little abruptly. Libby had the impression she'd been franker than she intended.

Libby's brain buzzed as she left. The head teacher's careful words had not quite concealed her disapproval of William Halfstead. Did that make him a more likely suspect, or was it simply a difference of opinion about teaching methods? Then, there was the MP, charming the headteacher and willing to use his position on behalf of his son. Had he any sort of hold over Mr Halfstead? And if so, what relevance would that have to Beryl Nightingale's death?

* * *

During Libby's interview with the head teacher, DCI Morrison had sent a text inviting Libby to a case conference to consider progress in Beryl Nightingale's murder enquiry. She arrived, breathless, in time to catch a full toxicology report that finally, and definitively, confirmed the cause of Beryl's death as nicotine poisoning.

DC Gemma Humberstone's glance at Libby was brief and unfriendly, and when Libby was asked to update the room on any information she'd gleaned in the past couple of days, the young officer's expression took on a hard edge. 'I'm aware that I need to be sensitive about any investigation into an MP,' Libby ended her report, and peeked at her watch. She'd arranged to spend the evening at a concert in Wells, where the performers included Mandy's boyfriend, Steve, an old pupil at the cathedral school.

DCI Morrison stepped in. 'A good point. Gemma, perhaps you could follow up Mrs Forest's excellent work.' The look Gemma shot in Libby's direction was pure fury.

Ian Smith looked from one to the other, a satisfied smile playing on his lips. At first Libby was puzzled, then a thought struck her. He really doesn't like women. He wants both Gemma and me to fall on our faces. If only Gemma didn't resent my involvement so much, I might be able to help her. I've come across many Ian Smiths before. Notably in the shape of her own husband, now deceased.

The DCI was still talking. 'We need to review our hypotheses at this point. We know Miss Nightingale was murdered, via something she ate or drank. She would not have been able to smoke sufficient cigarettes, or chew sufficient tobacco, to cause death. We need to consider whether there is the possibility of a self-inflicted poisoning, however unlikely a method this would appear to be. Mrs Forest, you knew the victim better than any of us. Would you believe her capable of suicide?'

Libby considered. 'She was a rather sad person, with a hidden drink problem. When I say hidden, I mean no one talked about it. However, residents all seem to be aware she drank. If she killed herself, I would ask, why now? The drink problem is long standing.'

Several nods in the room supported Libby's conclusion. Emboldened, she continued. 'A possible explanation may be the way she left her job. I've heard conflicting reports. Some say she retired – she was well over retirement age – while others hint at a query over accounting issues.'

Morrison nodded. 'Gemma, that's another one for you to follow up with the racing stables – the accounts belonged to them. Any other theories at this stage, anyone?'

Gemma Humberstone jotted something in her notebook, saying, 'I'd like to know more about William Halfstead. We shouldn't write him off as a suspect, simply because he's since had a heart attack. He was at the castle, and responsible for the presence of the schoolchildren.'

Libby raised a hand, then lowered it, blushing like a child. 'His wife mentioned he was out of sight around the time of Beryl's death. She suggested he might have been pursuing one of the other volunteers at the time.'

Ian Smith spluttered coffee on the floor. 'At his age? Chance would be a fine thing.'

Morrison bestowed a cold stare on his subordinate, and Libby caught a glimpse of the steel beneath the senior officer's gentle exterior. 'Because you're such a catch, Ian?'

'Come on, sir. The man must be seventy. Who was he after? Another geriatric?' A couple of young male officers tittered, but DCI Morrison's eyes narrowed.

Ian Smith's heading for trouble.

Gemma glanced at Libby and raised her eyebrow the tiniest fraction. Warmed by this show of feminine solidarity, however mild, Libby explained Margery's theory that her husband might be having an affair with Annabel.

DCI Morrison nodded. 'He's still at the top of our list, then. We'll need a proper statement from his wife. I suppose she's in the clear?'

'Judging by the amount of nicotine in the victim's tissues,' Gemma was glancing through the pathologist's report, 'it's likely the poison was administered less than an hour before death. There was enough of it in her body to kill a horse. So, Margery Halfstead would have been able to administer it, as would anyone who knew the victim. If she hadn't been attacked, I'd want to keep her on the list. Could the stabbing have been a pretence?' She looked at Libby, eyebrows raised.

Libby doubted Margery's ability to plan and carry out such a deception. 'I heard the attack and it sounded genuine enough. But, it's possible.'

'We'll keep her in mind,' DCI Morrison confirmed, 'just in case.'

PC Smith had been nodding while Gemma spoke, as though he'd attained some insight. He sounded triumphant. 'The killer must have been in the castle.'

Morrison raised a weary eyebrow. 'No,' he said, with a show of patience. 'The poison could have been introduced into the victim's alcohol at any time.'

Even Ian Smith recognised the disdain in his boss's voice, and slouched down in a chair.

'By the way, sir,' Gemma was frowning. 'We haven't managed to trace a woman seen at the castle. Mrs Halfstead mentioned seeing her upstairs. On a normal day, it would be impossible to track her down, but as the castle was closed except for the students, she was either there officially, helping with the cleaning, or she sneaked in. So far, no one seems to know who she is. It may not be important, and she was upstairs when the victim died, but...'

Several heads had jerked up. A rare smile brightened DCI Morrison's face. 'Well done, Gemma. Quite right. She need have nothing to do with the murder, but I don't like loose ends. Chase that up, will you? Find out who else saw our mystery woman, and get me a name.'

DCI Morrison tapped papers on the table, indicating the conference was drawing to a close. 'No one's ruled out, yet. Anyone in the castle that morning could have done the deed. A friend or neighbour who had access to Miss Nightingale's house – they could have dropped the poison in a bottle of her favourite tipple at any time. What was her favourite, by the way?'

'Whisky.' Libby's response caused a general groan.

'Could have been there for years, then.' The muscles of Morrison's habitually glum face drooped even further. 'Still, we'll bear it in mind. Ian, start talking to the neighbours. Gemma, speak to the housekeeper at the castle. Don't forget to liaise, you two, as some neighbours may also be volunteers.' Gemma's grim expression betrayed her lack of enthusiasm for working with Ian Smith, but the boss made no comment. 'Mrs Forest, thank you for your help so far. Any more ideas are very welcome.'

Libby turned to leave, just as Ian Smith leered at Gemma. 'Come on then, babe. Let's liaise.'

No wonder Gemma Humberstone had a defensive attitude. If Smith wasn't careful, he'd get himself in trouble for comments like that.

17

ORANGE JUICE

Libby was glad to fill the evening with a concert and avoid the long lonely hours of darkness while Max was away. She slid into a wooden pew in Wells Cathedral, next to Mandy. Angela, Steve's aunt, sat on Libby's left side. Mandy's Goth makeup had reappeared, and she'd topped the look with a black velvet hat that Libby secretly coveted.

Awed by the splendour of the cathedral's arches and the expectant hush from the audience, Libby waited until the orchestra began tuning their instruments before whispering, under the cover of the noise, 'I've heard from Max. He's fine, so I'll leave him alone to get on with his enquiries. He managed perfectly well before he knew me. I don't know why I was so anxious.'

'Wedding nerves?'

'Maybe. No news of Bear, I'm afraid.'

'Look on the bright side,' Mandy urged. 'The gang aren't killing dogs, they're stealing valuable animals. Max is on the case. He'll find him.'

'Hope you're right.' Libby wriggled. 'Anyway, I'm determined not to worry about Bear, or anything else, this evening. I'm going to enjoy the music.'

Mandy giggled. 'I won't tell you what I heard on the grapevine, then.'

The conductor tapped his baton and the orchestra began to play.

'What did you hear?'

A woman in the row behind shushed her. Mandy shrugged. 'Sorry, tell you at the interval.'

Libby's brain raced and she listened with only half an ear to the music. What could Mandy know? Was it about Bear? She discarded that idea. If Mandy had known something, she would have been bursting to tell. Perhaps she'd heard more gossip about Beryl or the Halfsteads.

At last, the final notes wafted to the ceiling. Libby grabbed Mandy's arm. 'You wretch, I've been on tenterhooks. What do you know?'

Mandy wrinkled her nose. 'Sorry, that was bad timing. When I was in the bakery, we had a visit from the man who's just moved into that big house that's been empty for months. You know, up in Millionaire's Rise?' Libby nodded. Everyone knew that street in Exham. Every house in it was way above the average resident's budget.

'He stayed in the shop for ages. Seems like he wants to get to know people. A bit smarmy, if you know what I mean, but Gladys from the flower shop seemed to like him.'

'She likes all men.'

'Whatever.' Libby winced at the expression as Mandy continued. 'Anyway, this isn't just gossip about her. The man – called himself Henderson, I think. That's right, Patrick Henderson.'

Libby wanted to scream. Would Mandy never get to the point? She bit her lip and waited.

'He said he'd come to see Beryl, because she used to work in his racing stables, but there was no reply at her house. Well, you can imagine. Gladys got all excited, telling him about Beryl dying at the castle, and how there was a rumour she'd left her job under a cloud, and did the man know anything about it?' She paused for breath.

'Go on,' Angela urged, as gripped as Libby, 'before they come back for the second half.'

'In a nutshell, this man said he supposed he could tell her because, he said "Beryl's dead and you can't slander the dead, can you, ha ha"' Mandy wrinkled her nose in disgust. 'Anyway, that rumour was true. Beryl used money from the business to make investments, but they'd all gone wrong before she could replace the cash, and the end of year audit uncovered the discrepancies.'

Angela drew in a long breath. 'So, she was stealing from the firm. Who would ever have believed it of Beryl?'

'What's more,' Mandy finished in a rush, 'because she lost the money she was dismissed and she was stony broke apart from the few bob from the state pension.'

It was time for the second part of the concert, and Steve stepped forward with two colleagues to play a saxophone trio; a setting of Alexander's Ragtime Band that soon had the audience tapping their feet. Mandy switched her attention to her boyfriend, her mouth slightly ajar, cheeks pink with excitement. Libby glanced to her other side, where Angela's rapt expression mimicked Mandy's, and grinned. For the moment, both her companions had forgotten the murder victim and the missing dog.

At the end of the evening, Libby turned down Angela's invitation to celebrate at her house. 'I'd love to, but I need to think about Mandy's information. If Beryl was broke and worried, that might mean she was drinking more.'

'Drowning her sorrows,' Mandy murmured, most of her attention still on Steve. Libby grinned. An idea was forming at the back of her mind.

* * *

Next morning, Libby was alone as Mandy had stayed with her aunt. Her lonely breakfast of orange juice and toast was interrupted by a ring at the doorbell. Libby leapt to open the door, excited, expecting to see Max, with Bear in tow alongside Shipley.

She flung open the door and smothered a groan. Gemma Humberstone was the last person she wanted to see.

The detective constable opened her mouth, but closed it again. Libby knew her face was a wreck. She hadn't even showered or combed her hair. Trying to appear calm, she took a deep breath and fixed a welcoming smile to her face. 'You'd better come in.'

She led DC Humberstone through to the kitchen, but the young woman refused an offer of tea. She looked uncomfortable, fidgeting and biting her lip. 'I wanted to make a suggestion, Mrs Forest, but I don't want to intrude.'

'I could do with some good news, to be honest.'

'Well, I have an appointment with Jason Franklin's father. He's requested – well insisted on – a meeting. He's not happy. I thought you might like to come along.'

'I certainly would.' An interview with the MP was just the tonic she needed, whatever the excuse, and the DCs offer felt like a small olive branch. 'Give me just a minute.'

Escaping, Libby threw water on her face, whizzed a brush

over her teeth and dragged on trousers and a jumper. Feeling slightly more human, she returned to the kitchen. 'I'm sorry to make you wait. I overslept.' She bit her tongue, annoyed that she sounded defensive.

As she pulled on a coat, her phone pinged with another text from Max:

In Hereford. Hopeful. Talk soon xx

* * *

Thomas Franklin was in his constituency surgery, close to the castle. Of average height, he carried himself with the assurance of a man who'd studied at Eton or Harrow. His carefully maintained shock of thick hair, the colour a vivid chestnut, could not possibly be natural, and his skin was deeply tanned to a colour that, in this part of the world, must be due either to a succession of foreign holidays or chemical assistance.

He made a great show of checking his watch and threw a pointed glance at the small band of petitioners sitting, cramped, on crowded chairs round the edges of the room. 'Come into my office. I can only give you a few minutes.'

He settled himself into a leather office chair and waved his visitors to a pair of small, hard chairs. There was no offer of refreshment. 'I gather you wish to discuss this business at the castle. As you can imagine, I'm not at all happy about my son's involvement, and I've made my feelings clear to the headmistress. I expect schoolchildren to be kept safe, not exposed to upsetting matters. Where was the man in charge? He seems to have abandoned the party and left them with his totally unqualified wife. My son may well be traumatised.'

Gemma avoided Libby's eye. 'Be that as it may,' she said, 'my job is to find out what happened.'

'Jason told you. He was talking on that ridiculous speaker tube, when this woman died.' The man's voice rose. 'The poor lad was actually speaking to her.'

'Yes, he told me what happened when I spoke to him at the castle. Mrs Forest was also present. I would like to add that your son is not under any suspicion. The students are currently viewed as unfortunate bystanders.' Libby admired the police officer's diplomacy.

The MP's bluster faded a little. He leaned back in his chair, raised his eyes to the ceiling, and steepled short, stubby fingers together. 'I am keen this should all be cleared up as quickly as possible. I assume you have a suspect. I hear William Halfstead is under suspicion.'

Libby listened closely, her eyes on the floor.

'I'm so sorry, I'm afraid I can't share that information at this stage.' Gemma spoke formally.

The MP frowned, used to having his own way. 'I'd be grateful,' he went on, 'if you'd keep me abreast of your enquiries. On behalf of my constituents, you know.'

'I will make sure you're kept informed when appropriate, sir. May I say, we're most grateful for the interest you're taking in the matter. We want to clear it up as soon as possible.'

'Of course, of course.' He sounded tetchy. 'Who was this woman? Brenda, was it?'

'Beryl. Beryl Nightingale. A volunteer at the castle.'

'Well, I'm always pleased to hear of members of the public doing their bit for the community. She was a friend of Mr Halfstead's, I believe?'

Gemma said nothing. The MP looked at his watch again. 'Well, I must get on. Plenty of problems to solve in the constituency surgery today. Thank you for putting my mind at rest that you have matters in hand. Wouldn't like my son to be more nervous than he is already. He has important exams coming up.'

Libby and Gemma were waved out. As she left, Libby glanced back, to see the MP watching them intently. Libby replayed the conversation in her head. He seemed very interested in William Halfstead.

They climbed back into the police car. 'Well, what do you make of that?' Gemma asked.

'An over-protective father?' Libby suggested. 'And boiling for a fight with the police.'

Gemma nodded. 'Exactly.'

She twisted round, ready to reverse the car out of its space. 'Thank you for coming. I wanted to apologise.'

'Oh?' Libby stayed non-committal.

'Yes. Ian Smith told me you impeded his enquiries in the matter of the poisoned cyclists. It happened before I joined the local police service, so I didn't know the details. Yesterday, we had a little leaving do for DI Ramshore and he told me the true story.'

Libby took a deep breath, controlling a burst of anger. How dare Ian Smith tell lies about her? 'No problem. That man's a menace. I don't envy you, having to work with him. He's always been difficult, but he seems to be getting more misogynistic, recently.'

Gemma swung the car expertly round the narrow corners of the A39, clicking her tongue as she was forced to slow behind a tractor. 'His third wife left him in the summer. I think he has a problem with women. Anyway, I'd better get back. Thanks again.'

Libby's smile was grim. Ian Smith needed to be taught a lesson. She wasn't sure how to manage it, but one day...

Meanwhile, she had other plans. Tired of waiting to hear

from Max, she decided to follow Bear's trail herself. She wouldn't stay at home, doing nothing, any longer. As the tractor pulled over to let the line of traffic through, Libby made up her mind. She'd set off for Hereford as soon as she could.

18

SAUSAGE ROLLS

Libby followed a scenic route to Hereford that led beside the River Wye, picturesque woodland towering on either side, but she wasted no time admiring the view. Her thoughts were all of Bear.

A search of Facebook had uncovered posts from the missing dog's owner, with a picture of a dog who looked remarkably like Bear, playing with a small red-headed child outside a farmhouse. Libby, reaching the address Joe supplied, recognised the house. The farmyard was swept clean, and the barns and outhouses well cared for. A young woman opened the door, with not one but two red-haired children in tow. From their dungarees, identical in design, except that one was blue and the other green, Libby deduced they were boy twins. They looked about three years old.

'Mrs Brant?'

The woman nodded. 'Can I help?'

Libby read hope in the woman's eyes. 'I'm afraid I don't have any news of your dog.'

The spark died and Mrs Brant sighed. 'How do you know about him?'

'I've lost a similar animal.'

'Really? You'd better come in.' Libby followed as Mrs Brant shooed her two small boys into a cluttered room, the carpet spread with toys. She turned the sound on the television down to a murmur. 'Sorry. They love Peter Rabbit. It will keep them happy while we talk. Thank heaven for iPlayer.' She waved Libby to an ancient, squashy sofa. 'They're missing the dog terribly. Well, me and my husband, too, of course. Barry's away today, gone to buy a new ram.' She shot a quizzical glance at Libby. 'How did you know about us?'

Libby remembered she was here unofficially. 'Facebook. I wondered if you had any information?'

The woman moved over to a window that looked out towards the back of the house. 'Not really. Domino – that's the dog's name – was out in the garden one minute, and next time I looked, he was gone. We thought he'd just escaped, but we checked the fences, and there were no gaps. We hoped he'd show up in a day or two, but no one's seen him. We put his photo on Facebook, and everyone's sympathetic, but there's no information. We're starting to think he's gone for good.'

Libby told the young woman about Bear. 'It seems there's a market for Carpathians.'

'They're wonderful sheepdogs, but we keep Domino as a pet. He's so gentle with the boys. They crawl all over him, and pull his tail, and he never even growls.'

* * *

The farm visit hadn't taken Libby any further forward. She left Mrs Brant and her two boys, promising to keep in touch, and drove the few miles into the city. She'd refused coffee at the farm, guessing the busy mother had plenty to do, but she was gasping for coffee. It wouldn't do any harm to ask a few questions of local people.

Parking in the city turned out to be easier than she'd expected, and she was soon trekking from one shop to another, showing posters of Bear and asking everyone who'd listen if they'd heard about any missing dogs.

She drew a blank in her first target, a pharmacy, and had little better luck in the estate agency next door. 'I don't know about missing dogs, but I can show you the most likely area to keep one, if you're interested in moving?'

Libby gave the young man full marks for salesmanship, but had no time to waste. There was a small café nearby, so she elbowed the door open. It was deserted, apart from a blonde wait-ress who flicked crumbs from tables, from time to time admiring herself in the mirror at the back of the shop.

Libby settled at a table and showed her the photo, holding out little hope, but the blonde licked cream from her fingers, screwed up her nose in thought, and announced she had a friend who sometimes worked on a training farm. 'They have lots of different dogs. Shetlands, Old English sheepdogs, you name it. Some of them had a funny name – like carpet.'

Libby could hardly believe her luck. 'Carpathian?'

'That's it.'

'Do you have an address?'

'For my friend?'

Libby was patient. 'No, for the training place.'

'Oh.' The girl looked blank. 'Miles away. What was it? Some-thing farm.'

Libby waited.

'I know. Johnson's. Or was it Jenson's. Yes, that was it. Like the racing driver, you know?'

A woman peered round the door to the kitchens. 'Ready to serve the customer, Maria?'

'Yes, s'pose so.' Maria looked less than enthusiastic as Libby ordered coffee. 'Jenson's Farm. Thanks for your help.'

The woman came further into the room, frowning. 'Mind if I ask why you want that place?'

'I heard about their dogs.'

'Press, are you? Journalist? I don't like the press. Intruding on people. You leave them alone. They're new here, trying to make a living, setting up a sheepdog training business on their farm. No money in sheep alone, these days.'

'No, it's not that. I mean, I'm not from the newspapers. I – we have a dog. Like the ones they train.' Libby tried to get a grip. 'I mean, we've lost our dog and I wondered if they could help.'

'You're with that man, then.'

'A man?' Hope flickered in Libby's heart.

'Tall, grey hair. Nice blue eyes. Said something about a dog gone missing.'

Libby was following in Max's footsteps. That meant she was on the right track. 'Yes. He's my – well, it's our dog.'

'Then, I'll show you on the map, like I showed him when he came this way yesterday.' She drew roads on the back of a menu. 'There you are: Jenson's Farm. Quiet folk. Keep to themselves. Been tenants on the farm for a couple of years, but making a decent fist of it. Took one of their dogs to the local show, came second in their class, working the sheep.'

Grateful, Libby took the hastily scrawled map, gulped a cup of watery coffee, and set off for Jenson's Farm, looking forward to finding Max and talking to the sheepdog trainers.

* * *

Following the map, Libby came upon a sign heralding Jenson's farm. She turned the corner and slammed on the brake as she caught sight of a familiar vehicle. Max's car was half hidden in a small patch of woodland beside the farm lane. Libby turned her car until it was parallel with the Land Rover and climbed out.

The Land Rover was deserted. Squinting, she looked around, but there was no sign of Max or Shipley. Puzzled, she locked the Citroen and set off up the road leading to the farm. She'd hardly gone twenty yards when a loud hiss made her jump.

'Libby.' To her delight, it was Max's voice. 'Over here.'

'Where? I can't see you.'

'To your left.'

Libby slipped into a small copse of trees. There was Max, Shipley sitting obediently by his side. Libby hardly knew whether she was more impressed by Shipley's improved behaviour, or perturbed by Max's secrecy. 'What on earth is going on?' Max, dressed in a dark jacket and black jeans, wore a black beanie on his head. 'And why are you wearing that ridiculous hat? It's not in the least bit cold today.'

Max's beam split his face in two. 'I'm hiding – staking out the farmhouse. I've spent a couple of days talking to local people, gathering information, and I reckon Bear's likely to be here.'

For a second, Libby's heart leapt. Then, reason kicked in. 'This farm's legitimate, I believe. They're openly training dogs. I've just come from a café in Hereford, and they told me everyone knows. It's all above board. I was on my way to visit.'

'Ah, but where do they get the dogs? That's the point. There's at least half a dozen there, various breeds. If we go marching up to the farmhouse looking for a missing animal they'll know we're suspicious. I'm waiting for it to get dark and I'm going to investigate.'

'Aren't you jumping to conclusions?'

Max shook his head. 'I called at another farm, nearby. They told me this was a busy place with vans constantly arriving and leaving. That farmer was an old timer. He said he'd been suspicious about sheep rustling, as there's been a spate of that recently, but when he heard they were training dogs, he stopped worrying.'

'How do we know they're stealing the dogs?' Libby objected.

'We don't, but I'm going to give Shipley a chance to prove his worth. I put one of Bear's blankets in the Land Rover. It's full of dried dribble. I'm going to see if Shipley can pick up Bear's trail. Call it a test of his new skills.'

Libby looked up at the sky. 'It's going to be ages until it gets dark. What if someone drives past and sees the cars?'

'I've been here a few hours, now. Several cars have driven in and out and none of them noticed me.'

'What are we going to do from now until sunset?'

'What's this about we?' Max had his hands on his hips. 'I'm staying here with Shipley. You need to go home and let me get on with it.'

'And miss all the fun? You must be joking. You're not getting rid of me that easily.'

Max looked as though he'd like to argue, but after a moment, he shrugged. 'In that case let's get into the Land Rover. I brought plenty of provisions with me.'

They walked back to the cars. 'We need to move your car farther into the trees,' Max remarked. 'If you're going to join me on spying expeditions in future, you may want to rethink your vehicle. This purple affair's a little too visible for my liking.'

Libby scratched her head. 'Maybe we could cover it with branches?'

Max chuckled. 'You've been watching too many television programmes. This isn't World War II, you know. We'll just put your car behind mine for safety. You'll need to manoeuvre between the trees, but at least your ancient and battered vehicle is small.'

'And, of course, I'm a brilliant driver. Don't forget that.'

The cars out of sight, they settled comfortably in the Land Rover. 'Good job it's not midwinter,' Max pointed out. 'We can't use the engine, in case it draws attention to us, so there's no heating. If you're cold there's another rug here.' Libby turned towards the back seat. Max grabbed her arm. 'Not that one, that's Bear's.'

'I need food.' Libby was suddenly ravenous. 'What have you brought?'

'Some of your very own sausage rolls from my freezer, and some pies I bought in Hereford. Not especially healthy, I'm afraid, but it will fill us up.'

'The diet's on hold, then?'

While they ate, Shipley lying comfortably behind them, Libby filled Max in on progress in the search for Beryl's killer. 'I'm confused about William and Margery,' she confessed. 'His heart attack was genuine enough. I suspect Margery has quite a tongue on her, and if she accused him of adultery, I'm not surprised he became agitated. But, it rules him out from the attack on his wife. He was already in hospital when it happened.'

Max tapped a finger on the steering wheel. 'I see what you mean. Unless he hired someone to take out his wife.'

'Come on, Max. That's going a bit far.' She didn't admit to having had the same thought herself.

'Can't rule it out, though. Did his wife recognise her attacker?'

'She says not.'

'And do you believe her?'

Libby considered, her head on one side. 'Not sure, to be honest. Their relationship is pretty complicated.'

Max laughed. 'I don't know of any relationship that isn't, especially if they've been married for forty odd years. A lot can happen in that time.'

'So, we won't cross William off the list of suspects yet.'

'Who else could be involved?'

'Almost anyone,' Libby sighed, 'who's ever been inside Beryl's house.'

'Most people in Exham, then. Other society members, maybe? If it's one of them, it rules out a crime of passion. Everyone in the society's at least middle-aged – not that over forties can't be passionate, but you know what I mean. They're not hormonal teenagers carrying knives in their back pockets.'

'Actually, there are a couple of new recruits. Annabel Pearson is around your cut-off date of forty, I would think, but Joanna, the doctor's wife, is even younger. She let slip that Beryl wasn't the sweet little old lady she appeared to be, and Mandy heard gossip that confirmed it. There's something about shady dealings, involving using clients' money, quite apart from the drinking problem. That's why she left her job in the spring.'

Max was nodding. 'Sounds like there's still plenty of work to be done. Let's find Bear and then we can get back to it.'

'There's another thing.' Libby told him about Terence Marchant's new shop, due to open in two weeks time. 'Angela's setting up the biggest party Exham has ever seen. We're going to get everyone into the shop for a wine and chocolate party that will scare off Terence Marchant and his posh French pastries, before he even begins. Angela has some sort of secret up her sleeve. She won't tell me about it.'

Max looked at his watch. 'If you've had enough to eat, I suggest you settle down and catch forty winks while you can. It'll be dark soon and then the fun will start.'

Libby yawned. It was true, she did feel drowsy. It was good to be with Max again. She could relax for a while.

19

BISCUIT CRUMBS

It seemed she'd only been asleep for five minutes when Max shook her awake, but the light had gone. The trees around the car had become sinister shapes in the gloom. 'Come on, time to go sleuthing.' Max's voice resonated with excitement.

Once out of the car, he held Bear's blanket close to Shipley's nose. The dog wagged his tail and sniffed the ground, but made no sign of finding his old friend's trail. 'They'll have been keeping Bear hidden on the farm, and he would have arrived in some kind of vehicle. We need to get nearer before Shipley will pick up the scent.'

In the dark, Libby kept close to Max, sliding between the trees that led up to the house as he lit a narrow path with his torch. Shipley kept his nose to the ground, tail wagging. 'He was born for this sort of work,' Max murmured.

'I think all his over-excitement happens when he's bored,' Libby whispered.

Max touched her arm. 'Don't whisper. Talk in a deep voice. Whispers carry for miles.'

'I said, he was bored,' Libby intoned, in the deepest voice she could manage, making Max shake with helpless laughter.

Regaining self-control, he waved his hand under Libby's nose, and they trod towards a group of sheds to the right of the farmhouse. 'Are you sure there's no one in there?'

'I can't be certain. While I've been watching the place, everyone who arrived, also left.'

Max stopped and held up a finger. 'What's that?'

Libby listened. 'It's a dog. Dogs. Lots of them. They're here.' She watched Shipley, who was still working, zigzagging with his nose to the ground, but showing no sign of excitement. 'We need to know if Bear's here. If not, the place could be legitimate. You did give Shipley a good sniff at Bear's blanket, didn't you?'

'If Bear's nearby, I'm confident he'll pick up the scent.'

Out in the Herefordshire countryside, there were no street lamps. The moon was a crescent shaped sliver high in the sky, providing the faintest of light. It was easy to slip round the side of the barn keeping the building between themselves and the farmhouse, just in case they were mistaken and the owners were still at home.

Shipley had shown no sign of sensing Bear until they were close to the building. Suddenly, his head went up and he stopped dead, shaking with excitement, tail wagging madly. Libby gasped. 'He's here. Shipley can smell him. You were right to suspect this place.'

'This way,' said Max. 'I can see the door on the other side.' Gently he pushed the door, but nothing happened. 'It's locked.' He reached into a pocket. 'I'm so glad. I've been wanting to use this kit for a long time.' He jangled a handful of metal.

'What's that?'

'A set of burglars' skeleton keys. Give me a minute, and I'll have this lock open.'

Libby waited patiently as he fiddled with it. Her feet grew cold. 'How are you getting on?'

'Not as easy as I hoped,' he admitted. 'I've practised at home, but it's more difficult in the dark. Wait, I think I've got it.' Max shoved at the door, but the lock held. He swore.

'Let me have a go.' Libby took the keys from him, inserted one into the lock, and jiggled it. For a long moment, nothing happened, then the lock clicked open.

'I loosened it for you,' Max muttered.

He pulled the door open and slipped inside, Libby following with Shipley at her side.

An acrid smell of dogs, urine, and meat made Libby blink. The barn held at least twenty animals, each in a tiny pen equipped with a bowl of water and another dish, presumably for food. Most of the containers near Libby were empty, or held a few biscuit crumbs. 'This place is a disgrace,' she whispered.

'Be quick. Find Bear,' Max commanded, but Shipley stood close to the door, making no attempt to move. 'Come on, Shipley,' Max said. 'Don't tell me you can't find Bear in here.'

Libby searched the pens. As she passed each one, the dog inside whined and ran to the barrier, hopeful she would offer food. With every step, her heart fell further. 'He's not here.'

'He must be. Maybe he's asleep.'

'Look.' She pointed at Shipley. 'He's telling us Bear's not here.'

Her spirits were in her boots. 'We were wrong,' she groaned. 'There's every breed of dog here, but no Bear. What do we do now?'

'We'll get back to the car and go home with our tails between our legs.' Max's voice was flat with disappointment. 'In the morning, I'll talk to the police. We don't even know for sure if these dogs are stolen, but they're neglected and the police will investigate properly.' He kicked angrily at a railing. 'I'm sure Bear's been here. Shipley could smell him.'

Libby shared his anger at the plight of the dogs. 'No one should keep fully grown dogs in such tiny spaces, with nothing to eat or drink. Besides, if they're stolen, they all have fond owners, waiting at home—'

Shipley interrupted with a low growl. He stood at the door, his nose pointing back along the track that led to the farm. Libby followed him and looked out, just as a car swerved around the corner, headlights lighting up the farm buildings. She blinked in the glare and, suddenly scared, pulled Shipley to the side, away from the door. She dropped a warning hand on his head and held her breath, hoping the dog would remain silent.

'Max,' she hissed. 'Someone's coming.'

Max flicked off his torch. The door rattled and the dogs in the barn set up a cacophony of hysterical barking. Libby and Max froze, their backs against the wall, Libby praying no one would enter. To her dismay, a tall man with a bucket in one hand kicked the door wide open and walked in. 'No need for all that racket,' he shouted as the barking intensified. 'Quit your whining.'

He shoved open the gate to one of the pens and aimed a kick at the dog inside, a silky coated collie. Libby bit back a cry. He hadn't caught sight of her or Max in the gloom, and he walked between the pens, tossing lumps of meat over the railings, some falling in the dogs' dishes, some dropping randomly onto the dirty straw of the pens. Max touched Libby's elbow. Quietly, as the man reached the far end of the barn, they tiptoed to the door.

For a moment, Libby thought they'd made it, but just as Max had his hand on the door, the new arrival swung round, dropped the bucket, and shouted, 'Oy. You there. Stop where you are.'

Max and Libby ran outside, closely followed by Shipley, as the man bellowed, 'Scott! Get 'em!'

His companion stood by the car, scrabbling in the boot. At the sound of his accomplice's voice he turned and raised his arms. He had a shotgun.

Libby bit back a scream and ran, as a shot rang out and whistled past her head.

The man from the shed shouted, 'Get in the car, Scott. Run 'em down.'

He'd reckoned without Shipley.

Like lightning, the dog raced at Scott, leaped in the air with wide-open jaws and clamped his teeth tightly onto the man's arm.

'Get off me,' his prisoner screamed, struggling, but Shipley hung on, shaken from side to side, growling deep in his throat. The villain's gun flew out of his grasp.

His companion took one look, turned, and ran. He wasn't going anywhere near the wild dog.

'Get back to the car,' Max ordered, and gave Libby a push in the direction of the woods. She shook off his arm. She wasn't about to leave Shipley to the attention of those men.

Furious, she ran across, grabbed the gun and sprinted after Scott's accomplice.

Too late, the man heard her approach, spun round, and aimed a blow at her head, but she ducked, the blow missed, and with all her strength, she swung the gun. With a dull clunk, it thudded into the man's body.

He screamed, clutched his shoulder and fell. Libby kept the gun trained on him, holding it against her shoulder, hoping against hope she wouldn't need to fire it. She'd never fired any kind of gun.

Max shouted, 'Let him go, Shipley,' and to Libby's astonishment, the dog released Scott's arm and stood guard, still growling.

Max gestured to Scott. 'You'd better sit next to your friend.'

Scott screamed, furious. 'Your dog's broke my arm. I'll have the law on—' He stopped as Max talked into his phone.

'Quite.' Max smiled. 'The law is on its way.'

Libby nodded. 'So, let's just wait patiently until they arrive.'

* * *

'Now, that was fun.' Max's cheeks glowed. A couple of bemused police officers had driven off with the dog thieves in tow, with promises to Libby that they'd call the RSPCA to look after the dogs. Libby, Max, and Shipley were on the road back to Exham, Libby's car left hidden in the trees. They'd collect it tomorrow. For now, they wanted to be together.

Libby's hands hadn't stopped shaking. 'I'm not cut out for this sort of thing,' she admitted.

'Well, you insisted on coming along.' Max took one hand from the wheel and hugged her. 'Apart from beating that man with the gun, you're a natural with skeleton keys. Are you sure you weren't a burglar in your former life?'

Shipley barked from the back of the Land Rover. Libby leaned back to scratch his head. 'You were wonderful, Shipley.'

Max chuckled. 'Good thing I had you with me. I think I may be getting a bit old. My knees will punish me, tomorrow. I'll leave the fighting to you, in future.'

Libby's glow of achievement faded as the adrenaline wore off. 'The trouble is,' she said. 'We're no nearer to finding Bear. I was so sure he'd be there.'

'Me too. I'm sorry.'

Libby blew her nose, reaction setting in. 'What are we going to do?'

'For the moment, we'll go home, and then we'll start again.'

She looked out into the darkness. 'Poor Bear. He's out there, somewhere, all alone. He'll be so lonely.'

'Bear can cope.' But Max's voice was uncertain.

'I hope you're right.' The thought of her beloved animal, possibly in another dirty shed, short of food, and wondering if he'd been abandoned forever, was too much for Libby. 'If we find him, I won't ever let him out of my sight,' she wailed.

Max changed gear. 'Not if – when we find him. We won't give up, will we, Shipley?' In the back of the car, the spaniel gave a short, sharp bark, as if in agreement.

20

WINE AND CHOCOLATE

On the morning of the Brown's Bakery party, Libby planned to spend the rest of the day quietly. She visited Angela to check the arrangements and gossip about her adventures in Hereford, basking for a while in her friend's open-mouthed admiration. 'You mean, you whacked him yourself? With a gun? Good for you!'

Libby confessed she'd been shaking for hours afterwards. 'But the worst is, we're no farther forward.'

'Think about the animals you saved. Their owners will be thrilled.'

'I'd feel better if we had a starting point, but the Hereford farm was our only lead,' she confided. 'The thieves must have sold him off before we arrived.' With an effort, she changed the subject. 'Anyway, I didn't come here to moan. How are the preparations for our party going?'

Angela waved a file of notes. 'It's all in hand, and there's an extra item; a wine tasting.'

'Really? Who's going to run it? I can't think of anyone in Exham, now the off licence is closed.'

Angela grinned. 'Well, you'll see.'

Libby gave her friend a long look. 'You're looking bright eyed and bushy tailed, today. Has something good happened?'

Her friend's burst of giggles gave Libby a clue. Angela never giggled. 'It's that man, isn't it?'

'He's coming to the party, so you'll meet him.'

Libby hugged her friend. 'Come on, tell me everything.'

'He's the same age as me, and a widower. He's in the restaurant business, which is how we met. I had lunch with my nephew in London, in one of Owen's restaurants, and Steve knocked over the wine bottle. Owen sent one of waiters to help and gave us another table. Things went on from there.'

'I can't wait to meet him.' The penny dropped. 'Is he going to run the wine tasting?'

Angela beamed. 'He is, he's giving his services free and he's supplying the wine at cost.'

Libby's jaw dropped. 'That's so generous.'

'And that's not all...'

'What do you mean?'

Angela was hugging her arms with glee. 'You'll have to wait until tonight. Anyway, that's enough about me. How's the Beryl investigation going?'

'Slowly.' Libby groaned. 'I feel as though I'm going in circles. She didn't seem to have any enemies, just a bunch of supportive friends, any of whom could easily have poisoned her whisky. The police have cleared the students, at least, because none of them knew her and they weren't anywhere near her at the castle. All we're left with is her alcohol problem.' She paused. 'I have one thought about that...'

'Go on,' Angela pleaded.

'Not yet. It's just an idea. Tell me, what do you notice happens when people drink too much?'

Her friend thought for a moment. 'They get talkative, and then miserable and maudlin, and then they fall asleep.'

'That's exactly right.'

'How does that help find Beryl's killer?'

'Wait until this evening. I have an idea, and it's going to be quite a night.'

* * *

The Exham on Sea Community Centre had never looked so cheerful. After hours of heart searching, and in consultation with Frank, Angela had suggested moving the party away from the bakery, because it seemed everyone in town wanted to be there. Libby was bemused. 'How have you persuaded people to stump up for a ticket?'

Angela winked. 'The tickets include a glass of wine and snacks, and everyone will get a few free chocolates. Frank's agreed it's about building support, rather than making a profit. He'll be happy if we just break even, and the goodwill should last a long time.'

'I hope you're right. Terence Marchant's patisserie will be a novelty, and I'm worried people won't be able to resist his mille-feuilles and macarons. Still,' determined not to be a misery, Libby stuck out her chin, 'there's plenty of custom for everyone.'

She hoped the wine would loosen tongues, and the unspoken Exham habit of keeping secrets might be overcome. She had a mental list of people she intended to question.

Mandy climbed a step-ladder, holding the last garland. She was upbeat. 'At least Terence Marchant's not going to sell chocolates.'

'You're right. Let's enjoy the evening. It's a good opportunity for a celebration, anyway.'

Angela giggled. 'We can always use one of those, and you need cheering up, Libby.' Her cheeks were suddenly suffused with colour. Libby followed her gaze to the door. A short, round man had arrived. He wore John Lennon spectacles and a beaming smile.

As he advanced up the room, Libby looked from him to Angela. The expression on Angela's face, her eyes warm with pleasure as she watched him arrive, told Libby all she needed to know. This wasn't at all how she'd expected elegant Angela's new man to look, but there was no doubting her friend's happiness.

'Libby,' Angela said. 'This is Owen. He's going to run the wine tasting for us.'

Owen's smile spread endearingly across his face, almost stretching from ear to ear. 'I've heard all about you and your exploits, and I'm honoured to meet you. Angela's set me quite a task, matching wine and chocolate, but I hope you'll enjoy the result.'

Max's arrival at that moment, accompanied by Shipley, gave Libby a chance to recover her equilibrium. She liked Angela's man already.

Shipley lay down on command, only a twitching tail hinting that he was on full alert. Angela seemed mesmerised. 'I can't believe it's the same dog. I've never seen him so quiet.'

Max grinned. 'He's had some serious training, and I've brought him along this evening to prove he can behave properly when the room's full of people.'

Libby placed a bowl of water in one corner. 'There you are, Shipley. I'm glad you're here.' She loved the newly trained spaniel, but he was no replacement for Bear. Libby's last hope was Gemma Humberstone. The detective constable, maintaining their delicate truce, had promised to come to the party. She'd sat in with a colleague from West Mercia as he interviewed the owners of the farm, and with any luck, she'd have news.

'Balloons.' Mandy cut into Libby's thoughts. 'We need more, Mrs F. Get puffing, people.'

Libby discovered it was impossible to stay sad while blowing up balloons. Angela agreed. 'It's like singing. Something about using your lungs properly.'

At that, Mandy blew too hard and the balloon burst, with an explosion that would have sent the unreconstructed Shipley into a spin. This time, he barely moved. Max beamed, as though he'd undertaken the animal's training himself. 'Look at that reformed character.'

Libby glanced at her watch. 'Hurry up, it's almost time to open the doors. Angela, will you collect tickets while Mandy and I set out the chocolates? Max, you're in charge of making sure Shipley doesn't steal any.' Within moments, the room buzzed. Songs from the West Country's favourite rural band, The Wurzels, played through a loudspeaker in the intervals between Owen's observations on wine. Local people sat at gingham-covered tables, ate, drank, and sang along.

Libby manned the counter at the end of the room, selling Mrs Forest's Chocolates, and as the noise level rose and the wine levels fell, she secured dozens of orders.

Mandy took over at last, and Libby slipped away to join the history society, who'd commandeered a large round table in a corner. She squeezed in next to Joanna, who'd already drained one glass of wine and was half way down another. 'Quite an occasion, Mrs Forest. You must be thrilled.'

Libby placed a bowl of chocolates in the centre of the table. 'Help yourself,' she encouraged. Joanna did not need to be told twice. As she leaned forward, selected a chocolate in the shape of a champagne bottle, and popped it in her mouth, Libby asked, 'How are you settling in? I hope people are friendly.'

'Oh yes. Everyone's been most kind, and I make a point of visiting some of the older folk.'

'That's wonderful. I'm sure they appreciate it.'

'Mrs Halfstead, for instance.' Joanna's eyes were bright, and she seemed eager to talk. 'I popped in this morning, just to see how she is. It must be terrible, with her husband under suspicion for this dreadful murder, and then, someone tried to kill her. She seemed very calm.' Joanna leaned closer to Libby. 'A bit too calm, maybe? I did wonder, you know—' She cleared her throat and continued in a whisper, 'I wondered if some of her story might have been made up.'

'Well, she was definitely stabbed.'

'Yes, but not very hard. I mean, no real damage done. Maybe,' her voice was an almost inaudible hiss, 'maybe she and William were in it together.' Triumphant, Joanna nodded and took a long swig of wine.

Libby asked. 'What makes you think that?'

'Well, who knows what goes on within a marriage? I know I would always stand up for Jeremy, whatever he did, but not all wives are as patient as I am.' Her lip quivered a little. Perhaps her marriage to the doctor was not as perfect as she wanted Libby to believe. 'Anyway, I heard William left his teaching job, and then, there was that business with Beryl's drinking and the accounts.' She gave a little tinkling laugh that jangled on Libby's nerves. 'Maybe William and Beryl were in cahoots and Margery found out about it. If William had killed once, he might have become overconfident and had a shot at getting rid of his wife.'

'It's a theory,' Libby said. 'But it couldn't be William who stabbed his wife, because he was already in hospital.'

Joanna's face fell. 'So, he was. I'll have to leave the sleuthing to you, Mrs Forest. Come on, do tell me what you think. It's so exciting, isn't it, to have a real-life mystery to solve?'

'Well, I don't know much more than you, I'm afraid. Have another chocolate.'

Joanna took a chocolate, swallowed it, and stared into her glass. 'Oh, dear, this is finished. I'll just get a top-up. Can I get one for you?'

Libby shook her head. 'No thanks.'

She moved to sit between George Edwards and Mrs Moffat. George watched Joanna as she staggered a little. His voice was harsh. 'That young lady's a bit too fond of the bottle, if you ask me. You can't trust a woman who drinks too much, no matter how long you've known them.'

Mrs Moffat said, 'I don't think everything is as it should be at the doctor's house. I saw him lunching with the receptionist the other day, in Exham, and they seemed to be getting on awfully well.' She raised her eyebrows. 'If you know what I mean.'

Libby managed a polite smile and turned to George. 'Is your wife not well today?'

He sighed. 'No, another difficult day, I'm afraid. I'm about to go home – I promised to buy some chocolates. Deirdre likes the ones with coconut. I can't manage them. The coconut gets under my plate.' Libby started, confused, before realising he was talking about false teeth. She tried hard not to stare.

He was still talking. 'I'll be buying plenty of boxes. I'm going fishing early tomorrow and I always give Deirdre a little present on fishing days. She doesn't like me going, not since that business at the club, but I tell her, people can think what they like, I won those trophies, fair and square.'

His face flushed an unhealthy shade of dark red. 'How dare they accuse me of cheating.' He banged his fist on the table, then seemed to collect himself, the flash of temper over, 'Before I go, I like to take her breakfast in bed.'

Max had arrived in time to hear the last few words. 'There, Libby. Married life means breakfast in bed.'

'Every day?'

'Well, let's just say, sometimes. But I came to get you. Gemma Humberstone just arrived, and she's bursting to tell us something.' He added, 'I'm sorry to say, Ian Smith's here as well.'

Libby leapt to her feet, paying no attention to Ian Smith, who was making a bee-line for the stacks of chocolates for sale. She wanted to hear what Gemma had discovered. 'Has she found Bear?'

Max took her hand. 'Not yet, I'm afraid, but she has news.'

Gemma looked young and pretty, and several male heads turned her way. 'The workers at the farm don't own the place, and they were only too willing to talk to me. I think they're hoping to get credit in court for grassing up the man behind the thefts. They say their only job is to look after the dogs. They know nothing about where the animals come from.'

Max snorted. 'A likely story.'

Libby, heart racing, interrupted. 'Did they know anything about Bear?'

Gemma grinned. 'They said two Carpathian sheepdogs arrived at the farm a few days ago, but they travelled on the next day. At first, they denied knowing where the dogs went, but eventually they gave us some addresses. There aren't many animals like Bear in the country, so he'd fetch a decent price.'

'And it should be easy to find him?'

Libby's spirits rose, but Gemma grimaced. 'Unfortunately, Bear was a bit too clever for the thieves. They loaded him into the van but they didn't lock the doors. After they'd been on the road a while, they stopped at a service station, leaving the dogs alone in the van. Half an hour later, when the thieves returned to the vehicle, the doors were open and Bear and a couple of other animals had disappeared.'

Max raised his glass. 'Good for you, Bear.'

Libby groaned. 'But, that means he's wandering around somewhere. Lost. Where was the van?'

'Just this side of Worcester. One of our officers is on his way to speak to the prospective owners. We may have a case against them, if they know the dogs they're buying have been stolen.'

'That's all very well,' Libby wailed, 'but what about Bear? He's lost, and the nights are drawing in. Anything could happen to him, and we're no nearer finding him than we were before.'

She looked around the room. Everyone was having such a fun time, but all she wanted to do was get away. She'd hoped to unmask Beryl's murderer, and her suspicions had increased during the evening, but there was one more item of evidence she wanted to check. 'Max, I'm going to go home early. Angela and her new man have everything under control, here.'

'I'll come with you.' Max's concern was touching.

'No, I'm fine. I'll feel better if you're here to help Angela lock up.'

Max hesitated before agreeing. 'If that's what you want. I'll come over when this is all done. Cheer up. The evening's been an enormous success. If this doesn't scare Terence Marchant away, nothing will—'

A shriek broke in to the conversation. At the other end of the room, Mandy, fists clenched, was facing down Ian Smith, her face incandescent with fury.

'All right, all right. No need to make a fuss. I didn't mean any harm...' Smith backed away, hands in the air.

Someone nearby applauded. 'Good for you, Mandy.' Libby saw an open box of chocolates, lying half empty on the floor. She stared at Ian Smith. A chocolate cream had lodged, squashed and oozing, behind his ear.

'What happened?'

Mandy, red-faced with fury, pointed at the hapless figure. 'He pinched my bottom.'

'I did not,' Ian Smith blustered. 'I just gave you a little pat on the behind. Friendly, that was all. No need to throw things, silly little—'

'You'd better get out of here, Smith,' Max broke in. 'You're not welcome.'

'But I didn't do anything.'

As Mandy grabbed another box of chocolates and took a step forward, the PC shrugged. 'All right, I'm going,' he muttered. 'Can't take a joke, that's the trouble with you Goths. I could have you for assaulting a policeman.'

Gemma was close behind. 'Mandy, do you want to press charges? I'm sure there are plenty of witnesses here.'

Mandy shrugged. 'I'll think about it.'

21

STEAK

Libby's head pounded as she arrived at the cottage. Ian Smith's behaviour had been the last straw. She opened the back door and called for Bear, as she'd done every time she returned home since his disappearance. There was no sign of him. She must learn to accept he was gone.

Aspirin, that was what she needed for this headache. She opened the cabinet in the kitchen, where she kept a first aid kit and a small supply of medicines, and sorted through the contents. She found the aspirin, and some vitamins she never remembered to take. She turned on the tap to fill a glass with water.

What was that?

She held her breath and listened. Another dull thud sounded from above.

She called up the stairs, 'Fuzzy, what are you doing? If you're winding wool everywhere...' The cat sometimes played with the balls of wool from a basket in the upstairs study. Libby was an incompetent knitter, too impatient to take the time to enjoy the activity, so her basket was full of half-finished scarves and hats.

She'd once come home to find green double knitting wool wrapped tightly around her chair and desk.

She climbed the stairs, calling the cat's name, and found Fuzzy in the airing cupboard. 'Stopped you just in time, didn't I? It's no good trying to look innocent.'

Fuzzy stretched, scratched a towel into a heap, turned round three times, and settled down to sleep.

Libby entered her study. The information she needed was in her files. She was sure Margery had told her something vital.

She grasped the handle of the top drawer of her filing cabinet, and it slid open. 'That's odd. I thought it was locked.' She shrugged, pulled out all her notes from Beryl's case, and started to read, muttering as though Fuzzy was listening, 'I can't see anything odd after all, except for that person Margery saw. She thought it was a volunteer, someone she didn't know. The police never did discover who it was.'

She re-read the description and gasped, her heart racing.

She snatched up a different notebook, the one containing her notes from the history society meeting. 'That's it. I knew it...'

The words died in her mouth. 'What's that?' she cried out. The thud had come from her bedroom, and it wasn't Fuzzy.

Libby swallowed. 'Is there someone there?'

No reply.

Trying not to breathe, Libby got to her feet and took a step towards the open door. She leaned back, eyes fixed on the corridor, fingers walking across the desk until they tapped against the heavy lighthouse statue she used as a paperweight. She grasped it, hand damp with sweat, and licked her lips.

A shuffling sound came from the bedroom. There was someone there, and Libby was in no mood to run. She'd dealt with the dog thieves. She could deal with her burglar, especially if it was the person she suspected of killing Beryl.

She closed her eyes briefly, took a breath and strode out of the study. With two quick steps she was at her bedroom door. She flung it open, just as the louvred door of the wardrobe clicked shut.

'Come out, whoever you are.'

No one answered. Had she imagined it? No. She could hear breathing from the wardrobe.

With a jolt, Libby came to her senses. She was alone with only a paperweight as a weapon, and if her suspicions were correct, the person in hiding there had already killed once. She needed to get out of the house and phone for help. Slowly, she backed out of the room. 'I'm leaving,' she announced, trying to sound firm.

As she reached the door, she turned to run. The wardrobe door flew open as she spun round, the paperweight held aloft, and faced the most genial member of the history society, Beryl's lifelong friend, George Edwards.

'You shouldn't have come back.' He murmured. 'I didn't want to hurt you, but it's your own fault, Libby.' He took a step forward.

Libby edged back, out of the bedroom door. She stammered, 'I know you killed Beryl.'

He whimpered, 'I couldn't trust her any more. She was my oldest friend, the only person who ever guessed my secret. She promised she'd keep it safe, but she was drinking too much. Her tongue kept running away with her.' His eyes pleaded for understanding. 'I couldn't let her tell Deirdre about me. It would kill my wife.'

He took a step closer. 'How did you know?'

Libby backed away, judging the distance to the stairs with a glance. A memory flashed into her head of George's wife, lying back on a chair, shaking her head, the hair of her wig remaining perfectly groomed. 'At the society meeting, I realised Deirdre wore a wig. Then, Margery described both the woman she saw at the castle and the woman who attacked her. The descriptions matched so closely it had to be the same person.'

Deirdre was housebound and too fragile to be the killer, but George had easy access to his wife's wigs and bright clothes.

The solution had seemed crazy at first, but the facts fitted together, and Libby had remembered Joe's advice to follow where the evidence led. She looked George in the eye. 'You like to dress in women's clothes, don't you?'

If she could keep him talking, she could reach the stairs and get away. 'What did Beryl know?'

George's face worked as tears filled his eyes. 'About me? Everything. I had to tell someone, and she was my oldest friend. I trusted her, and she kept the secret for years, but after she lost her job, she was drinking more and more. I knew she'd give me away, one day.'

Libby took another step backwards.

George's face twisted. 'It started with Deirdre's dresses, soon after we married. I used to try them on when she went out. Then, it was her – her underwear. She never knew. After her first dose of chemotherapy, years ago, she lost her hair and bought a couple of wigs.'

His face crumbled into self-pity. 'You wouldn't understand, but wearing her clothes, dressing as a woman, made me feel true to myself, for the first time in my life.' His eyes gleamed at the memory, and Libby felt a pang of sympathy. He'd had to hide his real feelings for so many years.

'I often visited the castle. I felt safe there. The building was big enough for me to avoid anyone I knew. I could wear Deirdre's clothes, and lipstick.'

He chuckled, suddenly, and Libby's compassion drained away. 'I planned it all. I bet you didn't know how easy it is to extract nicotine. Just like making tea, but with cigarettes instead of teabags!'

His smug expression was sickening. He was boasting, now, following Libby as she inched towards the stairs. 'I visited Beryl one evening, and when she left the room, I put poison in her silver flask. Silly woman,' he sneered. 'She thought no one knew about that flask. She'd told me she was playing the maid next day. So proud, she was. Full of herself.'

His eyes narrowed to angry slits. 'I should have stayed away, but I couldn't resist seeing if my plan worked. Then, Margery Half-stead saw me. She didn't recognise me, but I couldn't take the risk.'

He shrugged. 'I went to the house to kill her, but I couldn't bring myself to do it. Not with a knife. It was easy enough to put poison in Beryl's whisky, though. No blood, you see. I read how to make the poison on the internet.' His voice had become conversational, as though he was chatting with Libby about the weather. She glanced behind. She was at the top of the stairs.

'Stop.' George's face changed. 'I can't let you go, now.' His eyes glittered. He raised his hands, fingers curled, and lunged.

Libby was younger than he, and faster. She fled down the stairs, running for her life, a scream in her throat.

George was almost on her. Terrified, she looked back and tripped, falling heavily.

With a growl that shook the walls, Bear jumped over Libby and leapt at George.

* * *

Suddenly, the house was full. Max grabbed George and held him on the floor, as Shipley brought up the rear, barking wildly.

Flanked by the dogs, their eyes following George's every

move, Max sat on the killer's chest as Libby phoned for the police. George had visibly shrivelled. He looked old and pathetic. 'I knew it would come out, one day, but I couldn't face everyone knowing.' His face crumpled, he dropped his head into his hands, shoulders shaking with sobs, and muttered, 'I never wanted to kill Beryl, but she knew about me. I couldn't trust her...' The rest of the sentence was lost in sobs.

Revulsion rose in Libby's throat. 'You murdered one woman and tried to kill another, just to hide your weakness from your wife. How could you?'

Max looked from one to the other, puzzled, but before Libby could fill in the details, the police arrived.

Libby gave a short statement to a wide-eyed Gemma Humberstone, and, too tired to talk more that evening, agreed to go to the police station early the next day to give all the details. Meanwhile, another officer marched George to the car.

At last, Libby and Max were alone with their dogs.

Libby sat on the floor, her arm round the giant sheepdog. 'Where did Bear come from, at exactly the right moment?'

'One of my old mates, Alan Jenkins at the garage, saw Bear wandering through the lanes on his way home. He must have walked about twenty miles a day. Alan knew about your party, and brought Bear along, but they arrived about ten minutes after you left. I was going to ring you, but then I thought we'd come to the cottage and surprise you.'

'It's just as well you did, although I think I'm probably stronger than George. I could have beaten him off.' Libby tried not to recall the sheer panic she'd felt, as she fled down the stairs. She shivered. 'Imagine. Mild mannered George Edwards. What a mess he's made of his life.'

Max squatted, examining Bear's body with gentle hands. 'He

seems all right. His feet are sore, of course, but other than that, he looks pretty sprightly.'

'No wonder he's filthy, and thin, poor animal.' Bear lay with his head in Libby's lap, panting, as she talked. 'I suppose he hasn't had a square meal since he escaped from the van. I'll get him some food.' She staggered to her feet. 'You too, Shipley. You've both been wonderful.'

'We'll take him to the vet, tomorrow, but I think he's just tired. Come on, Bear, you'll sleep well tonight.' Max followed them to the kitchen. 'I'm not sure I understand why George broke into your house. He didn't come to kill you, did he?'

'No. He hadn't brought his knife. He'd come to raid my filing cabinet, to see what I'd found out, I suppose. I had planned to unmask him at the party. I was pretty sure he was the killer, once I realised Margery's attacker, and the unknown person in the castle, wore a wig like Deirdre's.'

She attempted a smile. 'I was planning a little drama, but when Gemma told me Bear was lost again, I couldn't bring myself to do it. I made an excuse to myself, that I needed to check Margery's evidence first.' She shivered. 'I was at George's table earlier in the evening, when he talked about women who drink too much. It was there, in his eyes; the man was unhinged. He must have left the party soon afterwards, knowing I was away from the cottage. He's completely paranoid, of course. He killed Beryl to stop her telling people he liked dressing in women's clothes.'

'That was it? No conspiracy? Just because he was ashamed? In this day and age, it's almost unbelievable.' Max squatted, to fill the dogs' bowls with steak from Libby's fridge. 'There you are, dogs. You two are heroes. Like Libby.'

The next evening, Libby leaned her elbows on the dinner table. 'What could be nicer than a few friends sharing a meal?' She smiled at each guest in turn. Max, Angela, Mandy and her boyfriend, Steve: they were all there, along with Owen, Angela's new man. It should have been a celebration, but her friend looked worried. 'What's wrong, Angela?'

Deep furrows showed on Angela's forehead. She gave a half-hearted smile and sat up straighter. 'I'm sorry. I was just thinking about George and Beryl. How many times did they share a meal over the years?'

'Or, at least, a drink,' put in Mandy with a wicked giggle. 'They'd known each other for ever.'

Libby spoke softly. 'Imagine having a secret, one so shocking that you couldn't bear your friends and neighbours to discover it.' She looked from one face to another. 'Your lifelong friend knows your secret, and she keeps it safely. Maybe she's known it for years and never told anyone. You'd think it would bring you closer together, but it had the opposite effect. George didn't feel secure at all.'

Max joined in. 'Then, the friend's life turns upside down, she's fired from her job, and the drinking gets out of hand.'

'George was convinced Beryl would give him away,' said Libby.

Angela mused aloud. 'He was devoted to Deirdre. He'd hidden his feelings from her for years.'

'Beryl's drink problem made it easy to poison her,' Libby pointed out. 'People visited her at home. It would be easy to slip something into a whisky bottle, or even give her one as a present. Why should anyone suspect George? It was Margery Halfstead who led me to the answer.'

Angela still frowned. 'We had a kind of conspiracy to keep Beryl's drinking quiet, because in a small town like this, public disgrace is one of the worst things that could happen.'

Owen's voice cut into the sombre mood. 'Is it always so exciting in Exham?'

Angela raised her glass to Libby. 'Ever since Libby came to live here, there's never been a dull moment. Not that it's her fault, of course.'

'I do sometimes feel as though I'm attracting trouble,' Libby admitted, 'but there seem to be pathetic characters like George Edwards everywhere, these days. Not to mention Ian Smith. Well done, Mandy, by the way. He got what he deserved. Are you going to press charges?'

Mandy took a swig of wine, smacking her lips in appreciation. 'No need. He won't be pinching women's bottom's again. In any case, the story's bound to get around to DCI Morrison. I wouldn't want to be in PC Ian Smith's shoes, with Gemma as a witness. I'll be surprised if he keeps his job.'

'I'd better make sure all the skeletons in my cupboard are well hidden, if I'm going to stick around with you people,' Owen said.

'Are you working in the area?' Libby asked.

Owen and Angela shared a glance, but before they could speak, Mandy interrupted. 'Owen's been looking at Exham for his latest venture.'

Libby puffed air through her lips. 'I hope you're not setting up another bakery. We'll have enough competition from Terence Marchant. I'm hoping the party gave him a nasty shock and showed him what he's up against. People here are very loyal.' She grinned. 'Especially after all that chocolate and wine. What an evening!'

'Go on, tell her,' Mandy pleaded.

Libby looked from her to Angela. 'What are you all grinning about? You're up to something. Come on, don't keep me in suspense.'

'To cut a long story short,' Owen said, 'I've known Terence for years. He's a pretty unsavoury character, with a tendency to overreach himself. When he heard about your party, with everyone in town supporting you, he got cold feet over the new shop.'

Libby's pulse quickened. 'You mean, he's not going to open?'

Owen shook his head. 'Better than that. I offered to buy his business premises from him, and I've got an offer for you. How would you like the bakery, and your chocolates, to expand using those premises, and including a café?'

Libby gave her head a shake, trying to make sense of what she was hearing. 'You mean, buy Frank out? He'd never agree. Brown's Bakery is his life's work.'

'On the contrary. He wants to retire – apparently, he's been thinking about it for months, but he didn't know how to tell you, because of all the work you put into growing the bakery.'

'Am I that scary?'

Max raised an eyebrow. 'Terrifying. But the point is, Owen's offering to make the business viable in the long term.'

Libby turned to Mandy. 'What do you think?'

'I think it would be wonderful. We've been moaning about the size of the shop. It's a squash when all the customers are in at lunchtime. Here's the perfect opportunity to move out into a bigger space, still in the middle of Exham.'

Libby hesitated, tapping her finger on the table. 'I don't think I could run a café. I wouldn't have time, for one thing. I want to concentrate on the investigating, and we're about to get married.'

'Actually, Owen has another idea that takes care of that problem,' Angela said. Libby looked up, surprised, but her friend refused to meet her gaze.

Instead, Owen said, 'Angela's keen to take on that part of the business. She'll run the café for me.'

Libby's jaw hung open as her mind raced. 'That's – that's a brilliant idea. You'd be perfect. You're the best organiser in town.' She peered at Angela's face. 'You used the wine and chocolate event for practice, didn't you?' Her friend turned puce. 'Come on, admit it!'

Angela fiddled with a spoon on the table. 'It seemed a good opportunity for a dry run. See if I could cope.'

Mandy scoffed. 'Can't think of anyone who'd cope better. You can keep us organised – Mrs F's always forgetting to order ingredients.'

Libby tried to scowl. 'Thanks very much, young Mandy. You're right, though. I've been taking on far too much. This could be the answer to my worries.'

The friends spent hours planning the café until they were all too tired to talk any more.

As Libby and Max waved them off, full of tasty food and some of the best wine from Max's cellar, he took her hand, pulled her close and enveloped her in one of his wonderful bear hugs. 'Now. What about this wedding?'

Libby thought for a moment. 'When Bear was lost, I thought we ought to put it off – we wouldn't want to go ahead without him. But, now he's back, let's do it next week – but we'll keep it quiet.'

'Just us, our sons and their wives, Shipley and, of course, Bear. Perfect.'

23

MADEIRA CAKE

Sick with excitement, Margery drove William home from the hospital. It was the first time he'd ever agreed to be her passenger. He always insisted on driving. 'It's my job to look after you,' he'd said. Well, things were going to be a little different, now.

She chattered happily. As so often, William let her talk. 'You know Libby Forest, who found out George Edwards was the murderer?'

'Yes, dear.'

'Well, her missing dog turned up, out of the blue, the other evening.'

He grunted.

She went on, 'Turns out it escaped and walked all the way home. What do you think about that?'

'About what?'

'The dog coming home, all by himself.'

William muttered, 'Good for him.'

'You can trust a dog,' Margery said. 'By the way, why did you let Jason Franklin do the talking over the castle's speaking tube?'

She gave a secret smile at William's sharp intake of breath. 'He – er – he won it in a competition I organised. An essay.'

Margery snorted. 'Nonsense. You fixed it. Come on, William. Time to tell the truth. We've seen what happens when people keep secrets. Just so I know, what did you want from Franklin senior?'

She felt, rather than saw, William's sideways look. 'Planning permission,' he muttered. 'For that extension you set your heart on. I know the local planners will kick up a fuss and the neighbours will object. I thought I'd get the MP on our side before we start. Planners have to listen to the MP, don't they?'

Margery fell silent, her mind working feverishly. 'You were talking to Mr Franklin that day at the castle, weren't you, when you left me with the students? Sucking up to him? Telling him the boys were there, and you'd given his son a starring role?'

William turned his head away, but not before she caught a glimpse of heightened colour. 'I never should have got involved with that Thomas Franklin. You see, he suggested a payment to get our planning application through. Just a small one. He said it was common practice to grease the wheels, that's what he called it.'

He shot a quick glance at Margery. 'I paid him what he asked, but then he started demanding more and more. I had to give him half the money I'd saved. I'm not even sure there's enough left for the building work. I tried to stop, told him I wouldn't bother with the extension, but he turned nasty. He even threatened to tell everyone it was me who weighted the scales at the fishing competition.'

Tears filled his eyes. 'But it was George Edwards. I've been sure of it all the time. I wasn't surprised it was George who killed Beryl. I've never trusted him, since that fishing competition, but now I know he attacked you as well.'

His hands were clenched tight. 'I'm sure Franklin knew it too. He was probably getting money from George, too. He's a bad man, is Franklin, but he's so powerful...'

'Not so powerful he can escape the law.' Margery's voice rose in anger. Really, William could be heart-breakingly naïve. 'He's the one who'll be in trouble once the police know he's been extorting money from you.'

'But everyone will know I've been dishonest.'

'Who cares what people know? You're nothing of the sort at heart. We'll go to the police station tomorrow and explain everything. I'll bet it's not the first time that man's taken bribes. I expect the police will give you a good talking to, but he's the one who'll be in trouble. I feel sorry for his son.' She stopped talking. 'What?'

William's mouth hung open. He seemed to be gazing at his wife with new-found admiration. She rather liked it. 'Didn't you realise you were a suspect in Beryl's murder?'

His shoulders moved in a tiny shrug. 'I was hoping for the best. My head was in a spin, and they couldn't accuse me of attacking you, could they? I was in hospital.'

Margery touched his fingers. They felt cold. 'You silly old fool,' she said, but her voice was warm. 'Why don't you forget all about that extension? You never wanted it. You were organising it to make me happy, and I don't need it now.'

'You don't?' He sounded puzzled, confused.

Margery thought of the little box in his shed, full of memories, out of sight so as not to upset her. She sighed. Her husband was a stick-in-the mud and naïve, as well, getting caught up in a shady business he didn't properly understand. She smiled her secret smile once more. It no longer mattered that Father never approved of William. Margery loved her husband, and he returned her feelings. How could she ever have thought he was interested in that Annabel? Once they'd confessed everything to the police, she would keep her husband on the straight and narrow.

Her voice was matter-of-fact. 'An extension would be just another room to clean, anyway.'

'Good old Margery,' William muttered.

She tapped her husband's dear, familiar hand, and then let it go so she could steer the car neatly onto their drive. 'Now, let's get inside and have a nice cup of tea and a slice of Libby Forest's Madeira cake.'

ACKNOWLEDGMENTS

The biggest influence on these stories is Burnham on Sea in Somerset, the template for Exham-on-Sea.

We have eight miles of sandy beach here, the second biggest tidal range in the world and we can boast of the UK's smallest pier. In the summer donkeys trot up and down the beach and, occasionally, there's even a Punch and Judy show.

Somerset itself is crammed with interesting places, from a castle to a tiny cathedral and the wild and wonderful Exmoor National Park; brilliant settings for murder and mayhem.

My publishers, Boldwood Books, have done a great job with the recent make-over for the Exham-on-Sea series, and I'd like to thank all of the team for their help and support. And, then, there's my husband and children who never fail in their interest in and support of my writing. Thank you all.

MORE FROM FRANCES EVESHAM

We hope you enjoyed reading *Murder at the Bridge* and *Murder at the Castle*. If you did, please leave a review.

Sign up to become a Frances Evesham VIP and receive a free copy of the Lazy Gardener's Cheat Sheet. You will also receive news, competitions and updates on future books:

https://bit.ly/FrancesEveshamSignUp

ALSO BY FRANCES EVESHAM

ABOUT THE AUTHOR

Frances Evesham is the author of the hugely successful Exham-on-Sea Murder Mysteries set in her home county of Somerset. In her spare time, she collects poison recipes and other ways of dispatching her unfortunate victims. She likes to cook with a glass of wine in one hand and a bunch of chillies in the other, her head full of murder—fictional only.

Visit Frances' website: https://francesevesham.com/

Follow Frances on social media:

   twitter.com/francesevesham
   facebook.com/frances.evesham.writer
   bookbub.com/authors/frances-evesham
   instagram.com/francesevesham

ABOUT BOLDWOOD BOOKS

Boldwood Books is a fiction publishing company seeking out the best stories from around the world.

Find out more at www.boldwoodbooks.com

Sign up to the Book and Tonic newsletter for news, offers and competitions from Boldwood Books!

http://www.bit.ly/bookandtonic

We'd love to hear from you, follow us on social media:

 facebook.com/BookandTonic
twitter.com/BoldwoodBooks
 instagram.com/BookandTonic